Favorable
Conditions

Also by Kathleen Kole

Breaking Even

Dollars to Donuts

Favorable
Conditions

Kathleen Kole

Sublime Coyote Media

FAVORABLE CONDITIONS

ISBN-13: 978-0986895654
ISBN-10: 0986895652

This book is published by Sublime Coyote Media. For more information please visit www.sublimecoyote.com.

For Peter
Truly, madly, deeply.

CHAPTER ONE

Pat zipped clear packing tape across the top of the last cardboard box on her daughter's bedroom floor.

"Done," she groaned as she let the black dispenser slip from her hand, then pulled herself upright from her crouch beside the box. Man, her knees were not what they used to be.

Pat inhaled the fragrant, lily-like perfume of the Evening Stock she'd planted in the white window box outside and listened to snippets of conversation drifting in through the screen. The kids were loading the van in the driveway and they sounded so eager and excited, she had to smile. Despite it being a tough day for her, it was a thrilling one for Crystal.

She smoothed back the strands of brown hair that had escaped her ponytail and perched gingerly on the stripped double bed. *The time has arrived,* she thought, while taking stock of what remained in the room; not much.

The art posters had been pulled down to reveal faded pink walls in serious need of a fresh coat of paint. The purple shag throw rugs were rolled up and packed away, leaving nothing but pale hardwood and dust bunnies. And, all of the girl clutter that had decorated Crystal's dresser and nightstand had been carefully wrapped up, exposing worn surfaces and permanent water rings in the pine.

Pat sighed. *My youngest child, my baby girl, is moving away to College,* she thought, discovering in that very instant she was simultaneously happy and horrified. Happy for Crystal because she was expanding her horizons and venturing out into a life beyond her childhood doors, but horrified for herself in the face of the realization that her work in the Motherhood trenches had come to a halt. She was now officially on the sidelines; only to be contacted when advice, or money, was needed.

At least that was her experience with her son.

Michael, while a decent and kind young man, was pretty much typical of his gender. In the past two years since he'd moved out to College, he called when something triggered his memory; or when he had girl trouble; or needed extra cash. Pat couldn't help herself and smiled. God how she loved her kids, warts and all.

The first bars of Vivaldi, *The Four Seasons*, emanated from Pat's jean pocket, jarring her from her mental musing. She pulled out her phone and answered, "Hello?"

"Hey, you! How are things going? Getting it done?"

Pat grinned at the warm, kind voice in her ear. It was her best friend, Melanie. "Oh yeah, it's going," she replied, while silently debating upon standing back up, or letting herself fall back onto the mattress.

"Kent's a blonde blur of energy, tossing Crystal's stuff around like it's the weight of feathers and I'm..." She paused, yawned, and then chuckled into the phone before she admitted her truth. "Definitely *not* eighteen anymore."

Melanie laughed out loud.

"Seriously," Pat insisted, a bubble of humor just beneath the surface of her words. "I'm sitting here on Crystal's bed and I feel like all of my muscles have banded together in mutiny. It's like I'm suddenly sixty five, instead of forty five. Although, don't tell my Dad I said that. Otherwise, he'll be pulling up to my doorstep and challenging me to a push-up competition, just to prove that age is all in my head."

"Okay," Melanie said. "So, other than the fact that your body is giving out, how are *you* holding up?"

"Oh, well." Pat tugged on the hem of her green tee-shirt and even though Melanie couldn't see her, shrugged her tired shoulders. "I'm okay. Or, rather, I'll be okay."

"And that means what, exactly?"

"Oh, it's nothing. Never mind me. Just the same foolish stuff."

Melanie was quiet, waiting.

Pat sighed and let herself fall backward into the mattress. She could hear Kent, the aforementioned blonde blur and Crystal's long standing boyfriend, teasing Crystal in the driveway below and was struck once more by how time had flown by.

"I *know* I've done the job I was supposed to do. And, believe me, I'm thrilled that both Crystal and Michael have become amazing, self-sufficient adults."

"But?"

"*But,*" Pat admitted, letting her limbs go limp on the pillow-top. "I guess I'm just feeling a bit in over my head and trying to remember how to tread water and breath at the same time."

"Oh, Pat," Melanie soothed, her voice full of caring concern. "It's all going to be okay. It'll just take a bit of time and then things will be fine."

Pat nodded silently and swallowed over the lump that had formed in her throat the moment the truth was out.

"We've talked about this, right? You've had a lot of changes in the past year and a half - and I mean a *lot*. But, once you adapt to this new normal, things are going to be great. More than great."

"I know, I know. You're right. I think I'm just tired out and making this harder than I need to." Pat cleared her throat and took a breath. "Oh hell. I hear the kids. I don't want to freak them out with my theatrics."

"Enough said," Melanie replied. "Do you want me to come over later?"

"No. I think I need to do this first night on my own, you know?"

"Kind of like a rite of passage?"

Pat grinned. "Exactly. I'm going to be here by myself now whether I like it or not, I may as well jump in with both feet."

"Understood. But, you know you can call me later if you need to talk, right?"

Pat took another deep breath and exhaled. "Of course. Thanks, Mel."

"No need. Go look perky. Love you."

"You, too. Bye." Pat smiled at the phone and hung up, feeling a lot steadier than she had just moments earlier.

"Last one!" Kent strode purposefully into the bedroom, his enthusiastic voice echoing off the naked walls. He stopped dead when he saw Pat sprawled across the bed. "Whoa. You okay, Mrs. K?"

Pat laughed and ignored her protesting back muscles as she sat upright. "Yes, I'm fine. Just taking a breather and updating Melanie on our progress."

"Oh, okay," he said, before effortlessly hauling the final box from the floor up to his shoulder. Pat grimaced, sure her tired muscles were groaning in sympathy.

"What is it?" he asked, watching her face. "Are you sure you're okay?"

Pat nodded and stuffed her phone back into her pocket. "Fine. Really. Just wincing on your behalf."

Kent grinned, his friendly face so open and full of promise that Pat wanted to pinch his cheeks. "No need," he told her, his strong arm wrapped securely around the box. "This has been one of the easier moves I've helped on in a while."

"Well, la-di-da, rub it in," she teased, knowing full well that the box on his shoulder contained Crystal's weighty paperbacks. "The last thing I'm carrying today is going to be that tape dispenser."

Kent chuckled and shook his head, his short blonde hair gleaming in the sunshine streaming through the bedroom window. "Got it. No more lifting for you."

"Did everything fit okay in the van?" she asked as he turned to carry the box out to the door.

"Easily," he replied, over his shoulder, before he left the room. "Even have space for more, if we needed it."

Pat listened to the sound of his footsteps as he rapidly descended the staircase and sighed into the silence. She glanced briefly at the tape dispenser, then turned toward the window to distract herself by watching the squirrels in the tree branches leaning across the driveway. They were natural comedians; rushing around at speed and then stopping to chatter at Kent as he emerged from the house with the box perched on his shoulder.

"Mom?" Crystal's voice, full of concern, called to Pat from the bedroom doorway. "Kent said you were lying down? You okay?"

Speak of the devil, Pat thought, straightening her shoulders and smoothing the front of her tee-shirt. She'd been so internally absorbed, she hadn't heard her daughter's footsteps on the stairs.

Show time, she told herself and plastered a carefree smile onto her face. Her melancholy had absolutely no place there. It was Crystal's moment, her time to spread her wings and there was no way in hell Pat was going to clip them before her daughter had even had a chance to try them out.

"Of course I am," she replied, lightly, as she twisted away from the window. "I told Kent I was just taking a breather. What reason would I have to not be okay?"

"Well," Crystal hedged as she pushed her mussed auburn waves from her face. "I don't know. Nothing, I guess. You just seemed so solemn standing there."

Pat watched Crystal fidget and knew that going off to College, to live with Kent, was pushing her to her limits. She had always been a sensitive child, had always had difficulty with change and Pat imagined that the mere thought there was a chance her Mother might be in turmoil was more than Crystal could bear.

She need not have worried. Pat was strong enough for both of them.

"Okay, fine. If you must know," Pat said, crossing the room to join her in the doorway. "I was thinking about my gorgeous and talented daughter getting ready to take her first steps into the world, embarking upon her exciting adventure at College."

Crystal, her brown eyes bright with a mixture of anticipation and just a touch of nervous fear, grinned. Pat looked into her face and felt her heart clutch; she looked so much as she had when she'd gone off to her first day of school, it was almost painful. *Deep breaths,* she silently counseled herself. *Keep it together.*

"It *is* exciting," Crystal agreed, pulling at the bottom of her hot pink tee-shirt and shifting from one sandaled foot to the other.

Pat wrapped a loving arm around her daughter's slim shoulders. "I'm thrilled for you, Sweetie. Thrilled and a little jealous. Maybe I'll tag along, get Kent to pack me into the truck with your stuff."

"And, more than a little unnerving, too."

"Oh, phooey, you'll be just fine," Pat stated, confidently, gripping Crystal's shoulder. "Haven't you got Kent, your strong, sturdy, gorgeous hunk of a man right there with you? You'll be hard pressed to have to lift a finger. He'll help you every step of the way."

Crystal giggled at Pat's description of Kent and she knew she'd hit the right note. The pair of them had been an item for three years - since Crystal had started high school. Pat remembered very well the day that Crystal had zoomed enthusiastically into the house, her eyes dancing for the boy that had caused her heart to turn summersaults. Even her older brother hadn't been able to deflate her zeal with his taunts and teasing.

Of course, according to Kent - a grade ahead of Crystal at the time - the attraction had been completely mutual. He was fond of telling anyone who would listen that he had taken one look at Crystal at the school welcome assembly and had fallen hook, line and sinker. He had known he wouldn't rest until he'd asked her out on a date.

As though on cue, Kent bounded up the staircase two at a time, all smiles. Pat fully admitted to herself, and anyone else, she adored him like a second son and held sincere hope that he and Crystal's relationship would survive the new terrain of College.

"Alrighty, Darlin', that's got it all. Time to hit the road." Kent glanced from mother to daughter and hesitated. "Sorry, did I interrupt?"

"No, no." Pat waved her hand dismissively and gave Crystal's shoulder one last squeeze before she let her go. "I think we're done here. Right, Honey?"

Crystal nodded, her giggles subsiding to be replaced by pale lips gone tight with suppressed emotion. She tucked her long hair behind her ears, blinked furiously as her eyes began to brim with unshed tears and quickly looked away.

Pat ached to reach out and hug her tight, but knew it would only make it worse. Instead, she swallowed against the lump that had reformed in her throat, while Crystal sniffled and squared her shoulders and followed Kent back down the stairs.

Pat watched her go, both proud and heart broken. The stripped bedroom was still and silent, never again to be draped in an assortment of discarded clothes, shoes and candy wrappers; nor the giggles and whispers of girls up long past their slumber party bedtime. At least, not while Pat resided there.

Her nest was truly empty, nothing left but her and her thoughts to fill the rooms of the once full house.

***

"Dah-na-na-na, na-na-na." Pat hummed to herself as she stripped her sweatpants from her waist, stepped out of them and turned to rummage through the clothes in her wardrobe. She'd missed the light switch on her way into the bedroom, then the switch to illuminate her closet, so the room was in shadows, making her quest a bit more of a challenge.

"Ah-ha!" She exhaled, then grabbed the edge of the closet frame to save herself being knocked out by the fumes from her own whiskey laden breath. She wasn't exactly what you could call an experienced drinker - far from it. Pat even liked to joke that if you were to look in the dictionary next to the word 'teetotaler', it wouldn't be that much of a surprise to see her picture. Ha-ha.

"Okay, Patricia," she said, having decided a few months back that one of the perks of being husbandless was being able to talk to yourself out loud. "Your time has finally arrived. You're free, you have no responsibilities and it's show time."

Pat pulled a man-styled, pink dress shirt from its hanger, slipped it around her shoulders to cover her tee-shirt and white cotton underwear and fumbled clumsily with the buttons. Whew, maybe that last whiskey and cola had been a bit stronger than she'd intended.

"Well, whatever," she slurred slightly and gave each one of her white socked feet a small shake. "It's time to celebrate and damn it, that's what I'm gonna do."

Pat spun jerkily on her heel, marched through her bedroom doorway and down the stairs - narrowly avoiding a mishap on the bottom creaky step that could have sent her sliding feet first into the foyer - and listed unsteadily into the living room toward the stereo.

"Dah-na-na-na, na-na-na!" she sang loudly, then grabbed the stereo remote in one hand, took a large gulp from a water glass on the coffee table filled with whiskey and cola with the other and, finally, paused for dramatic effect.

"Ready?" she asked her invisible audience, before releasing a spectacular belch that sent her into a fit of giggles; sputtering and gasping. "Okay, okay," she said, trying to catch her breath. "Focus."

She frowned to make her face serious and pointed the remote at the stereo. "Three, two, one," she counted, then clicked play and waited a beat for the familiar piano keys to rumble loudly through the speakers.

At the sound of the first keys, Pat grabbed one of the tall white candle sticks atop her fireplace, whipped around and ran toward the living room entrance; letting her feet slide as she crossed the hardwood floorboards that marked the threshold.

"Just take those old records off the shelf!" she sang robustly along with Bob Seger, before almost losing her footing like a person slipping on a banana peel in an old black and white movie.

"Whoops!" she yelped, catching herself and narrowly missing planting her almost naked backside on the floor. She chortled, spun around and tried to march cockily with the beat toward her fireplace.

"Today's music ain't got the same soul!" she chanted the third line of the song as she grabbed hold of her mantle and stamped her candle stick forcefully back down. "I like that old time rock and roll!"

"Wooo!" she bellowed and whipped herself rockily around, ready to dance.

"Don't try to take me to a disco!" she tipsily harmonized, while trying to throw out her best *Saturday Night Fever* moves. Wrong choice.

As Bob sang, "You'll never even get me out on the floor," Pat overshot her disco arm and smacked her five foot, brushed nickel floor lamp upside its cream linen shade, sending it speedily to the floor with a noisy clatter.

"Ooh!" she exclaimed, shuffling backward in surprise. That was unexpected. So much so that, instead of being upset, the crash cracked her up.

Pat began to chuckle, then giggle, and finally, to laugh hysterically; causing her to lurch gracelessly around her coffee table like a dizzy toddler - all the while Bob Seger singing, "Still like that old time a-rock and roll. That kinda music just soothes the soul."

"*Okay.*" Pat self-counseled, teetering on unsteady legs and took a breath. "Back on the horse!" She started to chicken-strut to the beat, back and forth across the polished floor, letting her socked feet slide as she reveled in the feeling of the slick surface.

"Here it comes!" she cheered, getting ready to let fly as Bob's voice was replaced by the swell of the music.

"Dah-na-na-na, na-na-na-na," she mumbled as she twisted and shimmied, then awkwardly attempted to do a half-split on the floor. "Oh!" she yelped, when her barely covered butt hit the area rug with a solid thump and she had to half scoot and half crawl her way out of her maneuver.

Back on her feet, Pat shook it off and glanced at the sofa with a smile. *Oh yeah, you know it,* she thought, with a large cheesy grin. *If Tom could do it...*

She took a deep breath and while the guitars wailed and the crowd cheered, Pat launched herself joyously backward toward the cushions. She almost made it. Almost.

"Auggg!" she blurted, when her tailbone hit the sofa frame instead of the pillows and she flopped like a rag doll, half on and half off the furniture. She should have thought it out more, or had less to drink. Or, maybe more to drink. Who could tell?

Pat let her body go limp and oozed down the front of the sofa onto the rug. And, as the last cords of the song faded away to be replaced by silence, she reached for her glass and sighed.

"Cheers," she said, lifting her drink in a salute. For better or worse, life was turning a corner.

***

CHAPTER TWO

Main Street was the antithesis of hustling and bustling. Granted it was still early, a good half hour before most of the shopkeepers would open their doors, and for that Pat was grateful. She was on a quest for coffee - hot, strong coffee that she could stand a spoon in - and trying to negotiate through a steady stream of shoppers, while walking with a limp from the huge bruise that decorated her tailbone like a tramp stamp gone terribly wrong, sounded like more than she could bear.

Hidden under a baggy, beige jacket and peering from behind oversized sunglasses that both disguised and protected her bloodshot blue eyes from the early morning glare, Pat silently cursed herself for not parking closer to her destination.

"Not your brightest shining hour, Pat," she muttered under her breath, then caught herself before she spoke any further.

God, it was happening. She'd become so used to talking out loud to herself when she was in the house alone, she'd lost her social filter for when she walked out her front door. What was next? Accosting shelf stockers in the supermarket?

Wincing her way past the real estate office, Pat hesitated. It had been so long since she'd done it... *Ah, well, they say old habits die hard*, she thought, wryly, before leaning forward to squint at the bright orange piece of paper plastered onto the other side of the shiny glass; displaying the newest properties available on the market.

She and her ex-husband, in what felt like another lifetime, used to peruse the listings every weekend when they brought the kids out for some fresh air and ice cream. It had become an almost family ritual, to search for that one-of-a-kind find that might have the potential to shake up their safe world.

"Pah!" Pat exhaled sharply in defiance of the memories. Clearly, she hadn't needed a house to shake things up. Stephen, in his Houdini inspired, disappearing husband act, had done that all by himself.

Damn it, Pat thought, annoyed at herself for wasting any more thoughts on such an outdated subject. He'd left, eighteen months had passed, enough already. She stuffed her hands into her pockets and began to turn away, only to hesitant again when one listing on the bright paper seemed to jump out at her from the page.

"What's this?" she muttered, quietly, unable to stop herself stepping closer to the glass for one last peek... And then nearly jump out of her shoes when a handsome face suddenly appeared to loom large on the other side.

"Geez!" Pat jerked and stumbled backward, pulling her hand from her pocket and slapping it on her jacket, above her heart. Gerry, the owner of both the looming face and real estate office, as well as her dear friend, beamed at her from behind the glass.

"Pat!" He waved enthusiastically, his friendly features lit up with good humor. "Come inside!" he shouted and gestured grandly for her to move toward the door.

Pat caught her breath and nodded; then limped slowly toward the entrance.

"Good morning, Sunshine!" Gerry pulled open the door, with the name *G&T Real Estate* etched on the glass, with a flourish and stepped aside to let her pass.

Pat flinched at the volume of his voice as she crossed the threshold, doing her best to disguise her limp. "Maybe so, but you nearly made me jump out of my shoes there."

Gerry giggled and closed the door against the cool air. "Sorry," he said, his voice laced with affection. "But, I was just so surprised to see you out there so early! What are you doing up and out at this time of the morning, on a Saturday no less?"

Before Pat could come up with an answer he frowned, took a step back, swept his eyes over the disarray of her petite frame in her baggy jacket, faded jeans and scuffed sneakers, then weakly attempted to suppress a gasp. "Sweetie! What in Heaven's name?"

Pat sighed and slowly pulled her dark glasses from her face. "Let's just say," she began, then had to wait a beat when Gerry gave a tiny shriek after getting a look at her bloodshot eyes. "My business isn't nearly as *risky* as it once was."

"I don't know *what* that's supposed to mean," he said, rapidly pulling out a chocolate colored, leather-bound, padded chair that sat aside his desk. "But, I think you should take a load off before you tell me."

Pat snickered at his theatrics and nodded. "Probably a wise plan," she said in acknowledgement and began her wince-every-second-step walk over to the waiting chair.

Gerry plastered one of his large hands across his heart while he watched her ease herself gently into the seat. "Good lord, Girl! What the hell *happened* to you?"

"Do you have any coffee?"

"Of course!" He strode swiftly across the sage green carpet to a small, impeccably kept Mahogany kitchenette at the rear of his office. "The usual? Or, maybe some sugar today?" he asked, over his shoulder, as he retrieved a stainless steel carafe from the brown granite countertop.

"The usual, please," Pat replied and unzipped her jacket. Man she was tired. She leaned back into the chair with a sigh and closed her eyes. It felt good to be pampered for a moment.

"Okay, Missy," Gerry said, his voice firm as he placed a large teal mug on a Dachshund printed coaster in front of her. "Spill."

Pat straightened up and grinned. "Thank you," she said, reaching for the cup and bringing it to her lips for a long sip. "Ahhh, that's the stuff."

Gerry was nearly vibrating as he sat down in the chair behind his large desk. "You're killing me? You know that, right?"

Pat let out a bark of laughter and set her mug back on the coaster. "Sorry, I'm just so bagged." She smoothed her bangs from her forehead and added, wryly, "As though *that's* not blatantly evident."

"What on Earth happened?"

Pat cleared her throat and flashed another smile at him. He was such a peach of a friend. "Nothing that will make the papers, I assure you." She rolled her head back and forth on her neck. "*You* look fabulous, by the way."

Gerry narrowed his eyes at her. He knew what she was doing. "Don't even try it, Missy," he began.

"But, you do!" Pat pointed at him. "Look at you!"

He was the perfect complement to his chic office - tall and broad shouldered, not one short brown hair out of place; clad in an exquisitely cut pairs of tan trousers and a striped dress shirt; finished off with funky red and purple dress shoes that shone so perfectly they looked brand new. The man was styling.

"Thank you," he said, with a slight inclination of his head. "But, I meant it. Spill."

"Okay, but I'm keeping it brief."

Gerry leaned forward, all ears.

"It was Crystal's last day at home yesterday—"

"Oh-my-God!" Gerry interrupted, his forehead creasing with distress. "How could I forget that! I'm a terrible friend!"

"Oh, don't even." Pat waved her hand dismissively at him. "Let me finish."

Gerry gave her pained look, but pressed his lips together and nodded.

"So, anyway." Pat hesitated and adjusted her unkempt ponytail, unsure of just how much detail she wanted to share. "I decided to have a bit of a celebration of my new freedom, as it were, and ended up having a few too many cocktails."

"*You?*" Gerry blinked, his face a picture of surprise. "Were you with Melanie?"

"Yes, *me*," Pat acknowledged. "And, no, I was by myself..."

She held up her hand before he could moan again about what a crappy friend he was. "By choice. Melanie offered, but I wanted to be on my own. Anyway, it turns out drinking multiple strong cocktails is a large mistake when you're forty five and you don't recover with the same speed as when you were twenty five. Trust me on this one, don't go finding out for yourself."

Gerry looked put out when she stopped talking. "That's it? Seriously? You go on a bender, which you've never done in all the days I've known you. Then, come limping in here looking like my Uncle Bo when he was thrown from his horse, and that's all you're going to tell? Because I know there's more."

Pat leaned forward for her coffee, grimaced from the movement and took a sip from her cup. "For now, yes, that's all I've got."

"Paaah!" Gerry exhaled in disgust.

"Too bad," Pat told him as she tried and failed to cover up a large yawn. "When I'm feeling less *thrown from the horse*, maybe I'll be more forthcoming with details. Until then, forget about me; there are details I want from you."

"Me?" Gerry's eyebrows shot up on his forehead.

"Uh-huh." Pat turned to point at the florescent paper on the front window.

"Oh, *that*." Gerry smirked. "I know the color is hideous, but it really does grab people's attention. I try to angle myself so I don't see it when I'm working."

"No, not the paper. Although, yes, I'll give it to you, it does grab a person's attention. I'm talking about one of the properties on it."

"Oh?" His face screwed up in puzzlement. "Really? Which one?"

"The used bookstore. Is it still active?"

"Absolutely. The listing's brand new, in fact. John's decided to sell up. And, from what I hear, folks around here are pretty upset about it."

Pat bit her lip and suppressed a grin when Gerry said, 'folks'. For all of his sophistication, he still had his country boy's heart. "Well, they may not need to be upset for long."

Gerry cocked his head. "I don't follow. Do you know someone who'd be interested in it?"

"Uh-huh. I want to see it."

"Go ahead." He sipped his coffee, not following her train of thought. "He should be open by now."

"No." Pat shook her head and winced at the sudden movement. "I mean, I'm interested in *seeing* it. As in, to possibly purchase it."

"Excuse me?" Gerry looked at her in wide-eyed amazement. "Are you serious? Where's this coming from? First the kids leave, then the slippery slope into secret drunken episodes, and now this? What's gotten into you?"

Pat rolled her eyes. "Oh, stop. There's no *secret drunken episodes*. It was a one-off. I'm sorry I even told you about it."

"Oh, there it is." Gerry teased. "The defensiveness about the *episodes*..."

Pat laughed and pointed a stern finger while she said, "Moving on."

"Fine. Secrets aside, I'm reeling here with all this new information. I have to tell you, I have absolutely no memory of you expressing a passionate interest in used books."

"That's because I never have. And, it's not the used books I'm interested in, Ger. It's the business. The potential. The possibility."

"But, really?" He peered at her across the desk as though trying to see into her thoughts. "A bookstore? It's a huge amount of work. Not that I don't think you can make a go of it. I do."

Pat sighed and smoothed back the hair that had fallen into her eyes from her ponytail. "The facts are, I'm at a loose end. The kids are grown now, it's been over a year since Stephen and I split and, like it or not, it's time for me to start creating a new life. I'm only forty five, for crying out loud. It's time I got back in the game, wouldn't you say?"

Gerry nodded and his face broke into a huge smile. "Yes, I'd definitely say. As a matter-of-fact, Travis was just telling me the other day that he met the nicest guy and thought he would be perfect for you—"

"Whoa, whoa." Pat held up her hand to stop him in his verbal tracks.

Travis was Gerry's partner, both in business as the 'T' in *G&T Real Estate,* and in their personal life. They'd met at a dog show, their mutual love for wire-haired Dachshunds giving them all the opener they'd needed to begin chatting. Four years later, the pair were thick as thieves and breeding the spirited small dogs; presenting them at shows and having great fun in the process.

"Tell Travis that while I appreciate him thinking of me, he can cool his jets in that department. I'm looking at getting a life, not baggage."

"But, you just *said*—"

"Yes, I *know* I said it's time to get back in the game," Pat finished for him. "But, what I meant was the game of getting a life of my own. Not attaching myself to some man."

Gerry knew when he was beat. When Pat dug her heels in, forget it. "Okay, fine," he said, holding his hands up in surrender. "Moving on. Let's get over to that bookstore."

Pat straightened up, her face transforming from closed off, to eager. "Right. And, before I forget, after we see the shop I want to talk to you about my house."

Gerry did an exaggerated double-take. "Meaning?"

"Meaning, I've been giving it some thought and I really think it might be time to consider putting it on the market."

"Whoa." He held the edge of the desk for support. "Okay, that's another big one. You've always lived there, ever since you moved into town."

"I know." Pat nodded, shifted in her chair and winced when the bruise on her tailbone complained. "But, I knew once Crystal left it would feel absurdly huge and believe you me, was I right. I've only had one day fully on my own and already I feel like a tumbleweed blowing along the hallways and through the rooms."

Gerry giggled at her description. "So, do you have any sort of timeline in mind?"

"I'm not exactly sure, yet." Pat shrugged her shoulders. "But, I wanted to mention it because, *obviously*, I'd be with you to do it."

Gerry pressed his fingers to his lips and looked genuinely touched. "That means a lot."

"Oh, please." Pat grinned, transforming her entire face from worn down, to alive and perky. "Who else would I go to? If it wasn't you, Travis would hunt me down and let all of your dogs poop in my yard. Repeatedly."

Gerry threw his head back and laughed. "You've got a point."

"And, with that said." Pat cleared her throat and pulled herself up and out of the chair with a small groan. "I want to see that shop."

"Let's do it." Gerry pushed out his chair, stood up and walked around his desk. He was thrilled to see such enthusiasm from his dear friend. She'd been through so much in the past year and a half he was all about encouraging her, even if it took her into areas he'd never imagined she would go. But, he was philosophical. Wasn't that what life was all about? Stepping past your self-imposed boundaries?

"No time like the present," he added, grabbing his sport coat from the back of his chair and crossing the office to hold open the street door.

Pat had to stop herself from bouncing on the spot and clapping her hands like an excited child. She thrust her sunglasses back on her face and breezed by Gerry as fast as her aching backside would let her. She looked so raring to go, he couldn't help but chuckle as he pulled on his jacket and followed her out into the sunshine.

***

"Guess what I did today?" Pat singsonged into the telephone headset clasped firmly to her ear. She was moving around her white, country-styled kitchen, much as she always did at dinner time; the one glaring exception being she was cooking for one, instead of a family of four.

"Hello to you, too." Melanie volleyed back on the other end of the connection.

"Sorry," Pat apologized, while she opened the large doors of her side-by-side, stainless steel refrigerator; a model Stephen had brought into the house claiming it would revolutionize the kitchen. She retrieved fresh angel hair pasta from a shelf and closed the fridge door with a solid thud. "I'm just so excited, I wanted to share. How are *you*? How was your day?"

Melanie grinned at the unexpected energy in Pat's voice. After so many tactics to elicit even a smidgen of verve from her best friend, she was keenly interested to hear what had warranted such unbridled gusto.

"My day has been fine, thank you," she replied, laughing. "But, I was teasing! Go on, you've got me all curious. Tell me your exciting news!"

Pat dropped her pasta into a pot of water boiling on the stove and began to pace, albeit slowly due to her bruise, around the kitchen island. "I've bought something! Or, at least started the paperwork on buying something. Something big!"

"A car?"

"Nope!" Pat stopped pacing to pull out a bright yellow strainer from a kitchen drawer. "Not a car, but still something that will change where I am for a substantial part of my day."

"A camper van?" Melanie tried again, thoroughly enjoying her guesses. "To take you to new and exciting locations? That would change where you were during the daytime. I'll come along, if you invite me."

Pat laughed. The very idea of her in a camper van, it was too much. She loved nature; however, she preferred experiencing it from well-worn foot paths and patios.

"Oh yeah," she said, between giggles. "That's going to happen. Seriously, can you imagine?"

Melanie joined her in her giggles, it was pretty hysterical. "Okay, I give up," she said. "What's the big purchase?"

"A business!"

"Pardon me?" Melanie asked, confused. She glanced at her half full glass of wine on her kitchen table and wondered if she'd already had too much. "What does that mean, a business?"

"It means, I now can say *my business* and mean it."

"I still don't understand."

"You know the used bookstore in town?"

"Uh-huh." Melanie took a hefty sip of her wine. If she'd already had too much, what was a little more?

"I bought it!" Pat placed her strainer into her sink, poured in her pasta from the pot to drain and then did a small shuffling dance; her soft, red flannel pajama pants brushing along the tile floor as she moved.

"You bought it? Seriously? Get out!" Melanie squealed as the reality of what Pat told her finally sunk in. She stood up from her kitchen chair and also did a little dance on the spot. "Pat, do you realize what this means? You're a business *owner*! The boss lady!"

Pat laughed, delighted she'd so easily jumped on board. Not that she was overly surprised, Melanie was always willing to jump in with both feet without hesitation. That was how she'd met her, in fact.

Pat had been in town with her kids - towheaded Michael, aged six, and little Crystal of the long auburn tendrils, aged four - and had decided to take them to the ice cream shop for a treat.

Everything had been ticking along fine, until Michael had assumed a very serious expression and firmly stated he was too old for ice cream treats. Pat had stared at him, flummoxed. Her son was always surprising her, but what child - especially a six year old child - was too old for ice cream?

Thank goodness Melanie had been in the shop that day. Dressed in a bold, green and blue print dress that accentuated her Mediterranean curves, her chestnut colored hair piled messily on her head and her generous lips painted a deep red... She was a perfect example of a Greek Goddess if Pat had ever seen one.

Standing next to Melanie was her three year old daughter, Gina, a gorgeous mini version of her mother. The little girl was on her tip-toes, peering excitedly over the edge of the case that held the multiple containers of ice cream, choosing her favorite flavors.

Melanie had overheard the conversation going on between Pat and Michael, had listened to Pat trying to soften Michael's stance - because she knew, as any Mother did, if he didn't get an ice cream he would bitch and moan about it later - and without introduction, or hesitation, had jumped on board to help her out.

"Do you know what I love about ice cream?" Melanie had turned to address them, a huge grin on her strong, beautiful face.

Michael's blue eyes had grown wide as he stared at her, startled that the strange and vibrant woman - the exact opposite of his petite and rather staid mother -

was looking directly at him and waiting for a response to her question.

"What?" he'd replied, finally, when it was glaringly apparent she was willing to wait as long as it took for his feedback.

"It falls into the *any-age-zone*." Melanie had informed him with a knowing nod. "Do you know what that means?"

Michael shook his head, no.

"It means that while some things - hell most things - aren't that way, ice cream has managed to stay age free."

Michael had goggled at Melanie when she'd said 'hell' and Pat had to bite her cheek to keep from laughing at his mouth-gaping amazement.

"I'm telling you." Melanie had driven her point home as she wagged her finger in the air between them. "There are so many things that are deemed too young, or too old, bah!"

Michael had jumped a little at her vehement exhale of disgust.

"But, not ice cream. Right, Gina?" She'd turned to her daughter for back up and Gina had nodded happily. "That's correct, my smart girl. Ice cream falls into the any-age-zone. Young, middle or old, ice cream is the Switzerland of treats!"

Michael had mimicked Gina and began nodding enthusiastically, a reformed child. He'd then turned to his mother, suddenly ready to make his decision about which flavor he favored. Pat had had to repress the strong urge to grab Melanie in a hug of gratitude.

Melanie, on the other hand, had just grinned, winked one sparkly intelligent eye and given Pat her business card - with the insistent instructions to call her sometime when she had a free moment. It had been instant friendship.

"A shop keeper! A proprietor! A proprietress!" Melanie now sang, delightedly, making Pat laugh out loud. "Woo-hoo! I'm dancing around my kitchen!"

"I know, it's crazy!" Pat enthused as she shuffled back over to her strainer to scoop the long, thin pasta noodles into a bowl and lash on butter, freshly grated parmesan cheese and spices. For the first time in a long time, she felt hungry.

"So tell me," Melanie egged, once she'd caught her breath. "What on Earth prompted this sudden jump into the world of self-employment?" She had a strong hunch it was tied to Pat's last child leaving, but she wanted to let her tell it. Let her feel it. Let her own it.

"I think it was a combination of things," Pat said, forking up noodles and slurping them into her mouth.

"It always is," Melanie replied, philosophically.

"Sorry, I'm chewing in your ear," Pat added, between swallows.

"No worries," Melanie said. "Go on."

"The first thing, obviously, was Crystal finally moving out. Not that I wanted her to leave..."

"No, no," Melanie said. "I get it. You knew it was coming, but didn't have to fully face it until yesterday."

"Exactly." Pat placed her bowl on the kitchen island and eased herself gingerly onto one of the adjacent pub stools. "So, after spending the night here by myself, and being fully hit in the face this morning by the fact that no one was going to be coming in to break the silence... Well, let's just say that it really thrust my life - what little of it there still is - into glaring relief."

"What little of it there is?"

"Well, yeah. I'm single with no prospects, not that I want any. And, let's face it, it's not like I have multiple engagements piling up to take me out of this house." Pat started gesturing with her fork at the large, vacuous kitchen. "This overwhelming, echoing, not a creature is stirring large house—"

"Which you've made into a beautiful and inviting home."

And, she had. Melanie's admiration bordered upon hero worship in regards to how Pat had decorated her straight-forward, barn-style house; taking an ordinary structure and transforming it into a warm and welcoming oasis for whoever crossed the threshold.

"Okay, well, thank you for that," Pat acknowledged, while gazing at her warm, butter-yellow kitchen. Yes, with the crisp white cabinetry and dark granite, it was as beautiful to the eye as when she'd first designed it, but...

"But, even so," Pat elaborated. "Being here all alone, with the quiet so loud it's started to become deafening, I've realized that all of this invitation is lost on just me. I feel like I was hit - like I'd had a blow to the chest - with the thought, *what now?*"

She set her fork down next to her pasta bowl. "Am I making any sense?"

"Yes, perfect sense," Melanie assured her.

And, she was. Melanie had sat on the sidelines, watching things unfold in Pat's life, and had felt utterly helpless to do anything as she'd weathered blow after blow in a span of just two years.

First there was Michael, Pat's first born, going off to school and no longer needed his Mother as he once did.

Then, before Pat had had a chance to catch her breath and recover from that blow, Shitty Stephen - as Melanie privately called him - had upped and delivered his news. His cowardly, selfish news that he needed to discover who he was and what he wanted from the rest of his life and oh, by the way, not with the wife that had taken care of him and given him a life for twenty years. Melanie exhaled sharply in disgust at the memory. Prick.

And, finally, just as she'd been encouraging and coaxing Pat back onto her feet, trying to convince her that there was something worth getting up off of the proverbial mat for, her beloved dog had decided it was his time to retire from the planet. Little Puck, Pat's constant shadow... Good God, it had all been too much.

"Am I really?" Pat interrupted Melanie's dive into the past. "I don't sound like some whiny baby, some desperate middle aged woman looking for a purpose to fill in time until she has grandchildren, or dies? Whichever one comes first."

"Jeez! No!" Melanie frowned and wished she was at Pat's house to smack her across the shoulder.

"Wow. Good thing you're not here," Pat said, a smirk on her face that Melanie couldn't see. "That *no* sounded like a shoulder slapper."

"Damn rights!" Melanie replied, vehemently. "And, I don't want to hear you saying such foolish words again. *Desperate middle aged woman*, please! Do you have any idea of how many women I know who only wished they looked so *desperately middle aged*? There's too many, I can't even count."

"Fine, fine," Pat said, still grinning as she picked up her fork. "Consider me slapped. I take it back."

"Good. Because I'm going to be your cheering section, Patricia," Melanie stated, firmly. "You've had too many days stuck in your baggy pjs and way too much moping. It's time for you to take your daughter's example and spread your own wings. See how far you can fly."

Tears welled up in Pat's eyes and she paused, her fork in mid-air between her bowl of pasta and her mouth. Melanie had said the very thing that she'd been feeling, when she had signed the contracts for the bookstore. That she was getting a turn to step out of the nest.

"You're the best, do you know that?" Pat sniffled, dropping the fork back into her bowl.

"Tell me that again when you're asking me to stack bookshelves and I want to sit on my backside and paint my nails."

Pat grinned and blotted her eyes with her pajama sleeve. "Grunt work aside, I do think this thing is all about timing. And, it's time for me to have something that's just mine."

Melanie's eyes sparkled as she listened. She couldn't have said it better. "Amen," she agreed, taking a large swallow of her wine. "And, I have a strong hunch my beautiful and generous sister-friend, it's all going to be fabulous."

"Me too," Pat agreed as excitement rose up from her toes and darted right through her entire body. "I think so, too. A fresh beginning."

"A fresh beginning *and* an opportunity for a whole lot of fun," Melanie added.

"Thanks, Mel."

"You're welcome."

***

CHAPTER THREE

"Achoo!" Pat's sneeze echoed, bouncing off of the bare, wood plank floors of the bookstore. She was attempting to dust, but it was slow going.

There was a whole lot of cleaning that had been neglected while under the wing of the previous owner, and she was starting to believe she was going to have to bring boxes and boxes of tissues in with her while trying to bring the shop back to its former, shiny glory.

"Bless you," Melanie called out as she pushed open the shop's door, making the tiny bell hanging above it ring merrily.

Pat spun on her heel, feather dusted held aloft. "Thank you! So, what do you think of the sign?"

"Love it!" Melanie enthused. "It catches your eye immediately."

Pat was pleased. She had chosen to rename the shop from *Main Street Used Books*, to *Possibilities* and had second guessed herself over and over until she'd forced herself to trust her instincts.

"You're absolutely sure? You don't think it's too—"

"No," Melanie said, firmly, cutting her off mid-sentence. "I don't think it's *too* anything. It's perfectly whimsical, yet practical. A name that will make people smile and remember your store."

Pat grinned. "Music to my ears," she said as she gave another swipe to the shelf she'd been dusting.

"You know," Melanie offered, while letting her eyes traverse the bookstore's space. "You really landed on your feet here."

"I know!" Pat enthused. "I've been thinking the same thing."

She followed Melanie's lead and admired her new shop. The huge bay window allowed for lots of natural light; highlighting the gorgeous solid oak shelves that lined the walls. The left side of the large, open room was home to a hulking desk that served as the checkout area - Pat had fallen in love with the desk the first time she'd laid eyes on it. It felt solid and sturdy, one of the few things that did in her life. And, finally, there was a narrow staircase at the back that led to the second floor - a slightly smaller area that Pat planned to remodel to allow her to sell all sorts of funky local wares, maybe the occasional coffee. All in all, it was like a little bit of Heaven in the dull landscape of her life. An oasis calling her back into the world of the living.

"You do need to add some comfy furniture and product of course," Melanie added, matter-of-factly. "You have catalogues, right? Because I've got lots of great places that I used for my store that I've kept, if you want them."

Pat nodded, then frowned when she noticed Melanie's awkward posture. She was standing with one hand on her hip, stretching out the black wrap she was wearing over a cream colored blouse, flouncy sky blue skirt and knee high burgundy boots. It was pathetically obvious she was attempting to hide something she was holding behind her back.

Pat pointed at her. "Whatchya got there?"

"Hmm?"

Pat walked over to the front desk and pointed again at Melanie's awkwardly angled arm. "You clearly have something behind you back, Mel. What's going on?"

"What? Oh, *this*?" Melanie's voice rose an octave, something it always did when she was hoping to avoid trouble, and Pat narrowed her eyes suspiciously.

"*Melanie.*" She cocked her head and placed her hands on her hips. "What. Is. Going. On?"

Melanie began to fidget and then her shoulders slumped. "Fine." She sighed and relaxed her rigid shoulders, giving up. "It was my intention to sell this with more finesse, but you've forced my hand."

She released her hold on her wrap and carefully pulled a small animal carrier from behind her back. Pat's eyes widened in surprise. "Now, listen," she said, immediately trying to placate. "Before you say anything—"

"No." Pat folded her arms tightly across her chest and shook her head.

"Hear me out," Melanie wheedled.

Pat's face grew rigid. "Seriously, whatever, or *whomever*, you've got in there. No."

"Okay, fine." Melanie relented and her face drooped. "But, it really is a tragic situation."

"Uh-huh." Pat's mouth had become a tense line on her face.

Melanie lifted the carrier up onto the granite topped desk and carefully unlatched and opened the wire door. "Poor little guy, he has nowhere else to go, but the shelter," she added, while reaching into the carrier's depths.

In the next instant, she pulled out one of the most adorable kittens Pat was sure she'd ever laid eyes on.

"Oh!" Pat exhaled, before she could help herself. He was just a little thing cradled in Melanie's hand, ginger colored - her favorite - with smoky grey eyes that blinked lazily at her as he yawned to reveal perfect, tiny white teeth.

"Do you want to hold him?" Melanie affected her best imploringly face and extended the small bundle of fur toward Pat.

Did she want to hold him? Well, of course she did! Pat had to restrain her hands from moving of their own volition toward the soft animal. "No," she said, unfolding her arms and smoothing the front of her dusty, purple shirt. "It's probably not a good idea."

Melanie continued to hold the kitten aloft, the light catching the shine off of his baby soft fur and Pat sighed. "Oh, hell," she muttered, quickly checking to make sure her hands were clean before extending them. "Go on then."

Melanie smiled, her whole face lit up, and she placed the warm kitten into Pat's embrace. Jackpot!

Pat could physically feel the slowing down of her breath as she accepted the butter soft feline into her grasp. He, too, seemed to sense the change in energy and immediately began to purr in appreciation of the loving hands that held him.

"Isn't he a peach?" Melanie asked, so pleased at the relaxed look that had taken over Pat's face she was hard pressed not to yip with glee. She hadn't seen that sort of ease from her friend in longer than she could remember.

"He really is," Pat agreed, contentedly, while she cuddled and stroked the kitten's fur. "He feels like cashmere and he's the color of a fine whiskey, wouldn't you say?"

"Ooh, I love that! It's a great name for him!" Melanie nodded her head in approval, making her silver earrings sway and sparkle in the overhead lights. "Whiskey. Perfect."

Pat closed her eyes and inwardly groaned. Great, now she'd gone and inadvertently named him. And, she knew how it went, once you've named it...

"Yes." She opened her eyes and sighed, resigned. "It suits him perfectly."

"Does that mean—?" Melanie hedged, not absolutely sure, but very hopeful.

"Yes, you terrible brat." Pat tried to look stern, but her pleasure at the arrival of such a lovely animal was really making it difficult. It had been so long since she'd cuddled any soft, four-legged creature, she hadn't realized how much she'd missed it until that very moment. "Of course I'll keep him."

"Yay!"

"However," Pat added, above Melanie's cheers. "I don't know how I'm going to do it, Mel. Where will he be when I'm here? I can't leave him by himself all day long." She gestured to the shop around them. "And, in case you haven't noticed, I still have a bit to do yet before I can open my doors to the public."

"Oh, that's nothing." Melanie waved her hand dismissively. "It's your shop and he's a cat, for goodness sake. He can come here with you every day and he'll adapt in an instant to the routine. In fact, he'll probably love trailing you around the place, hiding in the nooks and crannies. He'll get two territories, bookstore in the daytime and home at night. What cat could ask for more?"

Pat nodded as she watched the newly christened 'Whiskey' stretch and yawn before snuggling warmly against her torso for a nap. "He certainly seems easy going," she offered, already enchanted.

"He's like his mother. She's owned by one of my customers and one of the most even tempered cats I've ever met. I'm sure he'll be a treat to have around the place."

Pat placed Whiskey gently back into his carrier and without so much as a flicker of an eyelid, he sighed, curled up comfortably and began to purr gently in his sleep.

If only I could do the same, she thought, when a shiver that held notes of both excitement and nervousness traveled up her spine. First the new shop, now a new cat... She didn't dare ask what was next.

***

"You *what?*" Crystal's voice nearly blasted Pat's ear from of her head.

"Crystal, please!" Pat insisted, while frantically scrambling to turn down the volume on her headset. "More talking, less yelling."

"Well, I'm *sorry* Mother, but it's been three weeks, *three*, since I moved out. And, I figured that when I emailed to see how you were coping, I would read yes, you were COPING - not that you'd completely lost your mind!"

Pat winced and took a deep cleansing breath. She shifted her attention to Whiskey, watching him happily weave his way systematically through the legs of her kitchen chairs. Melanie had said his even temperament was just like his Mother's and, already, he was proving himself a treat to have around. That being said, she sincerely hoped such reflections of disposition only applied to animals and not people. Otherwise, what would Crystal's hysterics say about her as a parent?

"Hello? Are you even listening to me, Mother?" Crystal's voice held more than a smattering of indignation. "Or, in the space of three weeks since I left has that changed, too?"

Ah, the real truth, Pat thought, stifling a yawn. Her lovely daughter, all long legs and soft auburn hair, hated change. It did something strange to her; unnerved her in a manner that went further than just being unsettled. Always had. She was getting a better handle on it with age, but still, when push came to shove, Crystal resisted change like oil does water.

"Crystal, my lovely girl," Pat soothed as she pushed her bangs from her forehead. "I'm listening to every word you're saying and you don't need to worry one bit. I know exactly what I'm doing. Well, maybe not *exactly*, but—"

"You see!" Crystal was quick to interject. "You just admitted it, you *don't* know!"

"I was *going* to say," Pat said, firmly, while reaching into her fridge for a pitcher of orange juice. "I may not know every little thing about running a business - who really can. But, I have the guidance of good friends, fellow business owners like Melanie and Gerry, who are doing everything they can to help me as I find my footing in this new endeavor."

"*Gerry.*" Crystal practically spat the man's name. "This is his doing, isn't it?"

"Why are you attacking Gerry?" Pat asked, surprised. "You love Gerry."

"That's beside the point. I'm *attacking* him, as you put it, because I suspect he saw you looking at the listings page - which by the way I cannot believe you still do - and wanted to unload the bookstore—"

"Crystal." Pat stopped in her tracks, her voice developing a sharp, warning edge.

"Probably for a heavy commission, too." Crystal pressed, ignoring her Mother's tone. "And, he took one look at you, figured you needed a hobby and blamo! Welcome to self-employment!"

"Stop right there, young lady." Pat put the juice jug on the countertop and opened a cupboard for a glass.

"I mean, what's the trouble? Huh? Are he and Travis not selling enough dogs? Is that next, Mother? You're going to be purchasing a wire-haired Daschund?"

"That's enough!" Pat snapped, her hand clenching her glass so hard she had a half thought of worry she might break it. "I told you it was all my idea and I meant it. Although, I must admit I'm now having serious regrets that I told you at all. Foolishly, I thought you'd support me."

"Foolishly?" Crystal balked.

"As for Gerry," Pat continued, filling her glass with juice. "Don't you dare fault him. He's been nothing but a wonderful friend who's believed in my dream."

"But, *why?*" Crystal's confrontational tone melted into a whiny puddle. "Why do you have to do this at all? Why are you looking at listings at all? Is it because of Daddy? Did he rip you off in the divorce?"

Oh, Lord. Pat rolled her eyes. Why did it always have to go back to *Daddy*? It had been six months for goodness sake since their divorce had been finalized and while it had been a rocky road to travel to get where she was, it was time to drop that song from the catalogue.

Pat cleared her throat. "First of all, I'm only saying it one more time; I wasn't cajoled into anything. I always check the listings, which clearly you know because you just ridiculed it, and this time I finally found something."

"I did not ridicule," Crystal said, petulantly. "I was just saying that I was surprised you still did it, is all."

"Uh-huh. Well, whatever the case, it doesn't matter. What does matter is that life happens," Pat told her, matter-of-factly, and took a swig from her glass. "And, in regards to your comments about Daddy, no, this has absolutely nothing to do with him; nor the divorce; or money for that matter."

Pat sipped her juice and let the silence settle. She knew she wasn't being entirely truthful; Stephen's leaving did contribute in an indirect manner to her having to make decisions about the direction of the rest of her life. However, she also understood there was no way on Earth she would ever be able to easily explain that truth, not to mention convey the thought processes of a forty-five year old woman on the precipice of the unknown, to her fresh-faced, eighteen year old daughter. That was a whole other ball of yarn. Good luck.

"Then, what is it?" Crystal asked, insistently. "I just don't get how you would take this giant leap, this giant and risky-as-all-hell-leap, with so little thought."

Pat walked over to her kitchen table and sat down. "It wasn't as little thought as you might think."

"Well, it looks that way from where I'm sitting!"

Pat stretched her neck; then reached down to stroke her hand along Whiskey's back. They could go on like that all night. "So stand up," she said, sarcastically.

"Excuse me?"

Pat bit her lip and reined it in. "I'm just trying to say, regardless of how it may look to you, you're more than half my age. And, believe it or not, when you get to where I'm at you might discover that some decisions don't need nearly as much back and forth consideration as others. They just make sense, so you do it."

"What about your gardening and running and house projects?"

Pat rubbed her eyes. Crystal was stretching. Stretching to place her back into the comfortable box labeled "Mom" and close a reassuring lid on it until she made it home for a visit; where everything was the same, exactly as she left it, nothing changed.

"What about them?" Pat threw back, curious as to how her daughter would reply.

"How can you possibly keep doing those things, those things that you love, if you're tied up working yourself ragged in some bookstore in town?"

Pat smirked and shook her head. That 'some bookstore' was the same one Crystal had loved to visit all through her childhood.

"You know," Pat countered, choosing another path. She had no interest in defending her casual participation in her hobbies and definitely no desire to address her daughter's usage of the word 'ragged'. "I sort of had the thought that you might be pleased by all of this."

"*Pleased?*" Crystal asked, her tone incredulous. "You can't be serious. Why would you think I'd be pleased by you shifting everything around, without so much as a thought to anyone else?"

"Yes, *pleased*," Pat reiterated, ignoring the blatant barb and sticking with her theme. "I have so many happy memories of the two of us poking through the shelves of that place and then having to bribe you with the promise of ice cream to keep you from staying all day, tucked between the bookcases."

"So?" Crystal replied, warily. "I was a kid and I liked reading."

"Yes, but now you get to have it in the family. No more having to be lured away. I thought that would bring you some pleasure."

"Well..." Crystal faltered at the image her mother had created and Pat relaxed into her seat and took a long swallow of her juice. It would take time, but her daughter would come around. So much so, Pat was confident she would probably not just embrace the place, but want a summer job there.

Whiskey, still beneath Pat's chair, had had enough of playing between the wooden legs of the furniture and effortlessly jumped up into her lap. He gently kneaded her red fleece pants and settled himself into a purring ball for a nap.

"It's early days, Crys," Pat said as she smiled affectionately at the kitten. He was, for the moment, her secret indulgence and she was completely impressed at the brilliant job he'd done of adapting to his new lifestyle. Better than she had. She could learn from him.

"Just give it some time and, like all things, it will eventually feel normal."

"Has it, yet?"

"What? Feel normal?" Pat queried, surprised by her daughter's thoughtful question.

"Yeah." Crystal nodded, even though her mother couldn't see her.

"No," Pat admitted, glad she'd asked. "Not even close."

"So, *why...*" Crystal began to recycle her previous theme.

"*Because.*" Pat cut in to stop her from traveling back down the same path. "Unless I start to create some new ways of normal, I'll be stuck in limbo; neither here, nor there. And, let me tell ya, that's more frightening than taking some steps in a new direction and seeing where they lead."

Pat yawned and ran a hand across Whiskey's soft fur. "Can you understand that, Honey? Even just a little bit?"

"Uh-huh." Crystal's voice was subdued and Pat hoped she was applying what she'd learned from her own recent life choices and changes, to what was being said.

"I do get it, Mom." She sighed. "I may not totally understand it from your point of view, but I get it. Does that make sense?"

Pat smiled. "Perfectly."

***

CHAPTER FOUR

"Shoo you." Pat lightly tapped Whiskey's backside with a pen, making him dance on his tiny feet and turn round, ready to play. She laughed out loud at his reaction. He was such a silly animal and a delight to have around both her house and shop.

"That's not what I meant," she told him, her voice laced with affection when he began batting enthusiastically at her pen with his paw.

She broke off when the shop door chimed and in with the cool, damp autumn air came Melanie; striding confidently on a pair of wickedly pointed, high heeled, brown leather boots.

"Well, aren't you two getting on like a house on fire," she commented, all smiles as she placed a tray holding two takeout coffees onto cash desk countertop.

"What can I say, he's a charmer." Pat shrugged while Melanie reached out to scratch Whiskey gently under his chin. "Truth be told, I almost can't remember what it was like without him around."

Melanie gave Pat a quick hug, her purple wrap seductively wafting her perfume into the air around them. "Good, I'm glad," she said. "You deserve some fast friends who have nothing but cheer to bring into your world."

"You look gorgeous, by the way," Pat offered, admiring Melanie's dark chocolate, figure hugging, knee length skirt and matching blazer beneath her wrap. Her chosen accents of gold and amber earrings, necklace and bracelets added just a touch of the exotic to the look.

"Thanks." Melanie held out one of the two takeout coffee containers. "Two creams, no sugar."

"Mmmm, smells good. Thanks." Pat took the coffee and didn't elaborate further on Melanie's outfit. The woman had natural style and no matter how many times she tried to insist upon it - citing herself as the most glaringly obvious example of the opposite - Melanie refused to believe such style wasn't natural to everyone. The woman spent less time putting herself together than most people did styling their hair. It was pointless to gush, she would just dismiss it.

"I finally spoke to Crystal last night," Pat said, instead, and blew on her coffee.

"Oh?" Melanie raised an eyebrow and leaned her hip up against the desk. "How's she doing?"

"Pretty good all things considered." Pat lifted Whiskey around his middle and set him on the floor. "Settling in."

"Oh, dear." Melanie grimaced. "You don't sound very convincing. What's up?"

"I told her about my latest venture." Pat extended a hand to gesture at the bookstore.

"Oh, right." Melanie nodded in understanding. "I take it she wasn't over-the-top, excited about your news?"

Pat chuckled. Melanie had known Crystal from when she was just a little girl. She knew the lay of the land. "No, not exactly what you'd call all a-twitter."

"And?"

"And, she more or less made the proclamation that I've lost my mind, go figure."

"Because you've become a bookstore owner?"

"It's not so much *what* I've done, but the fact that I've done it. I've dared to step out of the carefully crafted mold of Mom, without polling the masses for permission, and add a new hat to my repertoire."

Pat leaned her elbows on the desk, set her coffee down and sighed. "The good news is that I managed to talk her round at least a little bit, to deter her from feeling she had to come rushing home to sort me out."

Melanie let out a bark of laughter. "My God, what *is* it with children when they first get out into the world? Every damned one of them suddenly gets so full of their own belief in their abilities. Then, they take it one step further and think their new found knowledge renders their parents incompetent. Such a bloody cliché."

"I know." Pat shrugged her shoulders as Whiskey jumped back onto the desktop and curled into a ball, his nose covered by his tail. "But, to be fair, we were no different."

"True. At least not until we had kids and found out the startling truth about how much we *don't* know."

Melanie picked up her coffee container. "God, I swear, with each passing year I find out I know less."

Pat snickered. "Preaching to the choir, my friend."

Melanie took a sip of coffee and swallowed. "So, you're confident she'll come around?"

"Uh-huh. In time. One thing about Crystal, she might resist change with a vengeance, but once she realizes she has no choice in the matter she's pretty good at getting on board with the program."

Before Melanie could reply, the bell above the door rang out, followed by the singsong harmony of two exuberant voices. "Hello, hello!"

Pat raised an eyebrow as she and Melanie turned to see Gerry, accompanied by his partner, Travis; the two of them practically tripping over each other as they burst through the door into the shop.

"My goodness, it's getting cool out there!" Travis effused, before stopping dramatically in his tracks and spinning on his heel in a full circle. "Oh! I love it! Love it! Gerr-Bear, you didn't under-sell it one bit!"

"I know," Gerry agreed, beaming with pride as he purposefully crossed the room toward Melanie and Pat. "Girls, you look gorgeous as usual," he told them, before wrapping them each in a warm hug.

Pat hugged him back and squelched her desire to respond 'Pfft!' to his compliment. Standing beside Melanie, in an outfit comprised of black dress pants, pale blue tailored shirt and brown hair pulled into a sloppy ponytail, Pat was under no illusions about how gorgeous she *didn't* look.

Instead, when he released her from his clutches, she asked, "What brings you boys by?"

"Really? Do you need to ask?" Gerry placed a hand over his heart and pulled an exaggerated, put-out face.

"Do we need an excuse to explore the *possibilities* being offered by our new neighbor?"

Pat, against her better judgment, snickered under her breath at his performance and over obvious play on the shop name. She knew better, knew that it would only encourage him; however...

"Akk!" Travis blurted, aghast. He narrowed his green eyes at Pat. "Did you actually snicker at that feeble attempt at humor?"

Pat shrugged, apologetically.

"Because, you know it will only encourage him!"

"She laughed," Gerry said, turning a smug smile toward Travis. "Because I'm naturally funny."

Travis rolled his eyes dramatically and Pat held up her hands in surrender. "Sorry, I'm tired. I had a moment of weakness."

Melanie let out a low wolf whistle, effectively stopping them in their conversation tracks. "Talk about gorgeous," she stated, while gesturing at the two men. "Look at you two! You look like you've come from a photo shoot."

Thankfully, Gerry and Travis took the bait; their bickering instantly dismissed to bask in the compliment. Gerry, all tall and dark and impeccably groomed in perfectly tailored dress pants and a charcoal grey sweater, did not offer any sort of 'Pfft!' at the comment. Instead, he grinned cheekily and pretended to smooth an imaginary goatee.

Travis, standing slightly shorter than Gerry, his blonde hair mussed to perfection and beard shaved to showcase his killer cheek bones, cocked an eyebrow as he smoothed his hands down his lean swimmer's build; clad in designer jeans and a cobalt blue turtle neck.

Pat shook her head and envied them their confidence to take the flattery and accept it. Granted, she'd witnessed firsthand the stir they could create just by walking into a room and figured, if she had that effect on strangers, she'd probably accept compliments without hesitation, too.

"Oh!" Travis gasped and pointed sharply at Whiskey, still curled up on the desk. "The ornament moved!"

"He's not an ornament," Pat began.

Gerry chortled. "Clearly not! Trav, you kill me!"

Travis ignored Gerry's ribbing and sidled across the hardwood floor to the desk. He carefully reached out a hand to gently stroke Whiskey's soft fur and made a swooning face. "Ooh, he feels just like cashmere. Heaven. How did this little lover come into the picture?"

"He was a gift," Pat told him, her face softening as she gazed at Whiskey. "From Melanie."

Melanie shrugged and held her coffee cup out in a salute. "What can I say? Some people bring flowers to warm a new business, I bring kittens."

"He's gorgeous," Travis stated, having picked Whiskey up to cuddle into his arms.

Gerry watched, an indulgent look on his face. "Don't get any ideas," he warned.

"No, no," Travis assured him. "We have our puppy kids. I'll just enjoy..." He paused and lifted his eyebrows questioningly at Pat.

"Whiskey."

"*Whiskey*." Travis grinned, making him look even more delicious than he already was. "Of course. That's perfect. I'll enjoy Whiskey as a treat when we see Pat."

"Funny," Melanie piped up. "I enjoy whiskey as a treat, too."

Travis snorted under his breath and stroked the contented kitten. "Now you see?" He pretended he was conversing with Whiskey. "*That's* funny."

Gerry cut his eyes at Travis then turned his attention to the store. "So," he said, nodding his approval. "Looks like the place is coming together."

Gone from the walls was the original, dingy, pea green paint and in its place was a smooth even coat of fresh buttercream. The floors and bookshelves, once in desperate need of TLC, had been given a rich cherrywood stain. Their new contrast to the light walls was startling, each bringing out the most favorable elements of the other. The final touches of shiny, bronze-toned light fixtures, freshly cleaned windows and a brand new shingle with *Possibilities* emblazoned across it tied the whole place together.

"All I need now is furniture. And, new books. And, a coffee station. And, impulse merchandise. And..." Pat tapered off, catching her breath.

"What's the timeline?" Melanie placed her coffee on the desk and accepted Whiskey into her arms from Travis. The kitten sighed and let her adore him, showing his appreciation with a deep, rumbling purr.

"Most of it should arrive in the next day or two, at most," Pat said, doing her utmost to hide her nerves.

Melanie put down her coffee, smiled at her friend and patted her arm affectionately. "It's going to be fine, really. Better than fine."

Pat sighed and let Melanie's words soothe her. It was so nice to be on the receiving end, as opposed to the giving end, of comfort.

"Before you know it," Travis added, while picking cat hair from his clothes and placing them one by one on the desk top. "You'll be running this place like clockwork and wondering why you didn't do it a whole lot sooner."

"We'll be promoting you with every house we sell!" Gerry enthused.

Pat wanted to hug him for his unwavering support.

Melanie pulled up a stool from beside the desk, sat down and settled Whiskey into her lap. Pat couldn't help but marvel at how unconcerned she was by the fact that the ginger colored feline was leaving a generous amount of hair scattered across her dark skirt.

"I have a lint brush," she offered and started pulling out desk drawers in search of it.

"Don't worry about it." Melanie waved her hand dismissively. "It will come off."

"*I'll* take it," Travis said, pleadingly.

Melanie rolled her eyes at him. "So, tell us, have you had anyone coming by, snooping around to find out what you're doing?"

"Are you kidding?" Pat replied as she continued to search for the lint brush. "I think every person who lives around here has found some excuse to *pop in* and say hello."

She chuckled and pulled the lint brush from the back of her drawer with an "Ah-ha!" Travis swiftly snatched it from her hand and began systematically running it over his clothes. Pat watched him, an amused grin on her face and added, "I don't think I've talked so much in years!"

"I figured as much," Melanie said, sagely. "But, let's be honest, not much new goes on around here."

"Amen to that," Gerry agreed, while pointing out stray hairs that Travis had missed on his lint brush attack.

"Not to mention," Melanie continued. "The people in the community are probably thrilled to see you out and about again. You have to admit, you were a bit of a recluse in the last year."

"Mel's right about that," Travis said and smiled kindly at Pat as he handed back the lint brush.

"Hopefully," Melanie finished. "All of the friendly interest and chatter will turn into revenue as you're ringing up sales."

Pat shrugged. "One can certainly hope."

"Speaking of people being happy you're out." Melanie's face suddenly grew serious and Pat raised an eyebrow. "Has any of this been mentioned to Stephen?"

"Not that you need to!" Travis cut in.

"No," Melanie agreed. "You're under no obligation, but if the kids know..."

"Then, he'll know." Pat finished. "And, yes, he does know."

Gerry and Travis moved as one toward Pat and Melanie, their faces eager for the next bit of information.

"And," Gerry prompted. "What happened? Tell us!"

"Oy." Pat exhaled, then picked up her coffee and took a long swallow while she remembering the phone call that had come, rapid fire, after she'd hung up with Crystal. She hadn't mentioned it, because she didn't want to store it to memory.

"Oy?" Melanie pressed, her curiosity piqued. "What's 'oy'? Did he call?"

"Yup," Pat confirmed.

"I *knew* it! Crystal blabbed!" Melanie's sharp words made Whiskey startle on her lap, his grey eyes wide as he glanced around the shop. She placed him back on the desktop and he curled into a sleepy ball, one eye slightly open to watch the two women as they paced around one another.

"It wasn't that bad, actually." Pat started to explain.

"Uh-huh." Melanie's heels clicked sharply on the floor as she fought to keep the sneer from her face and the loathing from her tone. "He was less asinine than usual? *Mr. Supportive*, was he?"

"No, not quite that far," Pat admitted, her flat, ballet-styled shoes barely making a sound beneath her feet. "But, he wasn't as pushy and know-it-all as I might have expected, either."

"What did he say?" Travis took over the stool that Melanie had vacated and Gerry occupied Pat's chair.

"Do you remember when he was the opposite of who he is now?" Pat asked, struck fresh by the shock of Stephen's metamorphous from a decent guy into... A self-absorbed schmuck.

Gerry and Travis stayed mute, their eyebrows raised as they glanced at Melanie for guidance.

"Sort of," Melanie mumbled. She knew where Pat was headed and she didn't like to remember when Stephen was actually a nice guy. It messed with her comfortable reality where Stephen was a sniffling dirt bag.

"Sometimes I wonder if he had an alien encounter and his personality was switched." Pat frowned, contemplating the idea. It sure would explain a lot.

Melanie snickered and Gerry and Travis cleared their throats in an attempt not to chortle along with her. "It would explain a lot," she echoed Pat's thoughts.

Pat stopped pacing, put down her coffee and stood in front of a bookshelf. "When I first met him, he was kind." She reminisced while straightening an already perfectly horizontal set of used books. "He was spontaneous, he laughed so easily, he was generous to a fault and never at a loss for complimentary words."

"All men are like that in the beginning," Melanie said, deftly aiming to burst the romanticized bubble Pat had created.

"Umm-hmm," Travis murmured in agreement, then winked at Gerry when he raised an eyebrow.

"True," Pat acknowledged. "But, some men do stay that way. Look at Duncan, for example."

"Mmm-hmm," Travis murmured a second time, then made a zipper gesture across his lips when Gerry turned to glare at him.

Duncan, Melanie's longtime boyfriend, was a huge exception to the rule of men displaying their best side until they felt secure enough to really show who they were. The side he had offered to Melanie when they'd first met four years ago was him. No games, no bullshit, just the real deal.

"And, you have to admit, Stephen did stay true to the image he'd created until... Well, until almost the end of our marriage for crying out loud!"

"*Well*," Melanie hedged, continuing to be the voice of reason.

"Alright, fine." Pat sighed and pushed her bangs off her forehead. "Maybe I am romanticizing and he *may* have dropped his A game. But, not until at least the first half, or maybe three quarters, had gone by."

Melanie rolled her eyes. "Yeah, he led you *waaay* down the garden path, nobody's arguing that. But, in the end..."

"Yes, *in the end*." Pat nodded.

While she did have many good memories of Stephen, she also hadn't forgotten the last few years of their marriage; when he had transformed from a caring and attentive husband, into a withholding and distant, selfish and self-absorbed, all-around jerk.

"Whew!" Travis exhaled, loudly. "Getting rather thick with seriousness in here! Time to get on with the story, Patty-cake. Dish up some gossip!"

"Right, moving on," Melanie said, giving herself a shake. She'd promised herself she wasn't going to let Stephen be a buzz kill ever again and she was determined to stick to it. "What did Mr. Pole-Up-His-Butt have to say when he called?"

Pat grimaced. *That* was an image she didn't need in her head. She took a deep breath and revealed the rest of her story. "Well, in a nutshell, it was pretty much as you said. As soon as Crystal knew what was going on with me, she blabbed and called Stephen with the story of Mom going off half-cocked and sinking money I don't have - as though she has any idea about what I do and don't have - into a doomed business."

"Jeez!" Melanie huffed. "Talk about lighting a completely unnecessary fire!"

"I know," Pat agreed. "But, that's Crystal for you. Especially when she feels threatened."

"Oh, for the love of Dixie! What in the world does that child have to be threatened about?" Gerry piped up, uncharacteristically. "That her mother, God forbid, is actually getting some sort of life of her own?"

Travis swiveled in his chair, his face a picture of surprise. Gerry usually kept out of discussions of a personal nature, so for him to actually offer any feedback was cause for amazement.

"Yup. You've hit the nail on the head," Pat affirmed. "The poor girl is so convoluted sometimes, alternately supporting me when things are tough and then backtracking rapidly when she perceives her own security being threatened. Trust me, I've learned not to take any of it personally."

Melanie frowned. Pat may have learned not to take it personally, but *she* did. Even though Crystal hadn't done anything directly to her, Melanie still had the desire to give her a firm shake on Pat's behalf for being so damned self-absorbed.

Like father, like daughter, she thought, scornfully. Not that her own daughter, Gina, didn't do the same sort of thing all of the time. It was just that, somehow, since she never created any huge waves, it seemed less offensive. Most likely a case of Mother Blinders.

"So, what did you tell him?" Melanie rallied her thoughts and cocked her head, eager to hear that Pat had taken the wind out of his sails.

"Oh, don't you worry, I straightened him out in a heartbeat. And, I have to say, it wasn't that bad. He surprised me by actually being supportive of my decision."

"Hmmm," Melanie murmured.

"What?" Pat shook her head, not following.

"Oh, nothing." Melanie tapped her fingers on the desk as she elaborated. "I guess I just don't trust his motives."

"I don't blame you," Gerry threw in. "He's proven himself to be anything *but* trustworthy."

"Yeah, that's what I'm thinking. It feels like the reason he'd be supportive of your choice, is because it finally takes some of the heat off of him." Melanie sneered, not being able to help herself.

"It's been over six months since the papers were signed," Pat reminded her. "If he was guilty, I think he'd be over it by now."

"I don't think so." Melanie crossed her arms over her chest. "I think, until he sees concrete evidence that you've created a life of your own, that man is doomed to feel slightly guilty about the choice to jump ship without so much as a discussion, or backward glance. In fact, I wouldn't be surprised in the least to find out he's thrilled to pieces there's a new light at the end of the tunnel. That he doesn't have to carry the weight of responsibility for your altered life since he pulled the rug out from under you."

"Wow, Honey, those are a whole lot of metaphors mixed together." Travis grinned in an attempt to lighten the mood.

"Maybe," Melanie acknowledged, giving Travis a small smile for his effort. "But, Pat knows it's true."

Pat shrugged. Melanie was only speaking the truth. For all of his bravado, when he'd announced his choice to leave there was no question Stephen carried a huge weight of guilt about how he'd left her blowing in the wind without a tether. He'd tried to offer solutions, Pat recalled him clumsily suggesting she could get a job. But, ultimately, he'd been at a loss as to how he could lessen the blow.

Then, when Puck passed away just six months after he'd delivered his marriage destroying news, it went from bad to worse. Stephen had floated back and forth between the house and his new apartment in the city and even half-heartedly attempted to slot himself back into her life, so guilty was his conscience.

Pat grimaced at the memory.

It had only been because she'd been so heartbroken over Puck, and Stephen had seemed such a poor consolation prize, that they'd continued moving forward with the divorce; instead of attempting to reconcile. Thank God.

"It *is* true," Pat said, pushing her memories far aside. "And, truthfully, if he can let some of that go I say good on him. Eighteen months ago when we started divorce proceedings, you know I would have been thrilled to think he was drowning in his own guilt. But now, *finally*, I'm healthy enough to say I just can't be bothered."

"Right." Melanie took her friend's cue, straightened her shoulders and placed her hands on her hips. She wasn't about to continue dredging up the past and heaping its putrid contents onto Pat's shoulders. "Enough of the past! Time to focus upon the here and now. Tell me and the guys what we can do in the present to help keep things rolling along."

"Hear, hear!" Travis cheered.

***

CHAPTER FIVE

Pat inhaled the heady smells of damp Earth beneath her runners as she beat a steady rhythm on the wooded trail near her house. She missed the fragrance of the Evening Primrose flowers, their stalks tucked in-between the pine trees that studded the path, but knew it was too cool for them at the top of the day. They wouldn't open their bright yellow petals until later in the afternoon when the sunshine would call them out to display their wares.

She watched her breath leave her mouth in cloudy gusts, the chill air leaving no question about autumn reaching with cool, creeping fingers to effortlessly claim the mountainous landscape, and sighed. She always felt slightly melancholy about bidding farewell to summer; since her kids were small there was something about the inevitable shuffle into fall that felt bittersweet.

Pat slowed her footsteps over the decomposing, multi-colored, maple leaves on the path and acknowledged to herself that some of her feelings came from the fact she'd just experienced her first summer as a single woman. It had been happy, and sad, and eye-opening.

She also had to accept that, despite her best efforts, she'd been rattling around in her big house for the past month. Even the addition of the bookstore to go to in the daytime, and Whiskey to dart in and out of the rooms of the house in the evenings, hadn't been able to banish the truth - she'd outgrown it. Or, more accurately, with only her and the cat to occupy it, the house had outgrown her.

New dreams were materializing and the idea of a small house; something cozy and cottage-like in nature; something just hers, held great appeal. Pat could see it in her mind's eye; cute, homey, a stone path, lots of trees, trailing vines and flowers...

"Oh!" Pat cried out as she jogged around a blind curve in the path and ran right smack into the solid chest of a tall man.

"Whoa!" he shouted back as they collided and he tried, and failed, to catch her before she ricocheted off him and landed squarely on her backside on the dirt trail.

"Jeez!" he said, lunging toward her, offering his hand. "I'm so sorry! Are you okay? Let me help you up."

Pat looked up into his face, a very handsome face it might be noted, and blinked a few times while she caught up to what was happening.

"I think I'm fine," she said, taking note that nothing felt painful. "It was my fault," she added as she dusted off her hands and began to pull herself upright. "I was daydreaming, instead of watching ahead."

"Seriously, please, let me," he insisted, reaching out his large hand to grasp hers. He peered more closely at her as she stood up, still tightly clutching her hand as though he was afraid she'd fall back over if he let go. "Are you absolutely sure you're okay? Because, if you don't think you are, I can call someone."

"Honestly," Pat assured him, while gently extracting her hand from his and placing it on her sweatshirt, over her heart. "I swear, I feel fine. I was just startled, but I feel okay."

The man exhaled, clearly relieved, and then his face broke into a huge smile.

Oh, my, Pat thought, nearly losing her breath in the face of all of that chisel, white teeth and dark blonde hair. She blinked a couple of times when, on the heels of that thought, she became almost painfully aware of just how untidy she looked. Grey, baggy sweatshirt, hair scraped back into a messy ponytail, stretched and shapeless black yoga pants, not a smudge of makeup... Good God, it was desperate.

"I'm Ian." The man extended his hand a second time; to shake, not to aid.

Pat smiled shyly and enjoyed the heat coming from his palm as their hands joined together in greeting. "Pat," she replied, suddenly tongue tied.

"Well, Pat," he said, and she enjoyed that his smile extended all the way to his clear hazel eyes. "I feel the need to say I'm sorry one more time, for lumbering into you like a charging ox."

Pat chuckled at his description and waved her hand dismissively. "As I said, I was daydreaming. I should have known better."

"Well, either way, I'll be sure to watch those curves from now on," he finished and allowed his eyes to drop briefly, for only a fraction of a second, to where Pat's hips would have been had she not been shrouded in baggy, shapeless clothes.

Pat watched it happen and felt her breath catch in her throat, wondering if she'd imagined it. Could he have been checking her out? She didn't have the opportunity to contemplate the notion as the man, *Ian*, was already stepping around her to resume his jog.

"Take care," he said, giving her a small wave.

Pat grinned and waved back, unable to think of anything more to say before he'd disappeared around the bend. She stood alone, just her and the sounds of the birds in the trees and thought, *Well, isn't that a kick in the pants?*

***

"Do you think I should change my hair?" Pat gazed at her reflection in the bathroom mirror, dissatisfied with what she saw.

"Where's this coming from?" Melanie asked, intrigued by the question.

"I don't know." Pat held her headset firmly, so it wouldn't be tugged from her ear as she pulled off the blue elastic that held her hair back from her face. "I've let it go in the last year and now that I'm a business owner and all that, I've been thinking it might be good for me to have a change. Get refreshed so I look the part."

"That makes sense," Melanie said, shifting her telephone receiver from her left ear to her right and trying to hide the growing excitement she was feeling.

It was the first time in absolute ages that Pat had expressed any interest in how she looked. From the moment Stephen had packed a suitcase with the speed of a criminal fleeing the scene, Melanie had had an agonizing front seat from which to watch her once put together and smartly dressed friend, descend into baggy pajama pants and fleece pullovers; barely remembering she had hair to brush. Even the hint of an indication that she was possibly turning a corner was enough to send a shiver of hope up Melanie's spine.

"Not to mention," Pat said, lifting a strand of hair, then watching as it fell back limply to her shoulders. "I think it would be a good thing if, when I look in the mirror, I see a different me and a reminder that I've moved forward with my life."

She refrained from mentioning that she'd run into, *literally*, a handsome man on her jog and was embarrassed by how shoddy she'd looked. Melanie would make it into a bigger deal than necessary and Pat didn't want to start up that conversation.

"Sounds smart to me," Melanie said, calmly, even though what she wanted to do was cheer and yell, "Amen! About time!"

"It's been so long, I don't even know if my stylist will remember me." Pat laughed. "God, how pathetic is that? Travis and Gerry would be aghast."

"You went to *A Cut Above*, right?"

"Uh-huh," Pat said, distracted from her reflection by Whiskey's antics. He was tucking himself together, then springing forward to bat at the toilet paper roll on the wall. "I also think I should probably do some shopping. When I was out on a run this morning I suddenly realized it's been ages, possibly before Stephen left, that I've bought any new jogging clothes, or any clothes for that matter."

"We could go to the city," Melanie ventured, tentatively. "I can leave the shop for the day, the girls can handle it."

She was referring to her own business just a block over from *Possibilities* door, where she sold nothing but the best in women's lingerie. It had been a risky move for her to set up a second shop, but since her first in the city was thriving, Melanie had thrown caution to the wind and taken the plunge. It had turned out to be exactly the right move - the smaller store was going from strength to strength, with a surplus of customers both local and tourist.

"Maybe," Pat hesitated, suddenly feeling nervous. Perhaps if she started with her hair, a baby step, she might feel more brave to take the next one and tackle her wardrobe.

"*Or*, we could leave it for a bit," Melanie added, hearing Pat's hesitation and immediately backing off to give her space. "Give you a chance to look through your stuff and see what you want to update."

"That's probably better," Pat agreed, simultaneously relieved and annoyed with herself. She was reminding herself of someone, someone she did *not* want to become; her Grandmother.

It was a trait of her Grandmother's - talking about making plans and then backing out of them. All through Pat's childhood she remembered her Grandmother doing it and, as a result, it made Pat and the rest of her family crazy with irritation. She did not want to walk in *those* footsteps, no thank you.

Pat squared her shoulders, pushed her hair from her face and fixed herself with a firm stare in the mirror as she spoke into her headset. "But, we are going to do it.

That's a promise, okay? First the hair, then the clothes. Step one, then step two."

Melanie smiled on the other end of the phone, impressed by her friend's strong spirit. She'd been knocked back, but she was far from out. "Deal," she said, matching Pat's firm tone. "First hair, then clothes. One thing at a time."

***

CHAPTER SIX

"Sandra?" Pat called out from behind the cash desk as she shifted some papers and books to peer beneath them. "Have you seen my glasses?"

"Yes," Sandra replied, from the second story of the bookstore. "They were on a shelf up here, so I put them on the desk in your office."

Pat smiled and silently thanked the Heaven's for the umpteenth time for sending her the gem that was Sandra. Young and full of enthusiasm, scarily efficient, funny and kind with a mind as sharp as a tack, she could run the show if needed.

Pat's gratitude knew no bounds as she looked around the shop to admire the overstuffed, patchwork-patterned chairs tucked into nooks; the spotless and shining bookshelves precisely labeled and filled to capacity; plants strategically placed to add color and life to dead spaces and, finally, gorgeous book displays to entice even the most indecisive of customers. It had been Sandra who'd stepped into the breach and whipped everything into shape, allowing *Possibilities* to run like a well-oiled machine.

"Thank you," Pat said, laughter lacing her words when she was visited with the amusing image of a customer discovering her red-framed reading glasses while browsing the shelves, then wondering if they had been left for their convenience.

"They're still such a new thing for me." She went on. "I just can't seem to get used to having them. Soon enough, I'll need to get a granny chain for around my neck and then I'll really start to feel like the sands of time are slipping by."

The shop doorbell jingled merrily and Pat turned to see who was blowing in with the cool autumn air. It was a man and woman and, between them, a small boy.

"Isn't this lovely?" said the woman, all smiles as she stepped forward into the bookstore.

Pat surreptitiously watched as the woman smoothed back her fiery red curls, the rings on her third finger glittering wildly in the overhead lights.

The blonde man nodded and held the hand of the tow-headed boy at his side.

"Very nice," he said, his voice appreciative as he looked around. "I'm sure you'll be able to find something great for both Renee and Kris in here."

"I think so, too." The woman looked around eagerly, while Pat watched with a small grin playing at her lips. It was so obvious she was trying to keep herself from rapidly moving further inside and losing herself in the shop.

"Hey, how about this idea." The man's face lit up as he smiled at her. "Simon and I will go and find a treat and you can browse to your heart's content. Just come meet us when you're done."

The woman's face lit up to match his. "Perfect! Does that sound good to you, too, Simon?"

Simon, who Pat guessed to be around four, or five, nodded enthusiastically before turning to his father. "Can we get cookies, Daddy?"

The man grinned affectionately down at his son, smoothed his hair and looked at the woman with one eyebrow cocked. "I don't know. Can we, Mommy?"

"Cookies also sound perfect." She nodded, her red curls shining in the afternoon sunshine pouring through the front windows. She was so cute, Pat wanted to squeeze her. "Ben, why don't you ask the woman at the desk where you can go nearby."

Pat hurriedly busied herself at the desk, shuffling papers and opening and closing drawers. Anything to make it look like she was distracted, as opposed to shamelessly eavesdropping on their family conversation.

Ben kept hold of Simon's hand and the two of them approached the desk. "Excuse me," he said, a polite smile on his handsome face.

Pat looked up to meet his eye with, what she hoped was, an expectant expression on her face - instead of one that revealed she'd been caught out. "Hi! How can I help you?"

"We were wondering if there might be a place nearby, say a cafe, where we could find some pastries—"

"*Cookies*, Daddy," Simon clarified, tugging on his father's hand.

"Right," he agreed. "Preferably cookies, if they have them."

Pat was delighted by the pair of them. Up close, she could see that the boy had not only his father's fair hair, but his generous mouth. His eyes, on the other hand, were large and a dark chocolate brown; probably a gift from his red-haired mother. They exuded happiness and Pat wished for just a moment she could bottle it.

"Of course." She gave her attention to Simon. "I know the perfect place." The little boy leaned forward eagerly, his eyes sparkling with eagerness, and Pat's heart clutched for a moment as she remembered her own son, Michael, when he was just that young and fresh.

"You tell your Daddy that you just have to turn left when you leave the store." Pat pointed at the shop door. "Then, you walk all the way down to the corner. When you get to the corner, look both ways and carefully cross the street. Then, all you need to do is keep walking and follow the sidewalk all the way around the next corner and a few doors down you'll find a lovely shop called *The Bakery*. They make all sorts of fresh pastries—"

"And, cookies," he reminded her.

"Yes, and cookies." Pat nodded. "I think you'll love it." She straightened up and while she looked at Ben, asked Simon, "Do you think you'll be able to lead your Daddy there?"

"Yes!"

Ben smiled appreciatively. "Make sure you remember your thank you, Simon," he said, meeting Pat's eyes warmly with his own.

"Thank you!" Simon enthused, tugging again on his father's hand as he did a little tap dance on the shiny floor.

"You're very welcome, Simon," Pat said, delighted all over again. "Please tell Phil that Pat from the bookstore, that's me, sent you."

"Hear that, Pen?" Ben turned around to call across to his wife. "Simon is going to take me to *The Bakery*. It's just one block down, cross over and follow the sidewalk around the block to the next street."

"Sounds perfect." Pen left the bookshelf she was inspecting to cross the floor back to them. "I won't be long," she said, giving first her husband a kiss, then bending down to squeeze Simon. "Save some cookies for me."

Simon and Ben waved as they exited the shop and Pat waved back. Before turning back to her browsing, Pen smiled at Pat. "Thanks so much," she said, adjusting the belt on her bright blue pea coat.

"My pleasure." Pat nodded. "Your son is lovely."

Pen's face glowed with pleasure at the kind words. "He's a wonderful boy."

Pat understood. She'd had a wonderful little boy who'd grown into an even more amazing young man. She cleared her throat. "Please, if you're looking for anything in particular, just give me a shout and I'll be happy to help."

"Thanks," Pen agreed, her focus already being pulled back toward the waiting shelves.

The bell above the door rang out again and Pat turned toward the sound, half expecting to see Ben and Simon returning for a repeat of her directions. She couldn't have been more far off.

A strong and strapping specimen of a man, judging by the width of the brown leather jacket that spanned his broad shoulders, stood inside the entrance; looking intently around the shop. Pat squinted, then startled in surprise as she realized it was the same man she'd careened into last week on the path near her house. *Ian.*

Ian's face lit up when he met Pat's eye and she grabbed the desk for support when her knees went weak. What on Earth was he doing there? In her shop of all places? She'd never laid eyes on him in all of her years living in the town and, suddenly, there he was for the second time in the space of one week. It was madness.

"Hey!" Ian said, his face alive with good cheer as he moved toward the desk. "It's you! Pat, right?"

Pat blinked and stared, speechless that he'd recognized her. When she thought back to how she'd looked that morning it was, as far as she was concerned, nothing short of a miracle. Ian cocked his head slightly and began to look uncomfortable.

"Uh..." He cleared his throat and stuffed his hands into his jacket pockets. "Sorry, maybe you don't actually remember *me*..."

"Oh!" Pat exhaled, giving herself a mental shake. "No! Sorry for going blank there, of course I do. I do remember you. Honest. It's Ian, right?"

He grinned and the smile traveled all the way up from his mouth to light up his gorgeous hazel eyes. "Yes." He nodded and his shoulders visibly relaxed beneath the fabric of his jacket.

Pat felt her breath leave her lungs in a whoosh at that smile. She remembered it from the trail by her house and she'd been just as disarmed then, too. She played with her amethyst earring and tried to steady her voice. "I guess I'm just a little surprised that you remembered me, is all."

Ian's smile transformed into a puzzled frown. "Why wouldn't I?"

"Oh," Pat said, flustered by his direct question and slightly embarrassed that she seemed to be repeating herself in the most monosyllabic way.

What was she going to tell him? That as a result of running into him, she'd had an entire make over and was surprised he was able to even remotely recognize she was the same woman from the trail? No. Definitely not.

"It's just that, umm," she stammered, while trying to get a grip on herself. "I guess I'd just say I don't think I was exactly memorable."

Ian's forehead cleared and the smile returned to his face as he held her eyes with his own. Pat felt lightheaded at the warmth there.

"Oh, I don't know about that," he said, his voice just on the edge of intimate.

Pat swallowed awkwardly, hoping he wasn't misunderstanding her and thinking she was fishing for compliments. She'd meant what she'd said, exactly as she'd said it. She had been so faded, so lackluster when they'd met, it was a miracle to her that the man remembered her at all.

"I mean, I'll grant you," Ian acknowledged, while he gestured to her tailored, houndstooth print dress pants, crisp white blouse and violet, high heeled pumps. "You aren't dressed in your workout clothes and colliding up against me. But, truth be told, that's not what stuck out most in my mind anyway."

Pat tried not to fidget under his appraisal, nor point out that she'd changed her hair as well. Gone was her faded and shapeless mop, and in its place was a choppy, chestnut colored shag. She was fairly certain that, being a man, it would be lost on him.

"The thing is, you've got the most amazing eyes. I don't think I've ever seen blue eyes like yours. They're so dark and have a touch of grey in them..." He paused and had the good grace to drop his gaze and chuckle. "Sorry, I hope that wasn't too direct."

"No." Pat breathed out with the word, making her reply husky as she received her first non-friend, or family, compliment in a very long time. "Not at all."

Ian looked up from his shoes and Pat, hearing the timber in her voice, flushed with self-conscious embarrassment. My God, what was she doing? Was she flirting? Oh, it was too much! The man had to be five, possibly even closer to ten years her junior. She was mortified at the thought he might be of the impression she was being, shudder, *cougar-esk*.

"So, have you worked here long?" Ian asked, changing the subject, seemingly unaware of her discomfort as he looked around the bookstore.

"Umm, not exactly." Pat coughed as she tried to regain her footing. "What I mean is, yes I work here, but we haven't been open that long and uhh..."

Ian raised an eyebrow and waited, forcing Pat to finish her sentence. She blazed through it. "More to the point, I don't just work here. I actually own the place."

It was Ian's turn to look embarrassed.

"Oh, God," he groaned and ran his fingers through his hair. "I'm sorry. I didn't mean to make it sound like I was..." He took a breath before finishing his thought. "I don't know what it is about you, but I seem to be inclined to put my foot right in it every time I see you."

Pat could feel a smile tugging at the corners of her mouth. He looked so apologetic, it was comical.

"An honest mistake," she said, making light of it. "Why would you assume I owned the place? It's not like I'm wearing a large badge emblazoned with the word *owner* on it. I could have just plain worked here, no shame in that."

Ian nodded and looked immensely relieved that she wasn't upset with his blunder. "Absolutely. I agree. No shame, one way or another. And, now that I've managed to make a complete mess of this, can we please start over?"

Pat, taken aback that he thought there was anything to 'start over', nodded.

"Excellent." He smiled his megawatt grin and leaned his elbows on the countertop, bringing him slightly closer to her. "So, now that we're moving on - yet we've established you own the place - I believe you're the absolute perfect person to ask about a gift for a woman."

Of course, Pat thought, hoping her disappointment didn't show on her face. *Of course he has a woman in his life.*

Men like him weren't single and, besides, she had no business caring. She'd only been officially divorced for a half year, not to mention the blazingly obvious fact that he was too young to even be on her radar; it would be akin to robbing the cradle.

"What did you have in mind?" She cocked her head and attempted to put them back on a professional footing. Shop keeper to customer.

"My brother's wife's birthday, my sister-in-law, is in a few days and he suggested getting her a book and..." He shrugged and looked at her imploringly. "Truth be told, I'm at a total loss."

His brother's wife. Well, whadda-ya-know.

Pat surreptitiously glanced at his left hand and noted an absence of any sort of jewelry. Not that that was a guarantee that he was single, but still, if he *was* involved with someone wouldn't she be here with him, helping him out?

Stop it, she silently chastised herself. *Focus*. She took a deep breath and exhaled.

"Okay," she said, cheerfully. "Let's start with the easy questions first. Do you have any ideas as to what her interests are?"

"That would make sense, wouldn't it?" Ian chastised himself. "But, I'm embarrassed to say I have no clue. I mean she's great, I love her, but she's always been Tom's wife. I've never given it any real thought."

"Need some help?" Sandra appeared at the top of the staircase to the second floor, Whiskey at her side, and called down to Pat.

Pat glanced up at her, ignored her big eyes as she took in the hunk that was Ian, and shook her head firmly. "No. Thank you, Sandra. There's another customer down here who I believe is looking for gifts, but I've got *this* covered."

Sandra smiled and her eyes held a glint of amusement that Pat refused to acknowledge. "Okay, *Ms. Keegan*, I'll be down in a moment. Please holler if you change your mind."

Ms. Keegan, indeed! The brat! Pat wanted to throw something at her, but instead fought to keep her expression neutral as she gave her attention back to Ian.

"I know!" Ian suddenly perked up, pointing at Whiskey. "Animals! Trish loves animals." He folded his arms across his chest and looked so pleased with himself that Pat decided not to badger him as to what sorts of animals. "Speaking of which, who's that?"

Pat followed his gaze to watch Whiskey meander down the staircase toward them. "Whiskey," she said.

Ian raised an eyebrow, then smiled. "I see," he said, as Whiskey padded off the bottom step, scrunched himself up like a slinky toy and shimmied sideways toward them across the floor.

Pat smirked at the cat as he leaped effortlessly onto the desktop. He was such a clown. "Happy there, Puss and Boots?" she said, affectionately, as she reached out a hand to stroke down his back. He closed his eyes contentedly and purred beneath her fingers.

Ian laughed. "That's hysterical," he commented. "He does look at lot like the cat from the movie."

Pat paused in her affections toward Whiskey, stilled by the deep timber of Ian's laugh. Wow. What a great sound. She could get used to that sound.

"So, anyway," she said, dropping her hand and clearing her throat. Ian took over affection duty with the cat and she was feeling slightly hypnotized by the long, even strokes he was playing down Whiskey's back. "We have books aplenty on animals, follow me."

Ian gave Whiskey a last scratch behind his ears, then moved aside as Pat stepped out from behind the counter. She felt the heat from his body as she brushed past him and if her own word *aplenty* hadn't been ringing in her ears, demanding to know where in the hell she'd pulled it from, she might have been unnerved by the sheer maleness of him. Instead, she was focused upon shoving her thoughts aside and attempting to keep a grasp on even a smidgen of her professional demeanor.

"I'm sure that horses are one of her favorites," Ian offered as he trailed closely behind her. "If you have anything in that direction, I'd be willing to give it a try."

"Fantastic. Absolutely," Pat said, leading him to a bookshelf tucked in a quiet corner of the shop. She'd never noticed it before, but was suddenly acutely aware of the intimacy of the space and had to question why on Earth they had placed the animal related books in an area that would have been more suited to erotica.

"Cozy back here," Ian said, glancing over her shoulder at the shelves.

Oh, hell, Pat thought, inwardly cringing. *Please don't let him think I'm trying to get him alone in dark corners*. He was the one who had said his bloody sister-in-law liked animals! She was just being a good shop keeper and taking him to what he was looking for!

"Yes," Pat began to awkwardly explain, feeling as though she was talking through a mouth full of marbles. "Well, the shop is old and has lots of irregular walls."

Before Ian could reply, she gestured with a sweeping arm at the selection in front of them and started backing out of the *cozy* corner. "There are the animal books. Have a look, see if anything catches your eye and I'll meet you back at the desk."

She turned swiftly on her heel, her face burning, and scurried like a startled rabbit back to the safety of the cash desk.

Ian watched her go, a puzzled look on his face, then turned his attention to the books on the shelves.

***

CHAPTER SEVEN

"You're overreacting," Melanie insisted as she stabbed at the salad on her plate with her fork.

She'd called her boyfriend, Duncan, and informed him she was joining Pat for dinner at her house; after receiving Pat's frantic call that she had to talk; lest she dissolve in a puddle of embarrassment from an encounter in her bookstore. Duncan, the generous and kindhearted spirit he was, had laughed and wished her a good evening. Now, hearing the extended version of Pat's tale, Melanie was thoroughly amused and delighted she'd changed her plans.

"Oh God, I wish," Pat countered, standing at her stove and pouring a bubbling pasta sauce and meatballs into a bowl. She reserved one meatball for Whiskey, leaving it on a side plate to cool. "But, I'm not. Not even a little bit. I was beyond out of my element and the worst part was that it was all in my own head in the first place!"

Melanie laughed and put her fork on the side of her plate. "First, I highly doubt that. Just like I told you this afternoon on the phone, a person doesn't feel that sort of attraction on their own. And, second, I doubt you were anywhere near as befuddled as you're making yourself out to be. He probably thought you were adorable and charming, which you are."

"More like pathetic and fumbling," Pat corrected, while carefully balancing the bowl in her hands and walking over to the table. "He's a baby, Mel," she moaned, setting the bowl on the table next to another holding freshly cooked rotini. "And, I was like an old cougar, licking my chops." Pat dropped heavily into her chair and grimaced. "God, the humiliation."

"Puh-leeze." Melanie snorted and rolled her eyes. "Youngish or not, he's not a child. Not by any stretch of the imagination."

Melanie wasn't sure how it had happened, but Pat seemed to have no idea of just how attractive, never mind how youthful, she was. And, it didn't seem to make one smidgen of a difference how many times she badgered her with the information. Pat just brushed the comments aside as pity compliments.

Pat began to spoon pasta onto her plate and narrowed her eyes suspiciously. "What are you talking about? How would you know how young, or old, he actually is?"

Melanie raised an eyebrow and Pat stopped spooning.

"What? What are you saying? Do you *know* something? Oh-my-God, don't tell me you actually *know* Ian?"

"Relax. No, I don't know him." Melanie shrugged and leaned back into her chair. "*However*, that doesn't mean I didn't find out about him."

"What!" Pat dropped the pasta spoon into the sauce bowl, sending a splatter of red to decorate the table. She jumped up to retrieve a wet cloth, making Whiskey scurry for his basket in the corner of the kitchen, and began to sputter, "What do you mean you found out about him? Between this afternoon when I called you and now, you've found out about him? How? From who?"

"Calm down." Melanie picked the spoon out of the sauce and shoveled pasta into her dish. "It was easy and, if you must know, the information basically fell into my lap this afternoon."

"Fell into your lap?" Pat repeated, returning to the table to wipe with broad sweeps of the cloth across the wood. "How does that happen, exactly?"

"Pretty darn simply, actually." Melanie dolloped a generous amount of sauce onto her pasta and reached for a container of parmesan cheese. "Ian has a brother, right?"

Pat pitched the cloth across the kitchen to land with a thump in the sink and nodded. "Uh-huh. He mentioned him at the bookstore."

"Right." Melanie dusted her pasta with parmesan, placed the container back on the table and picked up her fork. "Well, his brother, *Tom*, came into my shop shortly after I'd talked to you, looking for something last minute to get for his wife's birthday this weekend."

Pat picked up her fork. "So you thought..."

Melanie nodded and ate some pasta. "Uh-huh," she said, around her mouthful. "Since I'd just talked to you,

I put two and two together and, *tada*, started digging for the dirt on Ian."

"Jeez, Mel!" Pat exhaled and looked at her, incredulous. "Didn't Tom find it remotely odd that you were fishing for information about his brother?"

"Give me *some* credit." Melanie put down her fork and reached for her glass of red wine. "After being in the lingerie business for so many years, I've honed the skill for asking questions that don't seem prying, while at the same time gathering the information I need to make the perfect sale." She smirked and saluted Pat with her glass. "It really wasn't that difficult."

Pat put her fork down next to her bowl. Her appetite had suddenly disappeared. What she could really use was a glass of wine. A large one. She reached over to the sidebar and picked up a glass that matched Melanie's. "Hit me," she said, holding out the goblet.

"Absolutely." Melanie picked up the wine bottle and poured a generous measure into Pat's glass. She put the bottle back on the table then leaned forward, grinning like a Cheshire cat. "So, do you want to know what I found out, or not?"

***

Ian paced back and forth across the beige carpet in his brother's family room, too restless to sit down. Tom watched him with one eye, while trying to keep the other on the hockey game on the TV across from the couch.

"Ian, seriously," Tom finally said, when he'd grown tired of the distraction. "Sit down. You're making me sick to my stomach."

"Sorry," Ian apologized and flopped into the pillows on the adjacent leather chair.

"I have to admit," Tom commented, while grabbing a handful of popcorn from a bowl on the coffee table. "It's been a long time since I've seen you this way. Not since Marie."

Ian nodded. Marie was his ex-wife and the last woman to take his emotions for a spin. That was years ago and having those similar emotions rear up again, after so much time, he was feeling seriously out of his depth.

"I don't know what the problem is. You know where this woman works," Tom added, picking up his bottle of beer. "Just bite the bullet and go back and ask her out."

Ian released a bark of laughter. "Oh, sure," he said, sarcastically. "No big deal. Just waltz in and proceed to fall all over myself for a second time and cement her image of me as a complete, instead of partial, idiot."

Tom rolled his eyes, took a swig of his beer and said nothing.

"Did I tell you how I asked her if she worked in the bookstore and she had to correct me and tell me that she actually *owns* the damned place?" Ian ran a hand across the stubble on his chin and flinched at the memory. "God! Talk about putting my foot in it!"

"Yes," Tom said, trying to keep his patience. "You told me. And, just like I said before, I think you're making a way bigger deal out of it than it probably was."

"You weren't there," Ian insisted. "If you had been, you'd agree with me."

Tom put his bottle back down on the wooden coffee table and held up his hands in surrender. "Fine. I wasn't there. Now, can you do me a favor and let me watch the rest of this game without a blow by blow of the sorry tale of you supposedly making an ass of yourself?"

Ian frowned and stood up. "Fine. I'm going for a run. Then, I'm making my escape from this town as soon as Trisha's party is over tomorrow."

Tom nodded, only half listening as he focused on the TV. He didn't even notice when Ian left the room.

***

CHAPTER EIGHT

"What am I doing here? This is absurd," Pat stated as she fidgeted in her tight black skirt - or correction, *Melanie's* tight black skirt.

"No, it's not," Melanie insisted, then slapped Pat's hand. "Stop fussing like a teenager. It's just a skirt and you're legs look great in it."

The two women were standing outside Tom's front door - the guy Melanie had shaken down for information on Ian - and Pat was having trouble finding her breath. How had she managed to let Melanie talk her into such a stunt, she'd never know.

"This is ridiculous, Mel. I can't do this. I don't know these people and I feel too obvious." She started turning on the kitten heel of her black pump and Melanie reached out a hand to grab her wrist.

"*No*, it's not ridiculous. And, *yes,* you can do it," she soothed, while holding tight to Pat's wrist to keep her from fleeing the doorstep. "Keep your eye on the prize. And, if that doesn't work remember we were invited, so it's not like we're crashing the party."

Pat rolled her eyes. What Melanie called 'invited' translated to mean she'd chatted with Tom for such a long time in her store that he'd ended up feeling so comfortable with her he'd insisted she join the birthday barbecue. Not what Pat would call it. No, she'd call it pushing the envelope.

"Maybe *you* were invited," she countered, while trying to shake Melanie's hand from her wrist. "But, *I* most assuredly wasn't."

"Oh, *please*, as good as," Melanie stated as she rapped her knuckles firmly on the green front door. "Tom said to bring a friend, so that meant you. You're my friend."

"You could have counted Duncan as your friend." Pat started to argue, then shut her mouth when the front door swung open, music swelled forward to wrap around them and a barrel chested, cheerful looking man smiled broadly at them.

"Hey there!" he said, clearly delighted to see who was on his doorstep. "Melanie, you came! Trisha will be thrilled. I told her all about you and your shop—" He paused and nodded at Pat. "This must be your friend?"

"Yes!" Melanie matched his enthusiasm, while more or less dragging Pat inside the house alongside her. "This is Pat, my best friend in the world." She grinned encouragingly at Pat and pointed to Tom. "Pat, please meet Tom. Our wonderful host and the amazingly considerate husband I was telling you about."

Pat swallowed her nerves and smiled tightly. If nothing else, her mother had taught her manners.

"How nice to meet you, Tom," she said, extending her hand and trying not to yell at him above the thumping bass beat coming from the speakers tucked into the ceiling. "And, how kind of you to include us in your wife's special day."

"It's our pleasure." Tom beamed and gave Pat's hand a firm shake. "There's nothing like friends to make a celebration special."

Pat didn't know how to respond. Melanie had that effect on people. She went from being an acquaintance, to being thought of as a treasured friend, in what seemed a matter of moments. Pat had seen it happen time and again, but it still amazed her.

"Come on in, make yourself at home." Tom beckoned them to follow him forward. "I'll find Trisha and get you two some drinks."

"See?" Melanie whispered in Pat's ear as they walked down the hallway leading into the hub of the house. "Fine, perfectly fine."

"What?" Pat frowned and leaned in closer. She was going to need her hearing checked if she didn't move away from those speakers.

Melanie glanced around at the guests while they trailed Tom toward the kitchen. "Do you see him anywhere?"

Pat shook her head as her eyes traveled over the faces. "No," she practically shouted.

"Hey, guys!" Tom bellowed at the people near the entertainment unit. "Turn that down, will you?"

One of the young men nodded and, after a moment, the music dropped considerably.

"Oh, that's better," Melanie said, smiling at Tom. "Now we can talk without trashing our voices."

"I'll be right back with Trisha," Tom said, then left the kitchen and disappeared down another hallway.

"Listen," Pat said, the moment she and Melanie were alone. "Maybe he's not here... Oh!" She stopped dead and her knees tremored as she spotted Ian through the large kitchen window, outside in the backyard.

"What? Where?" Melanie was quick to grab the proverbial ball and started whipping her head back and forth.

"Stop it!" Pat spat in a hushed whisper. "Don't be so obvious!"

"Excuse *me*," Melanie replied, snickering under her breath.

"He's over *there*." Pat jerked her head in the direction of the window. "Through the window, in the yard. Dark blonde hair."

"*Whoa*." Melanie exhaled, impressed. The man was a seriously tall drink of water. "Way to go, Pat."

Pat flushed and finally managed to yank her arm from Melanie's grasp. "Don't!" she hissed, keeping her voice low and smoothing the sleeve of her blouse. Or, I'm outta here. Seriously, I'm gone."

"Okay, *okay*," Melanie placated as she straightened the collar of her zebra print, halter-styled top, worn beneath a black wrap draped casually across her shoulders. "Calm down, I won't embarrass you."

"There she is!" Tom reappeared in the hallway entrance and strode purposefully toward Pat and Melanie, holding the hand of a tall, sandy haired woman; clearly pregnant and clearly his wife. "Trisha meet Melanie, the woman I told you about." He smiled warmly at Pat. "And, not to be forgotten, her best friend in the world, Pat."

Trisha couldn't have been more lovely. Sweet and kind, she immediately began to extend herself to put them at ease in her home.

"I'm so glad you came." She blinked her big blue eyes as she gushed at Melanie. "When Tom told me about how much you helped him the other day, and then he gave me such lovely girlie things, I knew he wasn't exaggerating about you."

Melanie smiled and laid a hand on Trisha's forearm; rapidly becoming - whom Trisha would later describe as – 'my great friend Melanie'. Pat watched from the sidelines, bemused by the display, and didn't even notice when Ian came up beside her.

"Well, well," he said, his voice rich and warm like dark chocolate. "What a small world."

Pat felt the hairs on the back of her neck rise and a flush color her cheeks as she looked up to meet his eye. "It certainly is." She grinned and hoped she wasn't giving away the truth of her nerves right beneath the surface.

"I had no idea you knew Tom and Trisha," he said, seeming genuinely pleased. "Funny how the connection didn't come up in conversation at your store when I was looking for her gift, isn't it?"

Pat shrugged and thought, *Oh, hell.*

"Well," she said, thinking on her feet and pointing a finger at Melanie. "My friend, Melanie, is more their friend. Probably the reason I didn't make the connection."

Pat swallowed awkwardly and fidgeted with the French cuffs on her white blouse. Her thoughts were creating havoc in her head. All of the information Melanie had thrown at her about him was flying forward and she was feeling guilty, as though she'd used a secret spy to find out about him in advance. She desperately wished she had a drink in her hand to give her somewhere else to focus.

Pat knew he'd been divorced for four years, that he didn't have any children and was a successful graphic artist and, finally, the kicker; he was much younger than her. By *nine* years.

That tidbit, more than any other, had aggressively taken the wind out of Pat's sails. Not that they should have been up in the first place, but nine years! He was only thirty six, for hell's sake! And, when Pat had said that very thing out loud, then sang a few bars of *Mrs. Robinson*, Melanie had become very agitated. She'd reiterated over and over, like a bothersome parrot, that it was just a number. Just a handful less than forty five. Not even worth mentioning.

Standing squarely in front of Ian in Tom's kitchen, looking into his hazel eyes and taking in his near perfect skin, Pat was haunted one more time by the strings of that famous song.

Coo, coo, ca-choo, she thought. Why would such a gorgeous, youthful man want to give her even a moment of his time?

And, yet, he seemed to want to. Without any sort of force or coercion, he seemed to enjoy her company. It was confusing and exciting... Mostly confusing.

"Trisha." Ian tapped his sister-in-law on the arm. "This is Pat."

"We've met." Trisha smiled warmly and gave Pat's arm a quick squeeze.

"Yeah, but something you didn't know," Ian told her. "Is that Pat is the woman who sold me the book."

"Oh," Tom said, his eyes lighting up as he nodded knowingly at his brother.

Ian raised his eyebrows, then shot Tom a look that silently said, *Shut up, or you'll pay.*

Tom, only two years Ian's senior and having once shared a room with him in their childhood years, knew the look.

"I know you think the book is the best present you received," Ian teased, then winked conspiratorially at Pat. "But, we'll just keep that on the down low to spare Tom's feelings."

"Ha!" Tom exhaled and straightened his shoulders. "You wish."

"My *second* best present, Ian." Trisha grinned and turned to Pat. "Sorry, but my husband would never let it lie if he thought a book, a gloriously wonderful book I might add, won out over his gift for my affections."

Pat laughed. "Perfectly understandable. I'm just glad to know that, while second in line, you liked it."

Ian looked from his sister-in-law to Pat, a huge grin on his face. "It's okay," he said, leaning close to Pat. "*We* know the truth, even if Tom can't handle it."

Melanie burst out laughing, thoroughly enjoying the show. There definitely was something about this Ian fellow that made her feel good about him standing next to Pat. As though he belonged there. She was delighted.

"*Ian, Tom...*"

Pat raised an eyebrow at the singsong sound floating inside with the breeze when the kitchen door opened. She didn't have long to wonder about its source; a young nubile woman, her long blonde hair trailing in wavy tendrils down her back, slunk out from behind Ian and placed herself proprietarily between he and Pat.

"The barbecue's ready boys," she said, her voice teasing and flirty as she reached up to squeeze Ian's bicep. "Time for the Gaffney men burger flip off."

Pat, startled, exchanged a look with Melanie. Jeez, was there a puzzle piece Melanie had failed to garner in her interrogation of Tom? A very blonde, slim, territorial and, from the looks of it, under thirty puzzle piece?

Melanie unlocked her gaze from Pat's and narrowed her eyes as she watched the young woman's body language. She was sure Tom would have mentioned *this* in his information, so what was the real deal?

"Oh, I'm *sorry*." The blonde cast an efficient, catty eye at Pat; looking her up and down before she smiled warmly at Ian and squeezed his arm a second time. "Did I interrupt something?"

Pat felt a flush climb up her neck and swallowed uncomfortably. She was the odd man out and she knew it. *God bless you please, Mrs. Robinson*, she thought. *What the hell am I doing here?*

In that one simple look the girl, clad in low slung, figure hugging jeans; a form fitting top that revealed a slash of toned flat stomach, and shell encrusted flip-flops, made it clear she thought Pat was an old lady, an old *tart*, in the room.

Suddenly, Pat's black pencil skirt no longer felt flirty, it felt matronly. Her pumps no longer seemed sexy, but desperate. And, as she became acutely aware that she was probably the oldest person in the house, she wanted to flee. She had no business being there, attempting to *flirt* for God's sake. She'd only been divorced for less than a year, hadn't been touched by a man for a hell of a lot longer than that, what was she thinking? She should have been at home, tucked up with her cat, dressed in her comfy flannel pjs and planning the next round of books she wanted to purchase for sale at the store.

Melanie, watching Pat and reading her like an open page, wished she could 'accidentally' slap the girl. Hard. She exhaled, pulled herself up to her full height and squared her shoulders in preparation to fight, albeit verbally, for her friend.

"Oh please, don't. We're *sorry*," Melanie mimicked, cocking her hip to the side and smiling coldly, the grin not meeting her eyes. "I don't think we've been introduced, *dear*."

Tom, missing all of the unspoken conversation, turned to the girl to include her in the group. Ian shifted away, making her drop her hand from his arm.

"Sorry, it's my error," Tom said, apologetically. "This is Trisha's sister, Alexa." He gestured to Melanie and Pat. "This is Melanie and Pat, new friends we just met a couple of days ago."

"Hiya." Alexa gave them a cutesy wave, then placed her slim, tanned hands on her narrow hips. The posture allowed her to push out her pert breasts, making them strain against her thin top.

"Nice to meet you," Pat began, then tapered off when Alexa turned away, clearly done with them.

"Still have that competition." She giggled and winked at Tom and Ian. "May the best man win."

Melanie blinked and clenched her teeth in irritation. If she was intolerant of anything, it was rudeness. She was about to dive in and give the girl a run for her money, hell bent to expose her childishness for what it was, but Alexa didn't give her a chance.

"Burgers aren't going to flip themselves," Alexa said, spinning around fast on her flip-flops and twitching her perky backside out of the kitchen. "I'll get the buns prepped," she called teasingly, over her shoulder, her voice fading as she disappeared through the door and into the yard.

Melanie exhaled and cleared her throat. Judging by Pat's shell shocked expression, it was time for alcohol. "So, Tom mentioned drinks? Have any wine?" she asked, turning to Trisha.

"Of course!" Trisha frowned at Tom. "Where are our manners?"

Tom completely missed his cue. "We'd better get out there and start flipping," he said, nudging Ian in the ribs. "She'll never let up. You know that, right? It must be a family trait."

Trisha rolled her eyes. "You're just lucky I don't give up and you know it." She grinned and leaned in to give him a quick kiss. "Otherwise, you'd be hosting this barbecue all by yourself. A sad and lonely excuse of a single man."

Ian shook his head at the pair of them. "Well, that's my cue," he said, with a laugh, and turned to Pat. "Care to join us in the yard, while we metaphorically duke it out?"

Pat fought to keep the tension from her face. It wasn't easy. The last thing she needed was to betray her quaking heart by revealing its humiliation.

"No," she said, hoping the flush had left her cheeks. "Maybe another time, when we know you all better. I'm not sure I can withstand the possible fight to the finish, brother against brother."

Melanie sidled up next to Pat and threw a friendly arm across her shoulders, offering unspoken support. "I'm with you. Too much possibility to get caught up in the action, taking sides. Not the best way to start friendships. Besides, Trisha is getting us wine."

Before he turned to go into the yard, Ian gave Pat a penetrating look. She raised her eyebrows in surprise, clueless as to what he might have been thinking. Not that it really mattered all that much. Her only concern at that point was watching for an opportunity to present itself whereby she could get the hell out of there and leave her awkwardness far behind.

***

CHAPTER NINE

"So, if it were me choosing, I'd say these three books are the best ones for your money," Pat said, standing patiently beside her customer in front of her bookshelves, while he frowned in a contemplative manner.

"I think you're probably right," he agreed, shifting the books from one hand to the other, as though weighing them.

The sound of the shop bell signaled the arrival of a new customer, giving Pat her getaway. "You think on it, no rush, and I'll attend to the person who just came in and give you some space for your thoughts."

The gentleman smiled appreciatively as she turned her attention toward the front desk, and then wished she hadn't. Ian. Still tall, still gaspingly gorgeous in his brown leather coat and faded jeans, was standing there; watching her with a hopeful expression on his face.

Oh, help, Pat thought, trying not to falter in her step as she walked across the shop floor toward him. It had been a week since her painful humiliation at the barbecue, why couldn't he disappear as quickly as he had arrived?

Melanie, Pat knew, would want to shake her for her thoughts. They had hashed and rehashed the whole incident and Melanie had insisted - would not be shaken from her position - that Pat was reading far too much into it.

Pat, on the other hand, had decided that Melanie was a perfect friend; trying to shield her from the hideous truth that she had looked like a desperate middle-aged woman, trying and failing to fit in with the younger crowd.

God, just revisiting it in her thoughts was almost enough to make her want to turn on her heel and flee in another direction, away from Ian. But, where would she go? She owned the business.

"Hi," she offered, keeping her voice neutral as she reached the desk, then quickly zipped behind it to keep a professional distance from him. "What brings you here? Another birthday?"

Ian gave her a wry grin and shook his head. "No, nothing like that."

Pat waited. He seemed to be collecting himself and she wasn't sure what was going to come out of his mouth next.

"What brings me here is you."

"Me?" Pat echoed, taken aback. She definitely hadn't seen that coming.

"Yes, *you*," he reiterated. "You're the reason I'm here."

Pat went mute. She didn't know what to say in response to his honesty. Probably just as well, he seemed ready to continue.

"Listen, Pat," he said, sighing and leaning on the desktop. "Things have gone really wonky here. We've started out on the wrong foot and I was wondering, can I take you for a coffee?"

"Coffee?" Pat echoed, a second time.

"Yes." He glanced around the shop. "Do you think it would be okay? Could you get away for a few moments?"

Pat followed his gaze and noted that, besides him, there were only three other customers in the shop. It was afternoon, it was slow and she was absolutely confident Sandra could handle things whether they stayed as they were, or increased dramatically.

"I suppose," she agreed, reluctantly, wiping her damp palms surreptitiously down the sides of her tan slacks. "But—"

"Great." Ian didn't let her finish. "Can you leave now, or do you need a few minutes?"

The bell rang and Pat looked away from his eager face, letting herself be distracted by the two women who came bustling into the shop; chattering to each other as they made a beeline for her window display.

"Hey, Pat!" One of the women, crimson haired, wearing hip-hugging jeans and a thick, tight white sweater that revealed every square inch of her generous curves, raised her hand in a friendly wave.

Her raven haired friend, also dressed in tight jeans, stiletto boots and a red trench coat, peered through the shop window; her head turning back and forth as she watched the street on the other side of the glass.

"Hi, Heidi," Pat replied to the redhead, then cocked her head to one side when the other woman, Denise, didn't bother to turn around. "Hey, Denise," she tried.

Denise swiftly turned on her heel, her perfectly made up, almond shaped eyes crinkled at the corners and a cheerful grin lit up her face. "Oh! Hey, Pat! Sorry, I was just so mesmerized by your … window display!"

"We both were," Heidi piped up, before nudging Denise with her hip. "We just had to come inside to get a better look."

"Uh-huh," Denise agreed, then twisted back toward the window.

"Love the new hairstyle, by the way," Heidi offered, nodding as she stared at Pat's head. "Really cute. Very peppy. Suits you to a tee. About time too, I'd say. You were starting to look pretty rough around the edges, girl, since your divorce."

Pat cringed and exhaled. Wow, talk about to the point. "Umm... thanks. I had it done at *A Cut Above*," she began, while Ian turned around and leaned his elbow on the desk, clearly interested to watch the rest of the show.

"*Heeey*," Heidi cooed, her voice curling with flirtatiousness as she cut Pat off and raised her eyebrows at Ian. "I know *you*. You're Tom's brother, right?"

Ian nodded and smiled politely in return. "Uh-huh, that's right. Have we met?"

"Rumor has it you're got plans on the front burner to move into our sleepy burg, isn't that right?"

Pat folded her arms across her chest, curious to hear Ian's reply. He, on the other hand, looked slightly uncomfortable at the blatantly interrogatory tone in Heidi's voice as she gave him the once-over. Pat wanted to tap him on the shoulder and tell him to get used to it.

Before he could think of a reply, Denise suddenly exclaimed, "Oh!" and whirled around to grab Heidi's forearm. "We've got to go! I saw, umm... *Another* window display that just went by that we have to check out."

Ian's eyebrows shot up on his forehead. "That *went by*—" he began, clearly confused.

"Yup!" Heidi nodded her head up and down at speed as Denise tugged at her arm, pulling her toward the doorway. "Gotta run! We'll be back again to see you Pat," she added, then smiled and winked at Ian. "And, hopefully, we'll see *you* around town as well. Bye-bye now!"

Pat pressed one hand across her mouth to repress her grin and waved with the other as the two women exited the shop in the same flurry that they'd arrived.

"Wow." Sandra's comment floated down the staircase and Pat turned around as she reached the bottom step. Her brown eyes were as wide as they'd been the day Ian had first crossed *Possibilities* threshold. "Everything okay down here?" she asked, blatant curiosity written all over her elfin face as she walked over to the cash desk.

"Yes," Pat told her, still giggling. "Just Heidi Becker and Denise Chang, following a *window display*. Probably of the tall, dark and broad shouldered variety."

Ian kept quiet. He had a strong hunch he didn't want to know anything more about either of those women. Smart man.

"*Pardon?*" Sandra asked, her eyebrows knotted together in a puzzled frown.

Pat didn't bother to elaborate. It wasn't worth the oxygen.

"Never mind," she said, instead. "Listen, I was hoping to step out for a moment if that's okay with you." She quickly added, "But, if not and you don't feel confident about me leaving, that's perfectly fine."

Sandra looked back and forth from her to Ian, then grinned. She pushed her tangle of chocolate colored curls away from her face and gestured to the quiet bookstore. "Please, I could do this in my sleep. Take your time, have fun."

Ian's face lit up and before Pat had another moment to consider, she found herself being shuttled out the door and into the street.

***

Ian smiled politely at the man behind the counter of *The Bakery,* while he picked up two take away coffee containers. The shop had been Pat's suggestion and they'd walked the short distance from her bookstore making chitchat. Now, he had their coffees and it was time for him to take the bull by the horns. Or, at least that's how his brother, Tom, had worded it when he'd told Ian a second time to man up.

"Thanks," he said, then swallowed against his nerves as he turned to face the shop, and Pat waiting at their table near the windows. Show time.

Pat grinned at him as he navigated between the tables and chairs and Ian was taken aback once more by her beauty. He had a strong hunch she had no idea of how disarmingly pretty she was, and intended to make it his mission to clue her in.

"Here you go," he said, placing her coffee in front of her and joining her at the table. "Cream, no sugar, right?"

Pat reached out to wrap her fingers around the warm cup. "Yes, perfect. Thanks."

"My pleasure," he replied, then took a deep breath to quell his nerves. He couldn't believe how tense he was; as though he was a teenager all over again. It was absurd.

"Nice guy at the counter," he added, while taking off his jacket and hanging it on the back of his chair. "Friendly."

Pat agreed. "Phil. Yes, he's a very nice man. He and his wife own the shop and make everything from scratch. It's a real Mom and Pop operation. I often refer my customers here, if they're looking for more than just a coffee."

Ian tried to keep his focus upon what she was saying, but his thoughts were being bothersome; racing and bellowing, *Get on with it!* He could hear Tom in his ear, telling him to grow a pair.

"Listen," he said, clearing his throat. "I'd imagine you're wondering why I wanted to talk with you privately, right?"

"Well, sure," Pat said, a small smile playing at her lips. "It had crossed my mind."

Encouraged by her friendly tone, Ian took a bracing sip of his coffee and dove in. "Okay, so I'll just get right to it then, if that's okay by you?"

"Absolutely." She took a deep breath, as though readying herself for whatever he had to say. "Fire away."

"You've been on my mind, Pat," he told her, holding her gaze with his own. "A lot. In fact, I'll even go out on a limb here and say you've been on my mind since the day I literally ran into you."

Pat chuckled, bit her bottom lip and looked down at her coffee cup.

"And, then," Ian continued, encouraged by her laughter. "When I saw you at your bookstore, and again at Trisha's party..." He took a breath and exhaled, steadying himself in the hope of preventing her perceiving him as desperate. "Well, in a nutshell, it seems you've taken up permanent residence in my brain."

Ian took a large swallow of his coffee to occupy his hands and his mouth. *There*, he thought. *I've said, it. Let the chips fall where they may.*

Pat lifted her eyes from her cup to meet his. She blinked and sat very still as though digesting his words. Ian watched her and his stomach flipped over. She didn't look pleased, or angry, or even put out. She looked stunned.

"Pat?" He ventured.

"Wow," she said.

Ian raised an eyebrow, unsure of how to gauge her response. He didn't know what he'd been expecting, but was pretty sure 'wow' wasn't it.

"Oh, and I also wanted to tell you," he said, figuring he was in for a penny, may as well be in for a pound. "I'm sorry for whatever went down at Trisha's party."

Pat shrugged and fidgeted with the tips of her dangling silver earrings, a sheepish smile on her face. "Oh, *that*. Never mind."

"No, I'm serious," he insisted, placing his cup back onto the table. "I'll be honest, I don't know exactly what happened, but regardless, I'm not an idiot and I know something did. Otherwise, the mood wouldn't have shifted so dramatically and you and Melanie wouldn't have disappeared without my seeing you go."

"Oh, *well*." Pat shifted in her seat and seemed uncomfortable with meeting his eye.

Not good.

"Anyway, what matters about that situation is that you didn't realize how gutted I was that I'd let you get away *yet again* without getting up the nerve to tell you how I was feeling."

"Oh." Pat met his eye, a small smile replacing the awkwardness on her face, and Ian had to stop himself cheering.

"So, in a sloppy and roundabout way, what I'm trying to tell you is that I'm really hoping we can put those things behind us and start fresh. And, if I can manage to keep from screwing up our further interactions, I'd like to get to know you better. *Much* better, if you'll let me."

Ian sat back in his seat, spent. He picked up his coffee and brought the container to his lips, giving her a chance to consider his information while watching her reaction like a hawk. She hadn't fled the shop screaming, so that was a plus.

"I, uh," Pat faltered, a frown on her face.

Ian's stomach clenched. *Oh, shit*, he thought. *Too much. I pushed too much.*

"Okay," Pat said, taking a deep breath and exhaling. "Here's the thing. I'm flattered, Ian. Hugely flattered. But, I don't know..."

"What?" He leaned forward toward the table. "What don't you know? Ask me anything you want. I'm an open book."

"No," she said, fidgeting with the lid on her cup. "It's not that. It's just..." She stopped fidgeting and wrapped her arms protectively around her torso. "I don't know how to do *this*!"

"*This?*" Ian asked, trying his damnedest to keep up. "I'm sorry, Pat. I'm not purposely trying to be clueless, but I don't follow."

"The thing is, I've been married," Pat elaborated, before a wry smile captured her lips. "But, I guess you already know that from Heidi's oh-so flattering commentary at my store about my looks and my divorce."

Ian shrugged, an amused grin threatening to take over his face. "Uh, yeah. She wasn't exactly subtle."

Pat rolled her eyes. "I don't think that word is in the woman's vocabulary."

"Yeah." Ian nodded, remembering the woman's blatant questions and leering once-over. "I got that impression."

"So, anyway, since Heidi started the ball rolling, you may as well know that I was married for a long time."

Ian nodded again and contemplated as to whether or not he should mention that he'd done his homework and already knew a few things about her past. Probably not. She might misunderstand and it could backfire in his face. Maybe another time.

"I mean a *really* long time," Pat said, looking him in the eye. "As in, I have grown children."

"So?" Ian said, matter-of-fact.

Pat paused and watched his face. He seemed genuinely unfazed that she had grown kids. "Well, it's just that it took me a while - close to a year in fact - to get my bearings again and..."

Ian waited. When she stayed silent, he prompted. "*And?*"

"And, to make this long story not short, it's been a hell of a long time since I've dealt with any of *this* sort of thing." She made a sweeping arc with her hand, back and forth between them. "I'm seriously like a fish out of water here."

Ian's face softened. He was enormously relieved. "Okay, this is good," he told her, putting his cup back on the table. "This is great. This, we can work with."

"We can?"

"Absolutely." He sat back in his seat and flashed her a winning smile. "You're telling me your hesitation isn't about me directly, right?"

"God, no!" she blurted, vehemently, then pressed her lips together and lowered her voice. "No, my hesitation is definitely not about you. You're, *well...*" She stopped talking, grinned and a soft pink flush appeared to color her cheeks.

Ian liked that. A lot. She may not have finished her sentence, but she didn't need to. Her emphatic response and body language said it all. He grinned, feeling as though he could overflow with good cheer.

"See?" he said, confidently. "Everything's perfect. So, you're a little rusty? So what. We can work on that. No problem."

Pat raised an eyebrow and retorted, "I don't know if I'd use the word *perfect.*"

"We'll just ease our way in and see what happens," Ian said, his hazel eyes sparkling in the overhead lights as he swept aside her worries. "No agenda, just two people getting to know each other, either destined to become friends, or... More."

Pat's eye's widened when he said 'more' and she pointed a finger at him. "Okay, so, there is *one* other thing."

"Okay." He leaned his elbows on the table and gave her his full attention. "Hit me."

Pat bit her lip, then cleared her throat. "It's your age."

Ian's eyebrows shot up on his forehead. *That*, he wasn't expecting. "Pardon me?"

"Your *age*," she repeated, wringing her hands together. "Please don't ask me how I know this, or I'll sound like some sort of creepy stalker. I'm just saying that I happen to know you're not even forty, Ian. Hell, if we're brutally honest about it, you're still a few *years* from forty."

"Wow. Okay. Gotta admit, *that* I wasn't expecting." He shrugged. "But, my surprise aside, please forgive my ignorance. I don't follow."

Pat sighed and went back to fidgeting with the lid on her coffee container. "The thing is, I *am* forty." She stopped fidgeting and threw up her hands in exasperation. "Okay, if we're going to split hairs, I'm *more* than forty."

Ahh, Ian thought, as the other shoe dropped and comprehension dawned. It wasn't just that she was divorced and rusty at being back in the dating game. He nodded to himself. Got it.

"Okay," he said, trying to placate. "I understand what you're saying, but so what? I'm under forty, you're slightly over, who cares. It's just a matter of a few years difference."

"You sound like Melanie." Pat rolled her eyes.

"Then, I'd say she's one smart cookie," Ian offered, suppressing his glee that she had talked about him with her friend.

"And, I'll say to you what I said to her. It's more than a just *few* years difference. It's nearly a decade!" Pat visibly winced when she said it out loud and Ian knew he had to jump in and do damage control.

"Alright, fair enough. But, in the grand scheme of things, does it really matter?" he asked, bypassing her clarifier. "I mean, neither one of us is exactly a child here, right? I honestly can't see what a small difference in age matters at this point in the game."

When Pat didn't give him an answer, Ian reached across the table and gently took her hand in his.

"Listen," he said, his voice warm and soothing as he ran his thumb gently back and forth across her knuckles. "I know that women have the whole age crap shoved down their throats practically from the time they reach adulthood. But, you really have to believe me; when I look at you, age is the last thing on my mind."

"You don't have to say that," Pat told him, looking a lot less stressed as he continued his methodical stroking. "I wasn't fishing for compliments."

"The fact is, I find you enchanting. You're smart, you're funny—"

"And, you know this *how*?"

"Trust me," he said, with a wink as he released her hand. "I've asked around, too."

Her face was a picture of surprise and Ian suppressed a chuckle. He wasn't finished. "And, you've got spunk, strength and stillness; all wrapped up in a gorgeous, make a man want to break any vow to get to you, package."

Pat grinned and blushed. "Okay," she said, her face finally lit up with enthusiasm. "Fine. I guess if that's how you really feel, who am I to say no to that?"

Ian threw back his head and let out a bark of laughter. Jackpot! He'd done it! He'd had a game plan and he'd executed it to perfection. He took a breath and looked into her gorgeous blue eyes, hoping she was prepared for what he had in store. He'd meant what he'd thought earlier, she had no idea of how special she was, nor her own beauty. He was making it his personal mission that she found out.

***

CHAPTER TEN

"Whew, there's a wicked nip in that air!" Melanie breezed through Pat's open kitchen door, dark hair askew and arms laden with bulging carrier bags.

"I know," Pat replied, closing her oven door and wiping her hands on a nearby dish towel. "It just suddenly turned and it's freezing." She reached out to take some of the bags from Melanie's grasp. "Here, let me help."

Melanie handed over the bags, stamped her feet and rubbed her hands together. "Yup, I think autumn is finally packing it in, moving aside for winter to do her thing."

"It actually feels like we could be in for snow." Duncan, Melanie's boyfriend, followed her inside the house; his booming voice bringing the kitchen to life.

"Then, please, close the door," Melanie insisted, flapping her arms when a gust of cool, damp air rushed in behind him. "It's not only freezing, it's ruining the gorgeous smells in here."

"Mel, you're the best," Pat said as she began unloading plastic containers of food from the bags and placing them on the kitchen island. "Mmm, brownies and cookies and pie, oh my!"

"Don't thank me," Melanie replied, while untangling her crimson wrap from around her shoulders. "It's all Duncan."

Pat looked up and smiled. She adored Duncan. Had pretty much adored him from the moment Melanie had started talking about him. He was a large, solid man, six foot four and easily two hundred and fifty pounds, and he treated Melanie with a gentle reverence; as though he still couldn't quite believe his luck in being with her.

Pat knew Melanie felt the same way. She and her ex-husband Richard, or *Dick* as she was fond of calling him, had split up when their daughter Gina had been just two years of age. He'd become a cliché, barely seeing Gina, only coming around when the mood struck him, or he was momentarily bored with one of his conquests and wanted to play happily families. Melanie had wanted none of it.

From the moment the divorce papers had been signed, she had thrown herself into raising her daughter on her own and building her lingerie business; never allowing herself time to date, or even contemplate adding a man into the mix.

That is, until Duncan showed up.

Thirteen years after Melanie had shut her relationship doors, Duncan had arrived via a secret fix-up from a friend. Larger than life and with a smile that would warm you to your toes, Melanie hadn't stood a chance. He was a steady and determined suitor and, in what she called a moment of weakness, she'd let him gently cajole her into believing him when he'd said he was thrilled she had a fifteen year old daughter and wasn't looking for anything too serious.

Brave man. Smart, too. It was two years later and they still carried on like a honeymooning couple.

"I was thinking the same thing about snow," Pat commented, while she set out the final container of food. "That's why I asked Michael to go out there and rake up the last of the leaves. Did you see him?"

"No. Must have missed him in my mad dash from the car to the house." Melanie inhaled the savory smell of turkey, vegetables, stuffing and fresh bread with appreciation. "My God, the house smells fantastic. I'm starving, I haven't eaten anything in preparation for this meal."

"There's munchies, and antipasto, and cheese and crackers, and veggies and dip on the table." Pat pointed to the dishes. "Help yourself."

Duncan placed the bags he'd carried inside with him onto the sidebar. "I saw Michael around the side of the house," he offered, then reached for Melanie's wrap and hung it on a hook by the door. "He looked like he was close to being done."

Such a gentleman, Pat thought, before he spun around to face her, a wide grin across his face.

"Happy Thanksgiving, gorgeous," he said, walking over to her and wrapping his arms around her in a warm hug. "Thanks for opening up the house to us."

Pat reveled in the feeling of his cozy green sweater against her cheek, squeezed him back and laughed. "It's my pleasure. What's Thanksgiving without family? Pour me a glass of red, will you?"

"Coming right up." Duncan let her go and went back to the sidebar to start unloading bottles of wine, arranging them in a neat row.

"Oooh, it must be Thanksgiving if you're requesting wine before dinner," Melanie teased.

"Or, your bad influence is rubbing off after all these years and I've finally succumbed." Pat made a motion of volleying a serve back toward Melanie.

Melanie snickered and stuck out her tongue. "Call it whatever you want, but I'd say it's progress. Red for me too, Honey," Melanie said to Duncan as she sat down on one of the roomy chairs next to the table.

"Absolutely, my lovely lady."

Duncan flashed Melanie an affectionate smile and Pat watched them, reveling in their togetherness. She had a hunch her reveling, as opposed to feelings of envy, were a direct result of her spending far less evenings alone over the past few weeks.

Ian had taken her by storm since their agreement to get to know one another, dropping into the bookstore on a whim, taking her for coffees and lunches, running with her in the mornings, teaching Whiskey tricks - yes, a cat learning tricks - and then slowly easing himself into a position whereby she allowed some gentle, then increasingly passionate kisses and...

"Are Crystal and Kent around?" Melanie reached out and grabbed a slice of Swiss cheese and a cracker from a plate on the table.

Pat inhaled sharply and refocused upon the room. She cleared her throat and hoped she didn't look too flushed by her wayward thoughts. It was becoming so easy for her to slip into her memories of the heat of Ian's skin under her fingers and the pleasure of his mouth on hers. She'd been so nervous about any sort of intimacy with a man other than Stephen and now, all she could think about was what it was going to be like when they consummated their relationship.

"Uh-huh," she said, sitting down in a chair opposite Melanie. "Upstairs. They should be down right away. I'm surprised Kent isn't underfoot like the cat. He's been sneaking in and out all afternoon grabbing snacks without Crystal seeing him."

"Sounds like a typical boy." Duncan smirked and began pouring the wine.

"Oh, I'm warning you, watch it. You can't call him that," Pat told him as she happily received the glass he held out to her. "Thank you," she added and inhaled the rich, earthy scent with a sigh.

Melanie laughed. "Speaking from recent experience?"

Duncan handed another glass of wine to Melanie, then pulled out a chair to sit down.

Pat rolled her eyes. "Yup. This afternoon. Crystal gave me a detailed lecture about how they're no longer kids, they're in college now and deserve to be treated as adults. Blah, blah, blah. I'm surprised I didn't get a PowerPoint presentation, too."

"Sooo, tell us." Melanie locked eyes with Pat over her wine glass. "Did you grow a pair since we spoke this morning and tell your gorgeous suitor he could come over?"

Pat pulled a face and shook her head. "No, I did not." She stretched her neck from side to side. "It didn't feel right."

Melanie sighed and looked at Pat in exasperation. She'd been privy to all the details of the budding romance and it made her crazy that Pat was always putting herself last.

"And, it's not because of the kids and I'm putting myself last," Pat insisted, reading Melanie's face.

"Oh, come *on*." Melanie huffed, tucking her legs beneath her on her seat. "It is, too. They're not babies, Pat. They'll handle it that you're seeing someone. And, who knows, maybe they'll surprise you and be glad. Happy that their old Mother is occupied and they don't have to worry about making their Sunday phone call to make sure you're still alive."

Pat laughed and reached out a hand to slap Melanie's shoulder. "Very funny. But, I'm serious. It really isn't about them. It's about the fact that Ian and I agreed, both of us together, it feels too soon to be parading our friendship around."

Duncan, reaching out for a cracker and some antipasto, snorted audibly when Pat said 'friendship'. She cut her eyes at him and he shrugged his shoulders in reply before filling his mouth with cracker. Honestly, she knew Melanie kept no secrets from him, but *still*.

"Oh, *please*." Melanie added to Duncan's snort and rolled her eyes. "Friendship, my ass." She pointed at finger directly at Pat and added, "I mean, look at you! An entire day of cooking and you still have a spring in your step and a healthy flush to your cheeks. Nobody's fooled."

"The spring is from too much coffee," Pat said, defensively, knowing she sounded full of baloney. "And, the so-called healthy flush is just because of the steam from cooking."

Melanie laughed out loud, then shook her head. She was fully convinced it had been entirely Pat's decision that Ian was absent from their gathering. He was blatantly smitten and would have said or done anything Pat wanted, if it meant keeping her happy.

"Whatever." Melanie waved her hand dismissively. "You two have been cavorting for weeks now, what's wrong with a bit of parading?"

Pat was about to protest again, but was saved from having to come up with more pathetically weak excuses by Michael pushing open the kitchen door.

"Who's parading? Someone's in a parade?" he asked, a large grin on his handsome face as he let a gust of cool, damp air into the room. "Really? Around here?"

Duncan laughed and stood up from his chair. "No," he said, extending a hand to pat Michael affectionately on the shoulder. "No parades, I'm afraid. Unless you and your friends have something planned we don't know about."

"That'd be the day," Michael replied, shutting the door; then pulling off his letterman jacket and hanging it on a hook beside Melanie's wrap. "They're like me, at home. With the probable exception that they're not working their tails off in their parents' yards."

"Did you manage to get the leaves all done?" Pat asked, hopefully.

He walked over to the table and bent forward to envelop Pat in a hug.

"Yes," he said, then added, teasingly, "And, you're lucky I'm guilt ridden for being away so long. Otherwise, there's no way in hell I would have tackled that yard. Those trees have gotten huge! There were so many leaves, I thought my arms were going to fall off."

"Oh, come on!" Melanie slapped the table with her palm and let out a bark of laughter. "Not only are you earning your keep, but you're young. Enjoy it!"

Michael fixed her with a flirty grin and moved around the table to hug her as warmly as he had his Mother.

"Speaking of young, what's with you and Mom? It is the water, or some secret elixir? You both look sensational. I'd say it could be the new hairstyle for Mom, but *you...*" He raised his eyebrows up and down suggestively. "I think your youthful grace must be due to the large man to my left."

Pat snorted derisively, stood up and affectionately ruffled his short hair; once blonde with youth and since turned brown with maturity. Combined with his bright blue eyes, generous mouth and high cheek bones, her son looked so much like a younger version of his father it was startling.

"Okay," she said, walking over to the oven to check on the turkey. "Whatever it is you're angling for, you can stop. Drinks are on the sidebar, help yourself."

"Me? Angling?" Michael affected an offended expression, then began peeking into the containers on the island.

"Leave those," Pat told him, while grabbing her oven mitts. "Have some chips, or some cheese and crackers."

Melanie sipped her wine and watched, giggling into her glass at Pat's attempt to steer the conversational waters in another direction. The very idea of how Michael would react if he was informed right then and there that it wasn't just his Mom's hairstyle that had been refreshed, nearly had her in fits.

"*Mel,*" Duncan warned, watching her with a wary eye. He knew her too well and recognized it was hit or miss as to whether or not she'd blurt something she couldn't cover up.

Melanie wrinkled her nose at him. "I'll be good," she whispered. "Even if it kills me."

"You are such a sweet thing." Crystal's cooing voice offered them a distraction as she trailed down the stairs, Whiskey draped contentedly in her arms.

She hadn't been so indulgent when she'd first met him, quite the opposite. However, just as Pat had predicted, he was impossible not to like and sure enough, in a matter of hours, he'd thawed her daughter out and cast his spell.

"*There* she is," Melanie said, placing her wine glass on the table.

"Oh, hey there!" Crystal's face lit up when she saw Melanie and Duncan. "I didn't hear you guys come in."

Pat pushed the roasting pan holding the turkey back into the oven, closed the door and watched Melanie stand up, smooth her burgundy trousers and wait for Crystal to gently set Whiskey on the floor before wrapping her in a warm hug.

"It's so good to see you," Melanie enthused, having forgiven her for almost causing trouble for Pat with Stephen when she'd first opened the bookstore. Water under the bridge. She pulled back and held Crystal by the shoulders to get a better look at her. "You look terrific! Doesn't she look great, Pat?"

"Gorgeous," Pat agreed and leaned against the island.

Kent bounded down the stairs a moment later. "Smelling good in here!" he said, rubbing his hands together. "I'm starving."

Crystal folded her arms across her chest and shook her head at him. "Please. Like you haven't been sneaking food all day, right?"

"Well," Kent began, raising his hands up like he was on the firing line. "That depends upon your definition."

"Of what?" Crystal countered. "Food?"

Duncan placed his wine glass beside Melanie's and stood up to offer Kent his hand. "If I might interrupt?"

"Absolutely!" Kent grinned so hard and sounded so relieved, both Crystal and Melanie snickered.

Michael, standing beside Pat, laughed as he shoveled potato chips from a bowl on the island into his mouth. "Good save," he said, between chews.

Duncan winked at him, then turned back to Kent. "How're you kids adapting to the new living arrangements?"

"Funny you should ask," Crystal began, reaching out to take Kent's hand as she spoke. They exchanged an intimate look and Pat immediately felt nervous.

Oh lord, she thought. *Something's going on. Please don't say you're pregnant.* Her pulse quickened and she wanted to reach out and take Melanie's hand. She settled for gripping the countertop.

"Man, that turkey smells amazing, Mom." Michael nudged Pat aside as he moved from the chip bowl to the fridge. Pat shot him a look, but he was so focused upon his stomach that he missed it. Instead, he opened the fridge door, stuck his head inside and asked loudly, "Is there anything else I can eat besides scraps, before we get to the real meal?"

"*Michael!*" Crystal's voice held more than a measure of exasperation.

He pulled his head out of the fridge. "What? It's fine. I'll still have more than enough room for dinner. God, chill Crys."

"I don't give a crap about your never ending appetite." Crystal practically spat between clenched teeth. "I'm trying to have a *moment* here, you buffoon."

Melanie and Duncan raised their eyebrows at one another and took a step back toward the table. Pat wondered if she dared move to retrieve her wine and even Kent, sensing correctly not to get in the way of the brother and sister dynamic, went mute.

"A *moment*? What're you talking about? For what? Why are you being so coy anyway?"

Crystal narrowed her eyes at him, took a deep breath and continued. "I'm not being coy! I'd just like a *moment*—"

Michael rolled his eyes and cut her off. "God, you're such a drama queen. If you have something to say, say it already."

Pat was about to step in and insist that Michael lay off, but Crystal didn't give her a chance.

"Fine!" she blurted, then turned loving eyes to Kent. "We have big news. We're engaged, okay? Are you happy? Was that fast and non-melodramatic enough for you?"

Melanie clapped her hands and yelped, "Engaged!"

Whiskey, startled by her sudden outburst, scattered out from under the table and took refuge in his basket tucked in a corner of the room.

Duncan beamed and said, "Congratulations!" before reaching out to envelop Crystal in a warm hug.

Michael paused, looked at his sister with wide, stunned eyes, then whooped and threw himself at Kent for a brotherly hug.

Pat stood motionless, her mouth slightly agape, and watched it all as though in a dream; hardly believing what she'd just heard.

Her eighteen year old daughter; just months into her first year of college; the same girl who had so childishly given Pat grief about the bookstore, was engaged to be married. Married!

Pat closed the distance between herself and the table, reached for her glass of wine, knocked it back in one and took a deep breath. She knew she had to show support, lest her daughter made a federal case out of the fact that her own mother wasn't overjoyed for her happiness.

"Here we go," she muttered under her breath, before a sharp knock interrupted her.

Oh, praise be, she thought and turned gratefully toward the opening door; inhaling the refreshing shot of cold night air as it rolled into the warm kitchen.

"Hello!" Travis called out cheerily, his blue eyes sparkling as he crossed the threshold into the house. "Happy Thanksgiving, all!"

Gerry, trailing closely behind, stepped inside as well and pushed the door firmly shut behind him. "What's going on?" he asked, eyebrows high on his forehead as he took in the tableau before him. "Why's everyone hugging?"

"Crystal and Kent are engaged!" Pat practically shrieked, her attempt to sound joyful tripping across the scales and diving into hysteria.

Thankfully, when Gerry and Travis let out squeals of their own, nobody noticed. Except for Melanie. She arched an eyebrow at Pat, lifted a wine bottle from the sideboard and held it questioningly in her direction.

Pat nodded and reached up to rub her temples. Something told her, her teetotaling days were swiftly going to become a thing of her past.

***

"You could have said no," Melanie commented as she wrapped her hands around her coffee cup and sipped the fresh brew.

Pat sat opposite her at the kitchen table and rubbed her eyes wearily; thoroughly drained from a day of cooking, an evening of excited chatter over wedding plans and, finally, the effort to remain outwardly calm in the face of all the new information on the table. So much for being infused with energy from her newly budding relationship. She was knackered.

Crystal and Kent had retired to their room; Travis and Gerry had vacated the house laden down with leftovers; Michael had gone off to see friends who were also home for the holiday and Duncan had made a beeline for the living room to relax on the sofa and sleep off the effects of too much turkey dinner. Only Pat and Melanie were left sitting in the glow of the kitchen's overhead lights; Whiskey curled up and fast asleep on an adjacent empty chair.

"I couldn't have," Pat said, with a sigh. "Both Travis and Gerry have their hearts set on being in the wedding party, how could I disappoint them?"

Melanie snorted at Pat's attempt at humor. "Or, being the wedding planners. God, at one point there I had to kick Gerry under the table to shut him up."

Pat grinned. "I appreciate it, but Travis picked up where Gerry left off. They were like a steam train and there was no diverting them from the matrimonial tracks."

Melanie grinned and sipped her coffee.

"I do have to say, though, I'm rather shocked Crystal would be so wedding gaga after everything she witnessed with me and Stephen."

"She's young and thinks you're old, so she doesn't connect the two," Melanie offered, sagely, as she picked up a brownie from a plate on the table. "But, as for having it here at the house, I still say you could have told her it wasn't an option."

Pat raised an eyebrow. "Oh, please, you know I couldn't have looked Crystal in the eye and dashed her fuzzy, cotton candy spun dream of having her wedding here in the home of her youth."

"All I'm saying is, if it had been me and Gina—"

"If it had been Gina," Pat butt in. "You would have been outside in the freezing cold and falling snow measuring the space for a gazebo and marriage alter."

Melanie snorted with amusement. Pat was right. "*Fine.*" She snickered. "You're probably right."

"No probably about it. I am right."

"But this isn't *me*, this is you we're talking about." Melanie insisted, making grand, sweeping gestures with her brownie. "And, *you,* my dear friend, had plans. Serious, unload this house and all of its upkeep, plans. Now, you have to put them all on hold until practically next summer."

"I know." Pat shrugged, then stood up to retrieve a glass from the cupboard. "But, it's probably my fault for not saying anything from the get go."

"No way!" Melanie was outraged at the very idea. She took a bite of her brownie, chewed vigorously and added, "It's absolutely not your fault."

"Okay, maybe *fault* is the wrong word," Pat said as she poured a tall drink of water from the tap and returned to her seat. "But, how was Crystal to know what I was thinking when I didn't tell her? As far as she's concerned, I'm going to grow old here."

"So, are you going to tell her?"

"No," Pat admitted, resigned. "I'm not."

"Seriously?" Melanie popped the remainder of her brownie in her mouth, pushed her long, dark hair from her face and gaped at Pat. "You're going to go on living in this empty house, for the next almost year, just so that Crystal and Kent can have their June wedding in the backyard?"

Pat could hear the disbelieving tone in Melanie's voice and wasn't surprised. She had been going on about how excited she was at the prospect of getting a smaller place and now it appeared she was throwing that dream away. But, she wasn't.

"I'm not backing out of my plans, Mel," Pat told her.

"Are you sure about that?" Melanie countered. "You've been telling me, repeatedly, that you can't wait to lift the burden of this house off your metaphorical shoulders and get a smaller, cottage home. And, now, you're going to just shove those dreams aside—"

"*Temporarily*," Pat interrupted, emphasizing the word. "I'm just putting them temporarily on hold and then, once the wedding is behind us, I'll get them back up and running."

Melanie did not look convinced.

"Besides," Pat added. "All things considered, it's probably better anyway."

"How so?" Melanie was skeptical.

"Obviously, I'm going to be called into service to help with the wedding arrangements. And, doing that and trying to sell the house at the same time *and* running the bookstore..." Pat shook her head and exhaled. "It's too much at once."

Melanie shrugged, Pat had a point. "If there's any question about it, you know I'll help as well, right?"

"Yes, I do. Thank you. But, good God, did you *hear* what I said?" Pat moaned, then reached down to the floor where Whiskey had begun weaving his way in and around her ankles. "I just said, 'the wedding' as though it's no big deal that my eighteen year old daughter is the bride to be."

Melanie gave her a sympathetic look. She could only begin to imagine how she would feel if it was Gina announcing her upcoming nuptials. Granted, Gina was only seventeen and far from serious about any one boy, but *still...* The very idea made her shudder on her friend's behalf.

Pat snuggled Whiskey into her lap and stroked his fur, attempting to soothe herself. "Listen to me," she said, a smirk on her face. "*Mother of the bride.*"

Melanie grinned, sharing her small stab at humor.

"And, did you hear Crystal?" Pat went on. "Trying to offer *me* words of comfort?"

"Well," Melanie said, desperately wracking her brain for something more than a trite platitude.

"*Don't worry, Mom,*" Pat quoted Crystal, her voice an octave higher than normal. "*Kent and I aren't doing anything rash, like quitting school.*"

Melanie lifted her coffee mug and took a long swallow. Pat was on a role, she was better off leaving the banalities and letting her finish.

"Like I'm supposed to be thinking, 'Whew, dodged *that* bullet. Whatever they're doing, at least they're not being rash'!"

Melanie couldn't help herself and giggled. It was all so sudden, so absurdly unexpected, she couldn't help but snicker in the face of it.

Pat caught her eye and, against her better judgment, her smirk became a grin. The grin swiftly gave way to a wide smile, and then rapidly journeyed into a full on giggle fit.

"It's ludicrous!" She sputtered, trying to speak through her laughter. "She's just barely out of high school for hell's sake! I'm not even in menopause! Couldn't she have at least had the decency to wait until I'm through *the change?*"

Melanie snorted and set her coffee cup back on the table. "I know! The gall!"

Pat chortled so hard at Melanie's reply, her eyes leaked tears down her cheeks. The phone trilled on its base, jarring her, and she swiped at her face with her fingertips while giving Whiskey a nudge to get him off her lap.

"What now?" she said, to Melanie, before catching her breath, reaching for the receiver and warbling, "Hello?"

"Pat?"

Ian's voice was so unexpected, Pat snorted into the handset and sent Melanie into a fresh round of giggles behind her.

"Yes," Pat said. "It's me. Sorry, Melanie and I seem to be having a meltdown. Too much wine, or coffee, or possibly both."

"As long as it's in the house," he said, amusement lacing his words. "Don't want to shock the neighbors."

Pat smiled and relished the wave of appreciation that swept over her as he spoke. He didn't question it, just rolled with it. After so many years with Stephen and his barely veiled exasperation at she and Melanie's giggle fits, it was terribly refreshing. Pat sighed. How wonderful it would have been to be next to him, preferably in his arms, at that moment.

"Hey." Duncan pushed open the door that separated the kitchen from the living room. "A lot of giggling and snorting going on in here, you girls okay?"

Pat watched as Melanie nodded her head and Duncan leaned into her for a kiss, then turned her back and gave Ian her full attention.

"How was your evening," she asked, feeling clear-headed in the face of Melanie and Duncan's affection.

"It was okay," Ian replied, his voice soft and intimate. "Would have been much better spent with you. Next time though, right?"

Pat swallowed as yet another wave of gratitude swept over her. He was so willing to take the journey at her discretion. "Absolutely," she agreed, warm and happy inside. "Christmas is definitely ours."

"I've marked it on my calendar," he told her and then asked, "How did your dinner go? Were your kids okay with Whiskey?"

Pat sighed, suddenly remembering what she had thought was going to be her biggest worry: the kids might balk at the addition of Whiskey to her life. It felt like ages ago, now that Crystal had dropped her engagement bomb.

"Just fine, actually." She stood up from her chair and walked over to lean against the kitchen island. "It turned out he wasn't the big news. We were given a bit of a surprise just before dinner."

"Oh?" Ian's voice was laced with curiosity. "Good or bad?"

"Pat," Melanie said, interrupting their conversation.

"Hang on a sec," Pat told Ian and pressed the phone to her chest.

"We're going to take off," Melanie said, slapping a hand across her mouth in an attempt to hide a large yawn.

"Okay."

"Leave all of this." Melanie gestured to the pots and pans soaking in the sink, the plates and cutlery on the countertops. "And, I'll come by tomorrow morning and we'll have strong coffee and a good chat and clean up. Okay?"

"Deal." Pat reached out and gave her a quick hug.

Duncan leaned around Melanie and planted a warm kiss on Pat's cheek. "Thanks again for the meal, the company, everything," he said, before walking across the kitchen to hold open the door.

Pat grinned. "Always a pleasure. I'll see you tomorrow."

"Tell Ian we said hello," Melanie called over her shoulder as she headed out into the night.

"Will do," Pat called back. "Night." She watched the door shut behind them, then lifted the waiting receiver from her chest. "Still there?"

"Always." Came Ian's reply.

***

CHAPTER ELEVEN

Pat sat on a tall stool behind the cash desk and wearily attempted to stifle yet another large yawn. She'd been the first one in to open the bookstore that morning and, as the day drifted into afternoon, the early start was catching up.

"Wow," Sandra commented as she made her way down the stairs to the main floor. "Time for a coffee?"

Pat grinned. "You may need to hook me up to an IV."

"Late night?"

"You don't know the half of it. And, then, with the non-stop wedding chatter, the entire weekend turned into one long late night."

"I still can't believe your daughter's getting married." Sandra shook her head and picked up a pile of books on the floor beside the cash desk. "You don't look old enough to have a daughter getting married."

"You're kind, but I'm sure that today I look more than haggard enough."

"Not even," Sandra insisted, carrying the books with her and disappearing behind a shelf.

Pat grinned. "Don't worry, you don't need to be kind to get your Christmas bonus."

Sandra's disembodied laughter drifted out from behind the rows of books on the shelves.

"Listen." Pat yawned, again. "I'm not sure what else I can muster up the energy for, unless I duck out and grab a seriously strong coffee."

"Just leave it then," Sandra told her as she reemerged empty handed, the books filed. "The day is winding down, you've been going like a whirling dervish since you got here, there's nothing that can't be left until tomorrow."

Pat chuckled and pulled her glasses, attached to their dreaded granny chain, from around her neck. "Whirling dervish?" she repeated, grinning. "Where does a woman of your youth get introduced to such an old expression?"

"I blame my Grandfather," Sandra said, smiling fondly as she talked. It was clear she had a soft spot, and a close relationship, with him.

Pat nodded and was about to ask further questions when the shop bell chimed, cutting their conversation short.

"Ooh. *Quaint.*"

Pat looked over, certain she'd heard the voice before. It sounded a lot like... Ah, yes, Alexa. The girl from the party Melanie had dragged her to, Ian's *sister-in-law*, stood confidently in the shop doorway. And, she wasn't alone. Accompanied by another equally slim and gorgeous young woman, Pat wondered fleetingly if Alexa had a brunette twin that hadn't been mentioned.

They were even dressed the same, both wearing skin tight jeans; knee high, leather boots and car coat length, leather jackets. Other than their scarves and the contrasting color of their hair, their similarities were just shy of being freaky.

"Well, look who's here! Pam!" Alexa blurted, as though she was utterly surprised to see Pat standing behind the desk. As if.

Sandra raised an eyebrow while she watched the interaction, acutely aware of Pat's body language. It wasn't good.

"*Pat*, actually," Pat told her, while inwardly seething at the obvious attempt at a power play. Two could play that game. "Alice, wasn't it?" she volleyed back, her voice and face neutral.

The dark haired friend snickered at the name and Pat inwardly cheered. Score one for 'Pam'.

Alexa's sneer deepened on her Pixie-like face. "*Alexa*," she said, flipping her long, blonde hair over her shoulders and glancing around the shop, trying to look bored with what she saw.

Her friend, apparently oblivious to the tension, went, "Oh!" and took off between the shelves without a backward glance.

"Bree!" Alexa called after her, clearly annoyed she'd been so swiftly deserted. So much for strength in numbers.

"Just looking," Bree called back. "I'll be right there."

"I'll help her," Sandra offered, grateful for the excuse to get the hell away from the two women so clearly at a standoff.

"So," Pat said, clearing her throat, suddenly more awake than she'd been all day. Amazing what a little adrenaline could do. "Is there something I can help you with? Or, are you just browsing, killing time?"

Alexa fiddled with the large, gold hoops in her ears and blinked her sky blue eyes at Pat. "Probably just browsing," she replied. "Bree was the one shopping and said she wanted a new book, so I told her she should just get an eReader. But, she wouldn't be swayed and insisted on a DTB..."

"DTB?" Pat frowned, hating that she had to ask. However, she wasn't going to get caught out on ignorance of an acronym.

"*Dead tree book*," Alexa replied, the small sneer back on her face.

"Seriously?" Pat was taken aback by the information. Not a flattering acronym at all.

"Uh-huh." Alexa cleared her throat and twirled a lock of hair around her index finger. "So, *anyway*, since Bree had her heart set on a DTB, I gave in and told her that a friend of Ian's worked here—"

"I *own* the shop, actually." Pat cut her off. She knew she shouldn't rise to the bait, but on the heels of the derogatory DTB information, it really irked her that Alexa was blatantly attempting to lower her status.

"Right." Alexa shrugged and affected a bored expression. "Whatever. So, anyway, that's why we're here." She exhaled and fingered a few of the bookmarks for sale beside the cash desk and then her face lit up. "I guess I should be polite and ask you, how was *your* Thanksgiving?"

Ahh, Pat thought. *And, there goes the other shoe.* "It was lovely," she said, simply.

Alexa smiled, the expression stopping half way up her face, nowhere near her eyes. "Ours was really great, too." She played with the ends of the green scarf she had wrapped artistically around her neck and added, "Ian really got into the spirit of it all this year, but I guess he probably already told you about it, right?"

"Right." Pat could feel her pulse speeding up, but would be damned if she was going to show it. The girl in front of her was just that, a *girl*. And, Pat wasn't about to lower herself to take part in her childish, schoolyard games.

"Okay, done." Bree strode back toward the cash desk, book in hand. "Found what I was looking for."

Sandra came quickly behind her, saw the naked hostility between Pat and Alexa and immediately stepped in behind the desk, nudging Pat aside. "I've got this," she said.

"Thanks." Pat nodded at her and took a step outside the cash area, meeting Alexa almost face to face. She allowed herself one small delight; she'd worn heels that day, giving her a height advantage.

Alexa took a small step back, clearly not prepared for the idea that Pat might be brave enough to meet her head on. "Bree," she said, affecting a nonchalant tone. "The smell in here is getting to me. I'm going to wait outside."

As Pat watched her turn on her heel to leave, she delivered to Alexa the same steely glare she'd often used on Crystal when she was young. Clearly, it worked on more than just her daughter.

"Oh," Alexa said, glancing over her shoulder before she made her exit. "Do me a favor, *Pam*. When you see Ian, tell him Alexa said she'll be his games partner any night of the week. No need to reserve just for the holidays."

And with that, she twitched her pert backside out the door, leaving Pat with no time to respond.

"Excuse me," Bree said, brushing by Pat to follow Alexa out the door. "Great shop," she said, smiling. "I'll be back, thanks."

Pat could only smile and wave, her voice had caught firmly in her throat and she was afraid that a roar, instead of coherent words, might come out if she dared open her mouth.

"Wow," Sandra commented, when the door closed. "Quite the little bitch."

Pat raised an eyebrow and had to grin. Quite.

***

"You okay," Ian asked, his voice full of concern as he snuggled up to Pat on the couch in her living room. "You've been really quiet, did I do something wrong?"

Pat swallowed, debating over her choice of words. While she wanted to just let the encounter with Alexa go, not give the girl the satisfaction of causing tremors, she also felt sudden extreme vulnerability.

"What are we doing here?" Pat asked him.

Ian raised his eyebrows in surprise. "I don't follow," he said.

Pat shifted her position on the couch to face him. "I mean, what *are* we?"

Ian nodded, thoughtfully. "Okay, I hear you. But, first I have to ask, what do you want to be?"

Pat was sure she could hear the audible 'thwack' as he volleyed the question back into her court. She took a breath and rubbed her hands across the soft fabric of her red fleece pajama bottoms. "I'm not exactly, sure. On the one hand I'd like to clearly define things, but at the same time, I'm afraid to define them. I'm nervous it might change everything and then the house of cards will come falling down around my feet."

"Wow," Ian said. "Okay, well, how about I'll be the one to take the leap and offer a definition?"

Pat nodded and wrapped her arms around her knees, hugging them to her chest.

Ian stroked her arm as he looked directly into her eyes. "I know we haven't been seeing each other, *dating*, for that long. But, even though it's only been a few weeks, I think about you every day."

Pat nodded again. She felt the same way.

"And, not only do I think about you, I think about how eager I am to see you." He watched her for some reaction and when she stayed silent, continued. "Basically, I'm crazy about you. And, I'd love to be able to call you my girlfriend, but if it's too soon for you, I'll wait."

He clamped his mouth shut and waited, his heart pounding in his chest.

Pat's breath caught in her throat when he used the word 'girlfriend'. She hadn't been anyone's girlfriend in over twenty years. She didn't care if she was too old for the word, the very idea delighted her. She smiled.

"I'd like that," she said, biting her lip to keep from giggling. "I'd like for you to call me your *girlfriend*."

Ian grinned widely, all of his straight, white teeth on display. "Excellent," he said, pleasure written all over his face.

"There's just one other thing." Pat ventured. "Trisha's sister came into the store today." She refused to use the girl's name.

"Alexa?"

Pat nodded and tried to keep from sneering at the sound of her name. From the look on Ian's face, he was thoroughly puzzled as to where she was going with her information.

"Did anything happen between you two, at Thanksgiving? Because," she clarified, lying through her teeth. "If it did, you can say so. We hadn't defined anything between us yet, so I'll stay cool and calm and keep my mouth shut."

Ian began to frown as she spoke and Pat sped up her words; finally finishing off, rapid fire, with, "I just think it would be good if I know, so I'm not the fool in the dark."

"Whoa." Ian raised a hand in the air to stop her. "Wait. Stop. No. Absolutely not. Nothing happened. Nothing has ever happened between Alexa and me. And, to put a fine point on it, nothing ever will."

He ran a hand through his hair and exhaled. "Why would you even think that?"

"Well..." Pat hesitated. "She happened to come into the bookstore, so..."

Ian's eyebrows knotted together and he tried to understand. "So? What? Did she say something to you, to make you think that?"

Pat was ready to let it drop. His shock at the very suggestion was so genuine, she believed him immediately. "Possibly," she said, and then added dismissively, "But, it doesn't matter. Not now."

Ian reached out and wrapped his hands around her forearms to gently tug her into his lap. "Pat," he said, his voice warm and welcoming as he embraced her. "I told you before, I'm enchanted by you." He started to kiss her neck and during the gaps when his lips left her skin, added, "I'm under your spell. There's no way out for me, except for in."

Pat's pulse kicked up and she turned her mouth to meet his. She believed him. Oh, how she believed him.

Ian moaned as she opened her mouth to him and ran his hands over her shoulders and down her back to pull her closer. Pat could feel his desire and her skin felt as though it was on fire under his touch.

Ian paused to find the edge of her tee-shirt and deftly pulled it up and over her head, leaving nothing but the thin silk of her bra as a barrier to his touch. Not for long. He ran his hands through her hair and back down her spine, his mouth leaving a hot trail along her collar bone as he found the clasp on her bra and tugged it open.

"Jeez, Pat," he said, his voice thick with desire as he tossed her bra aside, then cupped her breasts. "You make me crazy."

Pat gulped and nodded, tearing at the buttons on his shirt. He helped, pulling the fabric apart and baring his strong chest, making her shudder as he pressed himself against her.

"I don't know how long I can wait," he said. "I'm sorry, but—"

"No," Pat agreed, greedily. She didn't want to delay things either. She stood up and within seconds had pulled down her pajama bottoms, revealing nothing but naked flesh.

Ian's breath came out in a whoosh when he laid eyes on her. "Good God," he said, his chest rising and falling as he feasted upon her. "You're beautiful."

Pat almost blushed at his words. Almost. She had the brief impulse to cover herself, fearing she looked too old in comparison to the girls of his past. However, when she watched him, watching her, desire won out. She could torture herself later, but in that moment with Ian looking at her with unabashed desire, she decided to let herself be beautiful.

"Show me," she told him, locking eyes and challenging him. "Show me how you feel."

He didn't need any other invitation. In a heartbeat, he stood up beside her, stripped away the rest of his clothes and it was Pat's turn to catch her breath as she took in the blatant maleness of him. All strong lines, lean tight muscles, golden skin and hard desire; she couldn't have drawn him better.

"Again," Ian said, as he reached out for her and ran hungry fingers over her flesh. "Forgive me. This dance is going to be straight forward. Maybe the next one will have more finesse."

Pat laughed as they tumbled back onto the couch. She didn't need finesse, not after a drought of nearly two years. She was quite happy with honest, no holds barred passion. It had been so long, too long, and when he rocked himself into her, the heat between them rising and their breath coming together as they found their rhythm, she let herself go and dived right down to the bottom of the pool.

***

CHAPTER TWELVE

Ian took a deep breath and braced himself as he opened the door to Melanie's lingerie shop. He'd contemplated going elsewhere to avoid embarrassment, but talked himself out of it. It was a foregone, logical conclusion she would be the best person to help him pick out something for Pat, for Christmas.

"Hello! Welcome to *Goddess*!" Melanie's voice rang out, before she appeared in the archway at the back of the shop that led to the change rooms. When she saw who it was, her face lit up. "Ian! To what do I owe this unexpected pleasure?"

Ian grinned while she walked over to where he stood at the front of the shop. She was such a great person, he understood why Pat adored her and considered her her best friend.

"Just doing some early holiday shopping," he said, trying not to blush.

"Early is right," Melanie said, raising her eyebrows and nodding appreciatively. "Did Tom and Trisha strong arm you into coming here?"

"No!" He laughed and shook his head. "In fact, I didn't even mention it."

"Right. Gotchya. You were never here." She pushed her dark, wavy hair from her face, cocked a curvy hip and crossed her arms over her chest. "So, how can I help you? I'm assuming you're here looking for a certain friend of mine?"

Ian chuckled some more, then cleared his throat. "Got it in one. I want to find something that will make her feel as pretty as she is."

Melanie grinned. "I'm telling you, Ian, you're a man after my heart. In fact, just the other day, I was saying the same thing to Duncan."

Ian raised an eyebrow. "And, did he say he was going to have to slug me the next time he saw me?"

"No," she said, slapping his arm lightly. "He knew what I meant. Duncan's a very secure man, trust me."

Ian watched her face and saw the naked adoration there when she spoke of Duncan. No question, the man had no worries.

"And, speaking of trusting me," Melanie said, sweeping her arms outward like a spokesmodel to indicate the racks and racks of lingerie, in all the colors of the rainbow and beyond. "Do you have anything particular in mind? Anything that catches your eye that you think Pat would like?"

Ian shrugged. "Not to sound too much like a caveman here, but I really need your judgement call on this one."

Melanie nodded. "Okay, no problem. Any particular vibe you're going for?"

Ian blinked, struck dumb as he took in the baby-dolls and teddies; the matching bras and panties; the slips and corsets. "As I said, I want something that she'll feel beautiful in and, uhh... sexy. But, at the same time, doesn't look like I'm dressing her up for an adult movie."

Melanie threw her head back and laughed out loud, causing Ian to relax on the spot. He'd been cringing at his description and Melanie's laughter was the exact thing to take the edge off.

"Sorry," she apologized, still grinning as she straightened the sleeves of her purple silk blouse.

"No," he replied. "Don't be. I needed that. I'm guessing by your laughter that you understand what I'm saying?"

"Yes," Melanie agreed. "I totally get what you mean and your comment about dressing her up for an adult movie cracked me up." She shook her head while she straightened some teddies on an adjacent rack. "I wish more men were willing to tell me so honestly, it would save a lot of time and effort to finally get to the thing they were looking for."

"Okay, then." He rubbed his hands together. "We know what we're looking for, no beating around the bush..." Ian tapered off, cringing as soon as he said it.

Melanie pressed her lips together, refusing to laugh a second time. "You really are smitten with her," she said, instead, looking at him in admiration.

Ian stopped cringing and smiled. "Hook, line and sinker," he said, matter-of-factly.

"It's going to be a good Christmas," she offered.

"You bet." He nodded confidently. "The best."

***

CHAPTER THIRTEEN

Pat grabbed two baskets of freshly baked rolls from the white granite countertop in Travis and Gerry's kitchen and carried them into their ornately decorated dining room. The entire house had been crafted in a roman inspired theme and the dining room, with its pillars, thick draperies and elaborate chandelier, kept that theme going strong.

"Tell me again," Pat called out, while nestling the baskets in amidst the paraphernalia on the lavishly set, ten seater table. "Why are we having such an opulent spread, so close on the heels of Thanksgiving?"

Ian walked into the room behind her, an affectionate grin on his face. "Just can't leave it alone, huh?" he teased.

"We told you," Travis said, patiently, as he trailed behind Ian and began straightening linen napkins that looked like they'd been laid out with a ruler. "We loved your Thanksgiving gathering. Loved it!"

"Loved it!" Gerry called out from the adjoining family room, to further emphasis Travis' point.

"But?" Pat pressed, her head cocked while she waited for the answer.

"*But,*" Travis admitted, tentatively, and fidgeted with the pillar style candles. "We felt that there was so much talk about the kids and their wedding—"

"Which we're extremely excited about!" Gerry threw in.

"Yes, we are!" Travis bantered back.

"And?" Pat nudged, waving her hand in a circle like an egg beater to move things along.

"*And,* while they love the kids," Melanie butt in as she carried two bottles of wine to the table. "We didn't end up getting a chance to have any adult conversation."

Travis nodded, clearly relieved that Melanie was the one to say it.

"*And,*" Melanie added, jerking her head pointedly toward Ian. "One of our numbers was absent from *that* gathering. Which was a shame."

"Exactly." Travis brushed his hands together, nodded sharply in satisfaction that he'd been understood, then turned toward the family room. "Duncan, Gerry, move your gorgeous tushes in here now. Dinner's ready."

"Wow," Duncan remarked while he got up from his seat on a hunter green, chaise lounge. "Travis giving me butt compliments. I must be doing something right."

Ian laughed and found his seat next to Pat. They were such a laid back and fun group. He'd had his share of experiences trying to navigate awkward social groups, it was a huge relief to feel at home and at ease so quickly with Pat's friends.

"Giggle all you want there, *boy-toy*, but I'd be including yours as well if you weren't already right here." Travis waggled his eyebrows at Ian, then waved a hand insistently at Pat to shut her up before she confronted his label.

"Leave it!" he said, vehemently. "It's a compliment!"

Pat pursed her lips and forced herself to keep quiet. While 'boy-toy' made her cringe, it was coming from Travis, after all. He never spoke with malice, so there was no need to make a mountain out of a molehill.

"So, who wants wine?" Duncan lifted a bottle of red and a bottle white in each hand and began pouring, not waiting for the answer. Ian watched in amusement, it was clear they all knew the drill.

"Ian?" Duncan queried. "Sorry, I don't know your preference yet."

"Red, if you still have it. Thanks."

"Good man." Duncan nodded and poured the last of the red into Ian's glass.

"So, speaking of *toying* around," Gerry offered, winking at Pat. "Now that the two of you are officially an item, are you going to get a little more public with your romance?"

"Gerry!" Pat nearly choked on her wine and glared at him in annoyance.

"What?" Gerry gave her a wide-eyed look and threw his hands up in the classic 'don't shoot' position.

Pat took a breath and set her wine glass on the table. "Don't you think you might be making Ian a bit uncomfortable with such a question?"

Gerry looked at Ian. "Am I?"

"Nope." Ian picked up his glass and tipped it gently in a salute before bringing it to his lips.

"You see?" Gerry shot Pat a smug smile. "Not uncomfortable."

Melanie snorted into her glass and Duncan nudged her with his elbow. "Don't," he hissed, under his breath.

"I'm just *saying*." Pat elaborated, while cutting her eyes at Ian. "We'll get more public, soon enough."

"Or, it'll be done for you," Travis commented, leaning back in his seat and folding his arms across his chest.

Melanie perked up. "Meaning?"

"*Meaning*, trying to keep things on the down-low doesn't always work. Especially in this town."

Pat snapped her head around. "What are you saying, Trav?"

He shrugged. "Just don't get too attached to the idea that people around here haven't figured out there's some serious slap and tickle going on between you and your young buck, here."

"Travis!" Pat slapped a hand on the table and her face began to flush.

"What?" He gave her the same shocked expression Gerry had and Ian started to snicker, not helping at all.

"Oh, boy," Melanie muttered and exchanged a look with Duncan.

He raised his eyebrows and nodded.

"Okay!" she said, piping up like an over excited cheerleader. "We should start eating this delicious food before it needs to be sent off to the microwave, yes?"

"Absolutely," Duncan chimed in, helping her along.

"Hey, where are the dogs?" Melanie asked, sounding like a talk-show host as she further shoved the conversation into safer waters.

Duncan cleared his throat and repressed a chuckle.

"Out with their walker," Gerry replied, then passed over a large platter heaped with homemade fried chicken.

"What's that?" Duncan took the platter and stared at Gerry, incredulous. "Someone else walking the dogs? Are you serious? Since when?"

"Since it got too cold for us," Travis said, blowing a kiss to Pat and jumping on the bandwagon to return them all to less volatile conversation. "We're wimps and we know it."

Pat stuck out her tongue at Travis just as the doorbell rang and Gerry leaped up from his chair. "Speak of the devil! They're back!"

"Brace yourself," Pat whispered in Ian's ear, a split second before a cacophony of dog yips and sounds of nail tips on hardwood shattered the peace of their gathering.

"Come on, Darlings," Gerry cooed from the kitchen, before he strode into the dining room with four perky, tail-wagging, wire-haired Dachshunds close on his heels.

Ian watched, wide-eyed, as Travis greeted them each by name, then sharply snapped his fingers and sent them all trotting off to settle into four baskets lined up neatly against one wall in the adjoining family room.

"Wow," he remarked. "Impressive."

Travis grinned and crinkled his nose in appreciation of the admiration. "Thank you. They're wonderful and Gerry really must take most of the credit for their impeccable manners."

"You do your share," Gerry insisted and reached out to give Travis' hand an affectionate squeeze before he returned to his seat.

"Personally, I think you're both mad as Hatter's," Melanie cut in as she picked up her wine glass. "But, I wouldn't have you any other way. It's your madness that makes you interesting!" She lifted her glass in a salute and took a long swallow.

The rest of them cracked up and Pat let her shoulders ease down from up around her ears. Okay, so Travis was being... *Travis*. So what? She'd always love him, despite his penchant for stirring the pot.

She glanced at Ian, grinning and fitting right into the mix as though he's always been there, and sat back contentedly. Nothing but good times ahead.

***

CHAPTER FOURTEEN

Ian gently nuzzled the back of Pat's neck, causing shivers to run up her spine. "This couch must have magical powers," he commented, a smile in his voice.

Pat grinned and shifted her weight beside him, pressing the length of her back up against his chest and stomach. In the few weeks that had passed since they'd first consummated their relationship, they seemed to be drawn back again and again to the soft yielding sofa in the family room.

"Or," she teased. "Its appeal lies in the fact that it's a whole lot more accessible than making our way all the way upstairs."

"No," Ian disagreed, while running the tips of his fingers along the length of her bare thigh. "Magic. Definitely magic."

Pat laughed and stretched languidly, enjoying the feeling of him stirring again in response to her movements. She wasn't sure what had happened to her since their first night together, but whatever it was, she was thrilled.

Sex had become such a small part of her life with Stephen that the idea of being physical with him, especially in the last year of their marriage, hadn't interested her in the least. She'd just assumed that that was the nature of growing older and had accepted it with a resigned grace.

Boy, had she been wrong. One hundred percent wrong.

It was as though a switch had been turned on and the smallest touch, the quickest kiss from Ian had her body responding with an eagerness she only last remembered from her teens.

Ian stroked a hand down her arm and trailed it around her torso to cup her breast in his hand. While gently squeezing her flesh in his palm, he bit at the sensitive spots on her neck, causing a low deep moan to escape from Pat's lips.

She pushed her backside firmly into his groin, feeling the length of him hard and willing. "God," she breathed as she ran her hands along the cords in his muscled thigh. "I'm really, really glad I bought this couch."

Ian chuckled and deftly turned her body to face him, kissing her deeply on the mouth and drawing her further into the oblivion he offered.

Pat was amazed at how ready she was for him, so fast and so soon, and wrapped her arms and legs around him, pulling him closer to where she wanted him to be.

"OH! MY! GOD!"

Pat jolted so hard at the sound of the shrill voice, she nearly sent herself out of Ian's embrace and onto the floor. She whipped her head around to see Crystal, her face a picture of horror, standing in the family room doorway.

"Jeez!" Ian barked, pulling Pat closer and trying to shield her with the bulk of his body.

Pat was momentarily flattered by the gesture, it demonstrated what a gentleman he was; however, quickly banished the thought when Crystal spun on her the heel of her sneaker and fled from the room like she'd seen a ghost.

"Oh, hell! Bloody, crappy hell!" Pat exhaled and untangled herself from Ian, pulling herself from the depths of the couch.

"Who the hell *was* that? What's going on?" Ian asked, utterly bewildered and scrambling to keep up with the sudden turn of events. "Please tell me you know that person?"

"Yes," Pat said as she began fumbling her way around the family room floor, reaching for her discarded clothes. She wasn't able to locate her bra and hoped it was tucked under a piece of furniture, instead of waiting to be discovered hanging from a chair in the kitchen.

"Sorry I didn't get to make introductions," she added, between clenched teeth. "But, that was my *dear* daughter, Crystal."

Comprehension dawned on Ian's face and he grimaced. "Shit," he said, pulling Pat's bra from behind a pillow, then swiftly reaching for his jeans and sliding them up over his firm backside.

"Pretty much," Pat agreed and gratefully took the bra from his hand.

Ian picked up his grey, cable-knit sweater, while Pat fastened her bra around her ribcage and pulled the straps over her shoulders.

"Uh, underwear?" she added, pointing at his groin.

The sounds of her daughter in the next room - banging cupboard doors, slamming pots down and rattling cutlery - made Pat wince as she pulled on her blue tee-shirt, then tried in vain to straighten a serious case of sex hair. Oh, the drama.

Ian pulled his sweater over his head and nodded. "Right," he said, scanning the floor for his boxers.

"There!" Pat pointed to the edge of the couch where a flash of green was tucked between the pillows.

Ian snatched up the shorts, ran his fingers through his hair - of course it looked fine, men always did - and gave Pat a quizzical look. "Did you know she was going to show up?"

"Of course not!" Pat replied, exasperation making her sharp. "I had no idea and, quite frankly, I'm pissed off this is even happening. I shouldn't have to go in there and console my eighteen year old, *engaged* daughter, when *she* was the one who showed up unannounced in my home!"

Ian nodded, unsure of how to respond. He knew it was between Pat and her daughter and didn't want to get in the middle of it any more than he already was.

"Look," he said, picking up his leather jacket from a chair and tucking his boxers into one of the pockets. "I don't know what you think, but *I* think it's best if I keep out of this."

Pat sighed. "Yeah, it's probably best I put out this fire on my own."

"Right," Ian said, relieved she agreed. "Then, I'm going to take off through the front. I don't want to add anymore kindling to the pile."

Pat grinned, even though her thoughts were already traveling toward the scene she knew was waiting for her in the kitchen. "Thank you," she said, pausing for a breath and softening enough to lean into him for a lingering kiss. "I'll call you later, once I get this mess cleaned up."

She watched him quietly leave the house, then turned her attention to the task at hand. Her dear daughter.

***

"You're back early," Tom called out, turning his attention away from the TV show he and Trisha were watching.

Ian pulled off his jacket and hung it on a hook in the front hallway, then joined the couple in the family room.

"Yup," he said as he walked over to an easy chair and flopped down into it, making the cushions whoosh beneath him.

"Trouble in paradise?" Trisha offered, while shifting herself awkwardly beside Tom on the couch. The closer she came to her due date and the larger her belly grew, the more challenging it was becoming to get comfortable,

"I don't know what to call it," Ian replied, exhaling heavily. "But, it's not pretty."

Tom raised an eyebrow and turned down the sound on the TV. "Okay, now you even have me interested. Spill."

Ian groaned. He wanted to talk about it, but at the same time he wanted to forget it.

"Come on," Trisha coaxed. "You'll feel better if you do."

Ian scrubbed his face with his hands, then pulled himself forward and rested his elbows on his knees. "Okay, fine. So, I was at Pat's, right?"

Tom and Trisha nodded.

"And, we were..." He paused and coughed. "*Well...*"

"Enough said," Tom said, putting his hand up, palm forward, and rescuing him. "Got it."

"Right. So, everything was fine... Until her daughter walked in on us!" Ian grimaced. "Totally unexpected! Otherwise..."

"Oh, my, God!" Trisha grabbed at Tom's arm, while he fell over sideways on the couch with laughter, and attempted to push herself forward in her seat. She failed and, still chuckling, Tom kindly gave her a boost to help her along.

"Were you actually..." Trisha waved her hands in the air, trying to find the words. "Well, *you know*?"

"No." Ian shook his head. "But, near enough. And, shit, who knows what the hell she actually saw." He groaned again and dropped his head into his hands.

Tom exhaled, trying to get a hold of himself. "What I want to know is," he said, finally managing to recover an edge of his composure. "What the hell are you doing here?"

"That's true." Trisha pointed at Tom to show her agreement with his question. "Why aren't you still there, helping Pat get things worked out?"

"She said," Ian began, then clarified. "We *both* thought my presence in that moment might have caused further upheaval. So, we agreed it was best I vacate and let her deal with her daughter, one on one."

"Wow." Tom whistled long and low. "Gotta hand it to you, that's one for the family archives."

Ian shot him a filthy look.

"I remember the day that I met Mom's new boyfriend," Tom said, affecting a high and girly voice. "Wow, did I ever get an eye-full!"

"Tom! Stop it!" Trisha smacked his arm, while trying to keep a straight face. "Poor Ian, he's all tied up in knots and this is what he gets for brotherly support?"

"Oh!" Tom's face lit up. "Can you imagine if you'd had Pat tied up in knots when the daughter arrived on the scene?"

Trisha slapped Tom's arm a second time, while Ian shook his head and flopped back into the chair. "You're impossible!" Trisha proclaimed and hauled herself to her feet.

Tom grinned and tried to catch Ian's eye. When he finally did, Ian couldn't help himself and snickered.

"Ah, you see," Tom said, a satisfied expression on his face. "Once you can find the humor, it all becomes manageable."

Trisha looked from one brother to the other and threw her hands up in defeat. "You're both ridiculous, as far as I'm concerned."

She waddled away from them towards the kitchen and asked, over her shoulder, "I'm hungry, you guys want anything?"

Ian shrugged and looked at Tom. "What do you think?"

Tom nodded and stood up from the couch. "I could eat."

***

CHAPTER FIFTEEN

"Good God." Melanie exhaled, shaking her head.

It was early morning and she was in Pat's kitchen; Pat regaling her with the events surrounding Crystal's untimely arrival the previous evening.

"Your life is starting to play like a cheesy soap opera."

Pat stared at her coffee cup and screwed up her face in disgust. "Tell me about it."

"So what did you do? I mean, she *did* find you guys *in flagrante*, right?"

"Or, near enough to." Pat grimaced at the memory and lifted her cup to her mouth.

"How on Earth does a person come back from that?" Melanie leaned forward, her makeup free face earnest as she rested her elbows on the kitchen table.

"I can't speak for anyone else, but for me I just jumped right in."

"Well, that makes you braver than me," Melanie stated as she picked up her coffee cup. "If Gina walked in on me and Duncan..." She winced at the thought.

"Oh, please," Pat said, rolling her eyes. "You'd be a lot smoother in that situation than me."

"No way," Melanie insisted. "I'm fine in a lot of situations, but I know I'd be tongue tied and wanting to run away fast; just like Crystal did."

Pat shrugged. "Perhaps."

"So, never mind that. What happened after she bolted from the room?"

"She ran in here and then I had to deal with her histrionics." Pat paused and shook her head. "What *is* it with that girl? Did I do something wrong while raising her? Is it my fault? Is it because of the divorce?"

"Don't be stupid. Of course not." Melanie was immediately dismissive.

"Of course not to which thing?" Pat clarified. "The way I raised her? Or, to the divorce?"

"To both!" Melanie said, vehemently. "We do our best raising our kids and that's all we can do. We're no more responsible for the way our children finally choose to shape themselves, than our parents were for us. The whole *my parents made me this way* is a worn out, tired excuse that people use to get out of having to take responsibility for who they are."

Pat nodded, her face thoughtful. "Well, then, I certainly hope Crystal starts to figure that out. Especially before she heads down the aisle and into the marriage arena."

"So, what did you guys end up telling her?" Melanie turned the conversation back to the subject at hand, eager for the rest of the details.

"First, remember there was no *you guys*. Ian snuck out the front door." Melanie rolled her eyes and Pat held up her hand to stop her remarks. "Not that I blame him one bit for wanting to avoid being smack dab in the middle."

"Can't imagine why, seeing as he was quite comfortable being in that position just moments before." Melanie chuckled, the sound low and dirty.

Pat laughed and slapped her hand. "Stop it! Focus," she chastised.

Melanie snickered again, then cleared her throat. "Okay, okay, sorry. Go on. Ian fled the scene of the crime *and*—"

"I came in here to find my daughter, my supposedly mature enough to be planning a marriage daughter, all curled up in a chair with Whiskey tucked in her lap and a big pout on her face." Pat rolled her eyes. "That's when it all started."

Melanie cocked her head to one side and waited, while Pat reluctantly recreated the scene between her and Crystal.

***

"My God, Mother!" Crystal's first words had been spat at Pat the moment she'd pushed open the door to the kitchen. "What is going *on* around here? We leave you on your own for almost no time at all and I come back to find you... you..." Her face screwed up in disgust as she gave Pat the once-over. "*Writhing* on the family room couch with a total stranger!"

Pat held up her hand, her face steely. "Stop! Just stop and close your mouth."

And, she did. Crystal saw the look in her mother's eye, clamped her mouth shut and was momentarily silenced.

"First of all," Pat said, attempting to get things back on some sort of level footing. "May I be so bold as to ask what you're doing here in the first place? Aren't you supposed to be at school?"

"I thought I'd surprise you, it *is* the weekend after all." Crystal shot Pat a haughty look and continued. "Foolishly I thought we might have a lovely mother-daughter weekend, since we didn't get much time together, one on one, at Thanksgiving. But, clearly, the surprise was on me!"

Pat didn't buy it. There had to be more. "*And?*" She pressed.

"And?" Crystal echoed. "What do you mean, *and?*"

"You wanted a mother-daughter weekend *and* what else?"

Crystal attempted to look put out, but Pat had seen it all before. Of course there was an *and*. She walked across the kitchen to the fridge and pulled out a jug of orange juice.

"Want some?"

"Okay," Crystal agreed, her voice stiff as she tucked her hair behind her ears. "By the way, your shirt's on inside out."

Pat bit her lip and poured two glasses of juice, refusing to take the bait. She walked over to the table, sat down in the chair opposite Crystal, slid one glass across the table top and purposely kept her mouth shut; employing her tried and true strategy since her daughter was a little girl. Wait her out.

"I *thought* we could have some fun, planning for the wedding." Crystal finally gave in, her tone defensive and laced with annoyance as she picked up her glass of juice. "After all, I've got a lot on my plate Mother, with school and Kent..." She exhaled, set the glass back down and ran her fingers through her hair. "So, I *thought* if we could do this together—"

"Which is fine," Pat interrupted, sensing she was getting closer to the truth. "But, still, you didn't you call me first *because*...? You always call first to make sure I'll be here and that's the thing I'm having the most trouble with."

"Because I can never find you, okay?" Crystal's voice held a strong whine and Pat wanted to send her to her room as she had done when she was a child. "I call here, you're not at home. I call the bookstore, you're never there! You never seem to answer your cellphone—"

"I'm always at the bookstore." Pat interrupted, cutting off her spiel.

"No, not when I've called," Crystal insisted. "That Sandra girl has told me many times that you're with a customer, or you're out for lunch, or coffee." She paused to narrow her eyes at Pat.

Pat sipped her juice and waited for her to wind up.

"Probably with that *man*," Crystal added, her voice still whiny. "How old is he, by the way? From where I was standing, he looked really young. You're not doing some sort of cougar thing, are you? Because *that* would be embarrassing."

***

"She did NOT say that!" Melanie burst out, interrupting the tale and feeling hugely indignant on Pat's behalf. "Do not tell me she used that word and, besides, like she could tell! Anyone over thirty looks decrepit to someone her age."

Pat took a swallow of her coffee, then nodded. "Oh, I'm telling you, she said it alright. And, believe you me, I set her straight in a fat hurry."

"Jeez!" Melanie huffed and shook her head at the audacity. "I should hope so."

"I told her that whoever I chose to spend my time with was none of her concern. That I was living my life as I saw fit and I sure as hell didn't need anyone's permission, one way or another."

Melanie whooped and slapped her palm on the table in delight. "What did she say?"

"Oh, well." Pat waved her hand dismissively. "Something about me being defensive and cagey, two traits she never thought she'd ever see in her saint of a mother."

Melanie laughed and reaffixed the clip that held her tumble of dark hair loosely at the nape of her neck. "Priceless. The transparency of youth, ain't it grand?"

"Or, *something*," Pat said, wryly, as she got up to retrieve the coffee pot.

The fact was, while she wouldn't admit it out loud, Pat didn't think Crystal was far off the mark. She did feel she'd become more cagey since getting together with Ian and wanted it to stop. It was high time for her to relax and savor the full joy of being with him, and not just with close friends behind closed doors.

"So, did you get things resolved?" Melanie bent down to scoop up Whiskey from beneath her chair.

"More or less." Pat shrugged and brought the pot over to refill their cups. "She admitted she should have called first and admitted she was really feeling stressed and pulled in too many directions, juggling school and wedding plans. So, naturally I told her I'd help out more—"

"When?" Melanie balked. "With all that you cram into your schedule, what's your plan? To stop sleeping?"

"I'll find the time," Pat assured her, amazed that in such a short period of time she'd gone from being divorced with a wasteland of a life, to having overstuffed days filled with work and Ian and wedding plans... From famine to feast.

"Did you guys discuss Ian any further?" Melanie refused to leave it alone. She knew how important Ian was in Pat's life and the catalyst to her coming out of her cocoon. She wasn't about to sit back silently and let Pat get so swept up again in her children's lives that she let her own slide.

"We did," Pat said, a small smile on her face. "Not too many details, I think she'd had more than she'd ever bargained for."

Melanie snickered.

"But, I gave her the condensed version of things and told her she'd get a chance to know him at the holidays."

"Good for you." Melanie grinned. "You're turning a corner, Pat. A definite corner and..." She paused to catch her breath and try to keep the emotion from her voice. "I'm just so proud of you. Thrilled and proud."

Pat's eyes brimmed with unshed tears. She knew exactly what Melanie was saying and loved her for it. If anyone had her back, it was her best friend. She'd been there, above and beyond the call of duty, to help her crawl out of the dark abyss after her marriage had dissolved. Not to mention, she'd practically carried her through those first few months that were a blur of tears and anger. And, then, finally, she was her greatest cheering section when she'd finally straightened her shoulders to get on with it. A true, blue friend of an entire other caliber.

"Yeah." Pat sniffled, swallowed shakily and attempted to lighten the mood. "Well, you won't be so proud when I'm stuffed into my mother of the bride dress next June, probably flat out on my back in the grass, completely smashed from drinking too much in my relief that the whole damned thing is finally over."

"Sure I will," Melanie said, cheerfully. "I'll just be lying next to you, thanking my lucky stars that it was you, and not me, in the hideous dress!"

***

CHAPTER SIXTEEN

Pat stood stiffly beside Ian, their faces a sickly neon green from the glow of the sign above their heads that read *Lucky's*. She watched the bouncer at the door, easily as wide as he was tall, his steroid enhanced muscles on permanent flex, wave a couple of twenty-something, giggling girls in the line ahead of them through the entrance; the thumping bass beat so loud she could feel it in her chest.

"Oh, God," Pat groaned under her breath as she stamped her cold feet. How on Earth had she let Ian talk her into this?

"You okay?" Ian asked, leaning into her and wrapping an arm around her shoulders. "Warm enough?"

"Well, let's see," Pat replied, while taking in the rest of the young faces in the lineup around them. "Other than feeling like a chaperone at a high school dance,

I'm just...." She took a breath, shivered and exhaled. "Wondering how in the hell I let you talk me into this."

Ian grinned and squeezed her shoulder. "You *told* me you were ready for us to be more public about our relationship, right? You *said* you were tired of feeling like we were constantly behind closed doors, right? Well, you have to admit, you can't get much more public than this."

Pat cut her eyes at him. "Please. In this crowd I'm either invisible, or someone to pity."

"Come *on*," Ian protested. "You know that's not true and besides, we're doing this for Alexa. This is hardly going to become our weekend thing."

Alexa. Pat tucked her hands into her armpits and fought to keep a sneer from decorating her face at the sound of the girl's name. Okay, granted, it was her thirtieth birthday which made her older than a girl. But, she did such a great job of acting like one that Pat couldn't drop the label in her head.

"Once we get inside," Ian continued. "We'll not only be a hell of a lot warmer, but we'll be surrounded by our friends and peers. It'll be a buffer from the rest of place."

Pat raised an eyebrow. *His* friends and *his* peers. While she would have liked to correct him, she held her tongue. It wasn't the time, or place, to make an issue of it.

"PAT! PAT KEEGAN!"

Pat jumped at the sound of her name being bellowed from someone with the range of a foghorn. She whipped her head back and forth looking for the source of the sound, while Ian did the same.

"OVER HERE!" The woman's voice rang out again and Pat leaned to her left to look around the shoulder of a girl with over-teased hair.

"Oh, no," she said as she locked eyes with Heidi Moore, waving frantically from the other side of the nightclub entrance.

"HER!" Heidi pointed vehemently at Pat, while holding tight to the arm of the beefy bouncer. "And, the guy with her! Those two are with us, Dexter!"

Pat watched, wide eyed, as Dexter nodded his large, basketball sized head atop his thick neck, then waved his steak slab of a hand at she and Ian.

"You're in," he stated, firmly, reminding her of some of her Elementary school teachers.

"He does mean us, right?" Ian asked, while beginning to shuffle forward with Pat by his side.

"I believe so," Pat said, still a bit dumbfounded at the sudden turn of events.

"Yeah, you two," Dexter repeated, pointing directly at Pat while Heidi grinned maniacally and tugged excitedly on his arm like a child. "You're in."

The lineup of twenty-somethings parted like the red sea and Pat and Ian moved between them; all the while receiving looks of either respectful interest, or disgruntled irritation that they'd been singled out for entry.

"Thanks, Dex," Heidi effused and planted a kiss on his cheek. "I owe you one, babe."

He grinned at her, making him look less Bond villain and more like an uber inflated Ken doll.

Pat, with Ian in tow, smiled politely at *Dex* as they crossed the threshold of the club, then braced herself against the thumping bass beat. It had been bad enough while in the lineup, inside the space it nearly knocked her sideways.

"Thanks so much, Heidi," Pat said, rubbing her hands together in an attempt to warm them. And, that was as far as she got. The volume was so loud it was clear Heidi couldn't hear a word being said, not to mention she appeared to be a few sheets to the wind.

"IT'S SO GOOD TO SEE YOU!" Heidi bellowed over the music as she nodded in time to the beat. "DENISE IS HERE, TOO!"

She glanced around and Pat thought it might be a good opportunity to disentangle themselves from her. No such luck.

"THERE SHE IS!" Heidi waved a hand over her head. "WOOT! DENISE! OVER HERE! LOOK WHO I FOUND!"

Pat cringed at the volume Heidi was managing to pump out and exchanged a look with Ian. He looked as dumbfounded as she had felt when they'd been beckoned from the lineup.

Denise, dressed in similarly revealing, clingy party wear as Heidi, shimmied over. Her face lit up like Christmas when she saw them.

"PAT! YOU SEXY THANG! LOOK AT YOU!" She looked Pat up and down, touched the edge of Pat's cinnamon colored bolero jacket and let out a long, wolf whistle.

Pat shifted her weight uncomfortably from one foot to another in what Melanie's daughter had called her 'come and get it' stilettos. She wished she was in her sweatpants, as opposed to the leather skirt and low cut blouse she was wearing beneath her jacket. The regret at allowing Gina to be her fashion consultant for the evening was, in that moment, almost painful.

"OUR BOYS ARE HERE SOMEWHERE, TOO!" Denise informed them, while bopping to the beat thumping from the speakers. "WHEN WE FIND THEM, YOU MUST MEET THEM!"

Heidi nodded vigorously. "YES! THEY'RE SO MUCH FUN AND... THEY'RE TWINS!"

Denise grinned widely, exchanged a look with Heidi that Pat didn't want to understand, and the two of them broke into fits of giggles.

"Think that's our cue," Pat said to Ian, firmly grasping his hand and taking small steps away from the dynamic duo. "Okay, sounds good," she said, without a care as to whether or not they were hearing her. "We have to go and find our group."

Ian smiled and waved as Pat tugged him away into the crowd, her hopes high they wouldn't follow.

"Wow," Ian said into her ear as they made their way through the throng of people hanging around the edges of the dance floor. "Were those the same women in your store that time?"

Pat nodded and attempted to see around the young bodies swaying to the music.

"They seemed really comfortable, didn't they?"

"They did," she agreed, having no luck finding a familiar face and feeling adrift in a sea of hormones.

"Comfortable in a way that makes you think they're here a lot, is what I mean." Ian clarified. "Did you notice, the one that got us in knew the bouncer by name? That's a regular if I ever saw one."

"Yeah, they're something. From what I know, they've lived here their whole lives, have some sort of internet business and generally just party their way through life."

Ian raised an eyebrow and nodded slowly as he digested the information. "Then, I'd say they're doing a great job of keeping true to themselves, huh?"

Pat grinned. It certainly was one way of looking at it. "So, do you see your group anywhere?"

"*Our* group," Ian said, correcting her as he looked over her head around the room. He pointed to the left and grabbed her hand. "I see them over there. Let's go."

"Oh, yay," Pat muttered under her breath as she allowed herself to be lead through the gyrating bodies toward a sectioned off set of tables in the corner. Show time.

"Hey!" Tom's face lit up with pleasure when he spotted them approaching the group. "You made it!"

Pat smiled warmly at him, she'd really grown fond of Ian's brother and Trisha. It was just Alexa that made her want to do something childish - like *accidentally* slice off her hair. Ugg. Bad stuff.

Ian hugged Tom, then looked around. "Where's Trisha?"

"In the bathroom." Tom pointed in the general direction of the ladies room. "Every hour, on the hour."

Pat grinned. She remembered it well, when she had been at the very end of her pregnancies. "I'm impressed she came," she told Tom.

"Well, it is Alexa after all." Tom shrugged. "Trisha would never hear the end of it if she didn't show up."

Pat resisted rolling her eyes. God, the girl was too much.

"Ian!"

Speak of the devil, Pat thought, when the girl's high pitched squeal hit her ear.

"You came!"

Alexa undulated over to where they were standing, her blonde hair disheveled, eyes rimmed with dark eyeliner to make them stand out exotically against her pale face, and lips wetly glossed. She reached out and grabbed hold of Ian's arm as she swiveled her hips in time to the music and Pat repressed the urge to slap her.

"You have to dance with me, it's my birthday," she said, her voice confident. "And, the birthday girl always gets whatever she wants."

Ian blinked and ran his free hand through his hair, discomfort written across his features. Pat watched and suppressed a sigh. Could it get worse?

"Hey, Pam right?"

Apparently it could. Pat affixed a stiff smile to her face and turned to face the girl that Alexa had brought with her into the bookstore. What was her name?

"From the bookstore, right?" The girl smiled in a friendly manner.

"Right. But, it's *Pat*, actually." Pat corrected.

"Oh, God!" The girl had the good grace to blush. "I'm sorry! I don't know why I thought it was Pam. I'm sure Alexa said Ian and Pam were coming."

Pat raised an eyebrow and refrained from comment.

"Bree!" Alexa squealed, still holding tight to Ian's arm. "You silly Billy! I said Ian was bringing his friend, Pat. How much have you had to drink?"

Pat gritted her teeth and held her tongue further. *Friend*, indeed.

Alexa didn't bother to listen for Bree's reply, instead she switched her focus back to Ian. "Ooh! I love this song!"

"Listen," he began, but it fell on deaf ears.

"Time for my birthday dance!" She began to charge away from them, holding fast to Ian's arm and dragging him with her. He shot Pat an apologetic look as he was swallowed up into the crowd.

"Oh, my, God!"

Pat whirled around at the sound of alarm, just in time to see Trisha reaching out for Tom as she scuttled back from the bathroom.

"Tom! It's time!"

Pat blanched and watched Tom do the same.

"What? Are you serious? As in *time* time?" He grabbed her outstretched hand and Pat wasn't sure if it was for her support, or his.

"Yes! My water broke in the bathroom!"

Pat's heart swelled with pity. "It's okay, Trisha," she soothed, stepping in where Tom was faltering. "I've been through it. Twice. You'll be okay, you still have plenty of time."

Trisha held her stomach with her free hand and shot Pat a grateful look. "We need to get out of here, where's my sister?"

Pat shrugged. "Out on the dance floor, I think."

"Ian?" Trisha looked around, her voice developing an edge of panic.

"He's with her, I think," Pat offered and watched Trisha's eye get even wider. God, she was being no help whatsoever. She had to think.

"Okay, listen." She grabbed Tom's shoulder firmly to jar him out of his trance and spoke directly to them both. "They should be back right away. You guys go. I'll find them and tell them what's going on and we'll take care of everything else."

"Okay, okay," Tom said, repeating himself and nodding.

"Do you guys have a bag ready?"

It was Trisha's turn to nod. "In our closet. Ian knows where it is."

"Excellent," Pat said, trying to infuse them with confidence with her voice. "We'll get the bag and bring it to the hospital, all you guys have to do is go straight there. Okay?" She waited a beat for them to catch up. "*Okay?*"

Trisha was first. "Yes, okay." She turned to Tom. "We have to go. Now!"

Tom grabbed Pat in a sudden hug, startling her and sending her breath whooshing from her lungs. "Thanks, Pat. You're a star."

And then, they were gone. Pat waved them off as they were swallowed up into the sea of bodies, much as Ian had been moments before. She looked at Bree, who was slugging back her drink and clearly had no idea what was going on, and squared her shoulders. Evidently she was going to have to step in and actually *be* the chaperone. Good God.

***

CHAPTER SEVENTEEN

Ian's black BMW purred along in the freshly fallen snow and the closer they got to his brother's house, the quieter Pat became. It had been a week since Trisha had delivered her baby boy and while they'd put the circumstances, and subsequent argument, from that fateful evening behind them, she was still feeling apprehensive of what might lay ahead.

And, what an argument it had been. After Trisha and Tom had fled the nightclub, Pat had had a hell of a time finding Ian and Alexa. When the song Alexa had claimed to 'love' so much that it was justification for bodily dragging Ian onto the dance floor had ended, did they return? No.

Instead, the adored song had segued right into the next; then the next after that; until Pat had been on the verge of exploding when Ian came staggering back, Alexa tripping happily behind him.

And, it didn't end there. When she'd explained to them what had happened, Alexa had put on a huge pout at being upstaged by the imminent arrival of Trisha and Tom's baby. Pat had glared at the girl, then nearly walked out when Ian began making attempts to console her. The only thing that had kept her rooted to the spot was the fact that Ian had driven. The idea of wrangling a cab had sounded like more hassle than it was worth, so she'd just stood there and simmered.

"You okay," Ian asked as he parked the car next to the curb outside Trisha and Tom's house. "You're really quiet."

Pat, jarred from her memory of her anger and the resulting fight - their first - cleared her throat and attempted a cheery smile. She had to let it go and leave the past in the past.

"Yup," she said and shifted the gift bag she was holding from her right hand to her left. "Fine."

Ian frowned. In his experience, when Pat - or any woman for that matter - said she was 'fine', it usually meant just the opposite and something else was brewing beneath the surface. He wasn't sure if he should press further, but wasn't given the chance to ponder the option. Pat was out of the car and half way up the path to the house before he'd even pulled his keys from the ignition.

Pat took a breath, turned and waited for Ian to get out of the car. "Keep it together," she quietly counseled herself as soft snowflakes began to fall gently around her.

She knew the true reason she was feeling apprehensive. It was best summed up in one word, or person. Alexa. She hadn't seen the girl since the night of the baby's birth and if Pat was to be perfectly honest, she'd have been happy to never set eyes on her again. The girl spelled trouble, plain and simple, and Pat wished Ian could see it as clearly as she.

"Okay," Ian said, walking around the vehicle and joining Pat on the path. She looked so stiff, standing in the falling snow He gave her an imploring look and asked, "Sure you're all right?"

Pat had no chance to reply. The green front door to Tom's house opened with a whoosh and he stood in the entryway, waiting to beckon them inside.

"Ian!" Tom was exuberant as they walked up the steps. "Brother of mine! Uncle of my first born!" He reached out with one arm to envelop Ian in a hug, then stretched out the other to do the same to Pat. They were like bookends on either side of him. "And, Pat! Our quick thinking savior to whom we owe a world of gratitude! Come inside, have some cider and join the celebration!"

Pat and Ian were ushered across the threshold and barely had time to remove their wet shoes before being quickly drawn into the crowd that swelled throughout the family room. Pat was startled, she hadn't been expecting so many people. She remembered back to when she'd had Michael and she certainly hadn't had a full on party so soon afterward.

"I know," Tom confided in them as Pat unwound her scarf from her neck . "A lot of people, right? But, Trisha wanted it this way, to get it over with in one fell swoop. Then, once everyone has had their look at the boy, we can let things quiet down and have some intimate family gatherings."

Pat smiled and handed her scarf to Ian and the gift bag to Tom. "Something for the baby," she told him.

"You can thank Pat for that, too." Ian pointed at the bag as he dropped their coats and scarfs on a pile on a chair, then wrapped an arm around Pat's shoulders. "Don't give me any credit whatsoever."

Tom laughed and gestured for them to follow him into the living room. "No worries, I wasn't about to," he said, his face softening as he looked across the room at his wife. "Honey," he called out, walking away from them and weaving his way through the crowd. "More gifts!"

Trisha's face lit up and Pat noticed she wasn't holding her baby. She scanned the room, looking for an obvious bundle, and her eyes finally found him... Ahh, of course, there he was nestled comfortably in the arms of his Auntie Alexa.

Ian spotted him as well and Pat watched as he was drawn as though by a strong magnet to Alexa's side. She bit her lip and hung back, feeling slightly awkward; a part of things, yet not.

Alexa looked up at Ian as he leaned over her shoulder, a warm and welcoming smile on her face. Considering the fuss she'd made on her birthday night, Pat couldn't help but find her placid demeanor glaringly ironic.

Ian needed no further invitation and tucked himself in beside Alexa on the couch, greeting his nephew with a huge grin. He leaned in to look at him and inadvertently placed himself so close to Alexa's small, perky breasts that Pat felt her stomach churn at the sight. He was entranced by the child.

"Pat." Ian waved a hand to beckon her closer and she smiled in relief as she walked over to him. Okay, nothing to worry about, he was still aware she was in the room. "He's perfect, come see."

And, he was. Ian's nephew, Brock, was a tiny bundle of fair-haired purity. From his impossibly long, dark eyelashes, to his cherubic sleeping serenity, he was a vision.

Pat gazed at him, brought back for a moment to the births of her own children, and was thrilled for Trisha and Tom.

"Do you want to hold him," Alexa asked Ian, jarring Pat from her daydreams and thumping her soundly back into the present.

She watched as Ian nodded and held his arms out tentatively for the child, he and Alexa giggling as she pressed herself against him to pass Brock over to his embrace. Her stomach twisted for a second time.

"Okay." Ian sighed audible when Brock was safely in his arms. "I think I've got him."

"You're perfect, just like him. It must be genetic," Alexa told him, still so close her arm was rubbing against his, and her voice so sweet Pat didn't recognize it. "Although, I think the best stroke of perfection is that he decided to arrive early on *Auntie's* birthday night."

Pat's breath caught in her throat and she nearly choked. God, what a steaming pile of bullshit! The girl had made such a fuss that Ian had had to cajole her out of her tantrum and, suddenly, Brock's early arrival was being cast as a stroke of good fortune?

Pat tried to catch Ian's eye to share in the hypocrisy, but to no avail. He was still rapt, watching Brock's every breath in and out. Pat swallowed her annoyance and glanced around the room, wondering if Tom was handing out anything stronger than cider.

"So." Alexa made no move to welcome Pat onto the couch, just raised her voice to reach not only Pat's ears, but those of the guests around them. "This must bring back memories for you, huh, Pat?"

Pat watched the girl's mouth moving, heard the light tone and, yet, clearly felt the danger behind it. She squared her shoulders, preparing herself.

"Why it must seem like just yesterday you were holding your own babies." Alexa continued, her voice steadily increasing in volume. "When in fact it wasn't yesterday at all, was it? Your kids are grown now, right? In college?"

Pat was trying to find the words to reply, but Alexa wasn't finished.

"Just think," she said, her voice turning playful. "The next little ones in your house will probably be *grandchildren*."

The chatter in the room seemed to lessen in volume as Alexa's words rang around them. Pat blinked a few times, hardly believing she could be just that cruel. She knew that the girl had a competitive streak, but this... It crossed the line.

Ian looked up from the baby to see Pat's stricken face and his heart clutched. Tom, only a couple of feet away, saw the same thing and deftly pushed through the crowd to collect his son from his brother. Ian handed him over gratefully and swiftly rose from the sofa to wrap his arm securely around Pat's shoulders.

"Come on, gorgeous," he said, keeping his voice warm and intimate as he leaned in and kissed her cheek. "Let's grab some drinks and enjoy our freedom."

"Right, rub it in," Tom called out, helping Ian to lighten the atmosphere.

"You'd better believe it." Ian grinned and winked lasciviously. "We welcome *our* sleepless nights."

Trisha laughed loudly and stuck her tongue out at Ian, also seeking to move the awkward moment along. Pat had been so kind to them, she would do whatever she could to lessen the blow of her careless sister's words. It seemed to work. Their friends chuckled and quickly resumed their volume of chatter and, soon enough, there was some blatant teasing about wings clipped and libidos crushed going on around them.

Trisha narrowed her eyes at Alexa sitting solo on the couch, a large pout dragging her mouth down, and shook her head in disgust. She'd straighten her out later, after the guests had cleared out. Whatever her sister's agenda, Trisha wouldn't have such energy in her home around her child. Ready or not, Alexa was about to be seriously schooled.

***

CHAPTER EIGHTEEN

"So, how's Ian?" Melanie asked into her telephone as she made her way around her kitchen, wiping surfaces.

"Umm," Pat replied as she adjusted her headset on her ear, slightly distracted by the papers strewn across her kitchen island. "Fine. Yeah, he's fine."

Melanie dropped her cloth in her sink and sighed. Not a good sign. Pat usually took any opportunity to enthuse about the man and ever since the disastrous baby shower at Ian's brother's house, the effervescence of her enthusiasm had grown flat.

"*Pat*," she cajoled.

"What?" Pat's voice held a strong note of defensiveness. "I said he's *fine*, which he is. I've just been busy. This whole wedding thing seems to have gotten a whole hell of a lot more complicated since we first did it, in the stone ages."

"I just wish you'd talk to me," Melanie said, hoping she could nudge her best friend out of the shell to which she was retreating.

"About what?"

"I'm not the enemy," Melanie told her. "Even though you've been avoiding me for the past week."

Pat laid a sheet of paper down on one of her piles and sighed. She knew that. Of course she did. She just felt so damned raw since Alexa's smack down and it pissed her off.

"I just can't get the image out of my head," she finally muttered, embarrassed.

"What image?" Melanie asked, both encouraged and encouraging.

"Of Ian." Pat gripped the countertop and fought to keep the tremor from her voice. "Holding Brock. He looked so..."

Melanie held her breath and waited. When there was nothing but silence, she prompted. "*So?*"

"Content!" Pat exploded, throwing her hands in the air and startling Whiskey from his snooze on a chair, making him dash from the room. "So right! So perfect! So in need of a child of his own I wanted to throw up!"

Melanie gasped and grabbed her countertop for support as the dam around Pat's silence broke.

"And, why shouldn't he feel that way?" Pat babbled, almost tripping over her words as she stomped around her kitchen island. "He has no children of his own. God knows he's young enough to have them, of course he'd want them! But, I can't! I just CANNOT Melanie," she wailed, coming to a standstill.

"No, no," Melanie sputtered, trying to get her footing in the conversation.

"And, I'm so afraid," Pat said, her words almost a whimper as she sunk into the chair Whiskey had vacated. "So damned afraid, I just want to curl up and hide away and let him go off and have a litter of kids with *Alexa*." She almost spat the girl's name. "And, try and forget he ever existed and hope my heart can take it."

"Jeez, Pat," Melanie said, her heart pounding so much in reaction to Pat's revelation that she had to sit down, too. "You have to talk to him, you know that right? You can't run away. You have to face this and tell Ian just what you told me and let him decide. You can't make any sort of decisions for him, you know that."

Pat sobbed quietly on the other end of the phone, her head cradled in her hands on her table. "I know." She sniffled, letting her tears fall unchecked. "I'm just so scared of what he'll say."

"I don't think it will be what you're expecting," Melanie soothed, wishing she was there to wrap her in a hug. "The man is crazy about you, he's so gone he's almost disappeared."

Pat chuckled a bit in appreciation of the picture Melanie was painting. "Okay," she said, wiping the tears on her face with the backs of her hands. "I'll talk to him."

"Promise?"

"Promise."

***

"I don't know what to tell you," Tom said, shrugging his shoulders at Ian.

They were hanging out in their usual spots in Tom's family room, the glaring difference being the addition of Brock sleeping on Tom's chest and the baby paraphernalia scattered over every flat surface.

Ian sighed. "I know. It's just making me a bit nutty, trying to figure out why she's suddenly shut down."

"And, you think it might have something to do with Brock?" Tom glanced down at his sleeping son, his face becoming sappy at the sight of him.

"That's all I can figure," Ian said, shrugging. "It's like from the night he was born, Pat shifted."

"Shifted?"

"Yeah. We had our first fight that night."

"What?" Tom winced, glanced again at Brock and toned down the volume of his voice. "Are you serious? Why didn't you say anything?"

Ian rolled his eyes and slouched further down in his chair. "Yeah. Like I was going to tell you that. Besides, the fight wasn't about Brock, directly."

Tom raised his eyebrows and waited.

"It was more the situation of how everything went down and she felt she'd been left holding the ball."

Ian looked over at the muted TV screen and watched the images from some commercial about toothpaste, not wanting to directly meet Tom's eye. He didn't want to get into the fact that Pat had been furious at him for being MIA and, once he did turn up, giving his attention to Alexa; instead of getting his ass in gear for his brother and sister-in-law. He still felt uncomfortable about it, because he knew she was right. He'd dropped the ball.

"Okay," Tom said. "Fair enough. I can see how she'd feel that way. But, that was then and..."

"Yeah," Ian agreed. "This is now. And, since we came over for Brock's welcome party, it's like I've been dating a new, much less friendly, woman."

"Do you think it might have to do with her feeling nostalgic for her past, when her kids were little?"

Ian raised an eyebrow and looked at his brother. Very insightful.

"I'm just saying," Tom clarified as he laid a protective hand gently across Brock's back. "I can see, *now*, how a person could feel that way."

Ian rubbed his fingers along the stubble on his jaw. "It's entirely possible. And, if that's the case, how do I deal with that? How do I help her move past her funk?"

Tom exhaled and shook his head. "*That*, I don't know. And, we're right back at the beginning. Maybe you should talk about it with Trisha? Get a woman's perspective on things?"

"Maybe." Ian sighed and looked over at the TV again. "Maybe."

***

CHAPTER NINETEEN

"I've tried," Pat said, over her shoulder, as she alternately dusted shelves and straightened books.

It was Friday evening, she'd closed the store and was tidying up for the weekend to come.

"Try harder," Melanie insisted, sitting comfortably behind the cash desk on a high stool that allowed her to watch Pat, aka 'Ms. Never Slow Down'.

"I don't think I can," Pat remarked, her face thoughtful as she paused in front of a shelf.

"Why not?"

"It's been too long, Mel." Pat sighed and pushed her bangs off of her forehead. "It's been two weeks for goodness sake since the baby shower and I've left it too long. It would just seem awkward and out of context now and I'm just going to have to drop it."

"But, if Ian—"

"Ian's fine." Pat cut her off. "He's busy, I'm busy, he's never said anything—"

"Not to *you*," Melanie muttered, stopping Pat short.

"Pardon?" Pat turned on the heel of her black, ballet flat to face her.

Melanie swallowed and straightened her spine. She'd said it, she might as well own it. "I said not to *you*. As in, Ian hasn't said anything to *you* about how things have shifted, but that doesn't mean he hasn't said anything at all."

"What does that even mean? Are you saying he's talked to you? Is that what you're telling me?" Pat's voice had risen an octave.

"Yes," Melanie said, attempting to sound neutral.

"What? Seriously? When?" Pat put her hands on her hips. "When did he speak to you?"

"About a week ago." Melanie shrugged, noncommittally. "He came into the shop..."

"The shop? *Your* shop?" Pat said, incredulously. "And, you're just finally telling me now?"

Melanie sighed and fiddled with the cuff on the sleeve of her grey silk blouse. "I wasn't going to tell you at all. I didn't want to interfere."

"Not directly, maybe," Pat said, crossing her arms in front of her chest.

Melanie let the remark slide. "He was worried, Pat. He *is* worried, because you aren't talking to him."

"I talk to him all the time!" Pat threw her hands in the air in exasperation.

"You know what I mean," Melanie said, shifting on her stool. "I've watched you two, you're not the same. Sure you're pleasant and all that, but since the baby shower the warmth and intimacy you guys had going on, that's been locked up. I know you're worried, but it's not *me* who needs to know that. You have to break your silence, not to mention stop all the platitudes and obvious comments about your advancing age."

Pat glared. How *dare* Melanie tell her about her intimacy with Ian. They were fine. Just fine.

"We're in a rough patch." She defended. "That's all. It happens in relationships. We've both been busy with work, I've had the wedding crap, and now it's only a couple of weeks until Christmas and the gift buying fever is beginning. I'm up to my neck in not just getting the store ready, but the house as well for when the kids come. It's no big deal. It will work itself out."

Melanie bit her lip and decided to back off. Pat was so defensive, there was no point. She changed direction. "Right. So, the kids are definitely coming for Christmas?"

"Uh-huh." Pat breathed steadily in and out, letting her defenses die down. "I thought they were going to go to Stephen, but Crystal insisted that they all want to come home and meet Ian properly and apparently Stephen is fine with it."

Melanie nodded. It sounded great, on paper. "Well," she offered, trying to smooth things out a bit. "Maybe it will be the perfect thing to get everything back on track, as you said."

"That's pretty much exactly what I've been thinking," Pat agreed, her voice more cheerful. "We can have some family time, Ian can be at the heart of it; I'm really hoping it will give us a chance to relax and reconnect."

Melanie refrained from rolling her eyes. The way that Pat was talking, you'd think she and Ian had been together for years instead of months. They were still in the honeymoon stage of things and the very idea of them needing to reconnect... It was laughable.

"Do you really think you can let the baby worry thing go?" Melanie asked, in one last attempt to get some honesty out of her best friend.

"I guess I'll have to," Pat replied, matter-of-factly.

Melanie just nodded. She knew the proverbial sound of the door on a subject being slammed closed.

***

CHAPTER TWENTY

"Oh, crap! Damn it!"

"Pat?" Ian came rushing in from the family room, his face concerned. "What's wrong?"

"I burned my finger," Pat complained as she held it under the cold water tap in the kitchen. "That's what I get for trying to do ten things at once."

Ian leaned over her shoulder to have a look and Pat leaned into him, enjoying his warmth.

"Looks like it will be okay, just a scald," he said, gently lifting her hand to examine it closer.

Pat relished the feel of his strong hands and sighed. She'd been correct in keeping her mouth shut about her worries, despite what Melanie thought. Just as she'd anticipated, they'd moved past it, were reconnecting and looking forward to a lovely holiday together.

"You could have been a doctor," she told him, when he'd finished inspecting her finger. "You have the touch."

Ian grinned and gently turned her to face him, wrapping his arms securely around her waist. "I have the touch for *you*," he said, his eyes sparkling down at her. "Big difference."

Pat stretched upward, lifted her hands to stroke the back of his neck as he took her mouth in a deep, lingering kiss and let herself melt against him into his heat. Bliss.

"Whoa!" Michael exhaled dramatically as he burst through the kitchen door into the house.

The cold draft followed him in and Pat pulled swiftly away from Ian, laughing at his entrance. "Oh, stop it!" she said, insistently. "And, get in here and close that door! It's freezing!"

Ian plastered a pleasant expression on his face, squared his shoulders and took a deep breath to ready himself for his introduction. After the incident with Crystal, he held high hopes it would go well.

Michael didn't wait for Pat to introduce him. Instead, he flashed a huge, welcoming smile and quickly thrust his hand forward to shake Ian's.

"You must be Ian!" It's really great to meet you!" he said, exuding kindness as they shook hands. "I've heard nothing but great things about you and if Mom's newfound youth and enthusiasm are an indication of things to come, I say welcome to the family!"

***

CHAPTER TWENTY ONE

I am in Heaven, Pat thought, happily, feeling lit from within like the Christmas tree they had all gathered around to decorate.

The smell of fresh pine, the crackling fire, her cozy fleece pjs and some expensive port to warm her further; Pat was beside herself with the joy of feeling she'd landed smack dab in the middle of a Christmas special.

Seated comfortably on her family room sofa, watching the dynamic of the room, Pat was finally able to admit to herself she'd been more than a bit nervous about Ian meeting her kids. How awkward it would have been, had they all been stilted and uneasy with one another. A horrible thought.

Thankfully, just the opposite had happened. Her kids had immediately taken to Ian and in the few days they had all spent together, were getting on as though they'd been friends for years. Pat was thrilled beyond words.

"Oh, come on." Michael was teasing his sister. "It's been ages. Show everyone how well I taught you to fart with your armpit!"

Ian and Kent cracked up, while Crystal slapped her brother's arm. "Stop it! Or else, I'm going to make *you* demonstrate how well you walk in heels!"

"Ooh!" Kent, seated on the floor near the tree with Whiskey sprawled across his lap, fell sideways laughing.

Pat offered Ian a look of pure pleasure and he got up from where he was seated on the floor to join her on the couch.

"Beautiful tree," Pat told him, snuggling up close and admiring the lights and decorations.

"Beautiful woman," Ian replied, looking her over in much the same manner.

"Flatterer." She teased, pleased he'd said it.

"Hey, if it gets you pressed next to me beneath the sheets tonight..." He waggled his eyebrows suggestively.

"Well, I don't know about you guys, but I'm bushed," Kent announced. He lifted Whiskey from his lap, stood up and stretched his arms over his head. "Who knew decorating a tree could be so exhausting."

"The miles of sidewalk we shoveled earlier might also be a factor." Michael reminded him, yawning loudly.

Only Crystal remained motionless, as though ready to sit as long as needed. *Oy*, Pat thought. *My daughter, the intimacy police.*

"Come on, Crys." Kent grabbed her hand and hauled her to her feet. "Tell me a story to put me to sleep."

Crystal looked ready to protest, but Kent ignored her and pulled her behind him. "Night!" he called out as they disappeared up the stairs.

"I'm hitting the sheets, too," Michael told them, smiling. "See you guys in the morning."

"Night," Ian said, returning the grin. He really liked Michael and looked forward to getting to know him over time. He liked Kent, too... And, of course, Crystal. She was just proving to be a slightly tougher nut to crack.

"Night, Sweetie," Pat said as Michael left the room. She listened to his familiar whistle into the kitchen and then the sound of him taking the stairs two by two, as usual, to the second floor. She hadn't realized she'd missed those sounds, until just then.

"They are really something," Ian said, wrapping his arm around her shoulder. "*You're* really something."

"What do you mean?" Pat cocked her head to look at him.

Ian reflected upon the past few days and grinned. He had seen another side of Pat, her maternal side, and it was delicious. The way she whirled around everyone, making sure everything was done smoothly and effortlessly, he was really enjoying getting a glimpse of another side of her personality.

"You're a great Mom and a great homemaker," he told her. "It's been a treat to see another facet of your, forgive the lack of a better metaphor, already glorious portfolio."

Pat found herself stiffening as he spoke. "Well," she said, her voice neutral. "I guess so. After all, I've had a lot of years of practice."

Ian completely missed her cues. "And, you've perfected it. Made it an art. It's truly inspiring to see you in motion. You're beautiful."

Pat's stomach twisted. She didn't know how to respond, how to make it go away. She didn't want him to see her as a homemaker. She'd outgrown that part of her life and left it in her past. Yet, he seemed to be determined to pull it out, shake it off and throw it at her to slap back on.

"Oh," Ian continued, still utterly oblivious. "That reminds me. Tom and Trisha have invited us over for Boxing Day. They know we're here with your kids for Christmas, but they were hoping we could spare a couple of hours to stop in, share some family cheer, coo at Brock... *Jeez*, Pat."

Pat turned to look at him, surprised by the sudden irritation in his voice. "What?"

"What's *with* you?"

Pat's eyebrows knotted together in confusion. She was really in the dark. "I don't follow."

"Every damned time I mention my family, you make that *face*." He pushed himself away from her and twisted in his seat to look her directly in the eye.

"Face?" she asked, trying to understand.

"Yes," he insisted. "I mention my family, I mention Brock — You, see!" He pointed at her. "There it is!"

And, it was. Pat realized with horror that in the moment he mentioned Brock's name, her mouth pulled down into a frown. She hadn't even been aware she was doing it.

"Oh, God, you're right. I'm sorry," she muttered.

"What have you got against Brock?" Ian was looking at her as though she was crazy. "He's just a baby. And, yet, every damned time I mention his name you look like you want to either throw something, or just plain throw up."

It was bad. Really bad. In that moment, Pat knew she had to come clean. Melanie would have been so proud.

"It's not Brock," she said, her voice weary.

"Okay, then what?" Ian's face softened.

"It's what he represents," she admitted.

Ian just looked at her, completely at a loss. Pat prepared herself to explain further, but a firm knock at the door stopped her in her tracks. She raised her eyebrows and looked at Ian in surprise.

"I've got it," Ian said, standing up and walking toward the door. He swung it open and stood face to face with a grinning man he'd never met. "Can I help you?" he asked, ready for anything.

"Absolutely! You must be a friend of Michael's! Good to meet you, son! Can you direct me to my wife, or make that *ex*-wife and kids?"

"Stephen?" Pat came up behind Ian, her face a picture of incredulity. "What on Earth are you doing here?"

"Crystal invited me!" He stamped his feet on the mat, then held numerous bags filled with gift wrapped parcels aloft as he stepped across the threshold into the house. "Merry Christmas, Pat!"

Ian blinked. He hadn't been prepared for that.

***

"Kick. Him. Out." Melanie was doing her best to keep her voice even and not give in to the desire to shout at the top of her lungs.

"I can't," Pat whispered, having stolen a few moments away to stand outside in the freezing cold to call Melanie and relay the latest surprise.

"Why the hell not?" Melanie pressed. "You've been officially divorced for over half a year now and apart for even longer than that. He has no bloody right to barge in on you and Ian and your family."

"That's the clincher right there," Pat offered as she shivered on the back step. "Technically, they're his family, too."

"Pfft!" Melanie exhaled, sharply. "Details! Besides which, family or not, it's still your home and not his."

"Yes, but—"

"Do not tell me something stupid like, *technically, since the kids are there, the house may as well be his, too,* Patricia. Do. Not. Say. It. It's not true. So don't."

Pat couldn't help but smile when Melanie used her full name. It was like being reprimanded by her mother. Oh God, her mother.

"My Mom had an opinion, too," she said. "In case you were wondering."

"How does your mother know Stephen is there?"

"She called to wish us all a happy Christmas Eve, which she never does. I swear the woman has a sixth sense when there's chaos going on in my life. Thank God she and Dad went on that holiday cruise. Can you imagine if they'd descended upon us, as well?"

"And, so." Melanie braced herself. "Heaven help us, what did Shirley have to say?"

"She was shocked at first, but then she was of the opinion that I should give him a chance. Can you believe that? There I was, Ian in one corner, Stephen in the other, and she's blathering on about familiar pastures, or some such lovely adage."

"Fuck that!" Melanie spat and Pat burst out laughing. Language from her best friend was a rarity, she must have really been riled up.

"Slimy bugger." Melanie went on, fueled by a couple of hot toddies shared with Duncan. "He doesn't deserve you! He probably never deserved you from the time you met and he needs to get it through his tiny brain that you are no longer on the table." She took a breath and added, "He's afflicted with deserter's remorse, plain and simple. Well, too bloody bad."

"Hey, Mom?" Crystal poked her head out the door. "Are you coming back inside?"

Pat turned to her traitorous daughter and exhaled a plume of moist air into the night. "In a moment," she replied, stiffly. "Why, is there something wrong?"

"No, not exactly." Crystal shook her head. "It's just that I was hoping to go to bed and it feels weird to leave Dad and Ian alone."

God, Ian. Pat could only imagine what he was thinking.

"Listen," she said, to Melanie. "I have to go. I'll call you in the morning and, hopefully, I'll have sorted this out in some way that is agreeable for everyone."

"Agreeable be damned. I still say you should toss his sorry ass out the door," Melanie stated.

"It's Christmas."

"Bah, bloody humbug," Melanie replied and the connection went silent.

***

"You left?" Tom asked, his voice an incredulous whisper as he quietly ushered Ian into the house and locked the door behind him. "I thought you were staying the night, doing the whole wake up on Christmas morning thing, and you left?"

"That's what I said," Ian replied, through gritted teeth as he kicked off his shoes and hung his leather jacket on a hook by the door.

"I don't understand." Tom yawned widely and walked into the kitchen, his slippers making a shuffling sound on the tile floor.

Ian followed him, took a deep breath and blurted, "Her fucking ex-husband showed up!"

Tom whipped around, his eyes wide as saucers. "Shh!" he hissed, while feeling light headed by the rapid movement. "Holy shit! You're kidding me, right?"

Ian ran his fingers through his hair, tugging hard on it in an attempt to keep himself from bellowing. "I feel like my head's going to blow off," he groaned, sitting heavily on a bar stool at the kitchen island.

"Tom?"

"Oh, crap." Ian cringed at the sound of Trisha's voice, then winced when she came around the doorway into the kitchen, her hair mussed and dark circles vivid under her tired eyes.

"Oh, sorry, Hon," Tom apologized, gathering her into his arms for a hug. "Did we wake you?"

"No." Trisha covered her mouth with her hand as she yawned widely. "I wasn't fully asleep yet after Brock's last feed and I heard voices."

"Jeez, Trisha," Ian said, his voice thick with contrition as he took in the full sight of them; her in her sloppy pajamas and his brother, beside her, in his sweats and tee-shirt. "I'm so sorry for disturbing you guys. I know it's late, but I didn't know where else to go."

"What's wrong?" she asked, concerned. "I thought you were with Pat and her family tonight."

Ian swallowed, determined not to yell a second time. "I was, but she had an unexpected surprise show up on her doorstep. Her ex."

"What?" Trisha's eyes widened in much the same manner Tom's had. "Why? I mean, how on Earth?" She blinked rapidly as she tried to get her sleep deprived brain wrapped around the information.

Tom kept hold of her and led her gently toward the family room couch. "Come on, we may as well get comfortable if we're going to hear this."

Ian nodded and wearily pulled himself up from the kitchen stool to drag himself over to his stead-fast friend, the easy chair, and flop heavily into its cushions.

"Hello, friend," he muttered, wryly, letting his shoulders slump.

Trisha and Tom settled onto the couch and looked at him expectantly. "So, the guy showed up," Tom reiterated the information he'd been given. "And, I'm sorry I have to say it again, but, you *left*?"

"I didn't know what else to do!" Ian grimaced when his voice echoed. "Sorry."

Trisha waved a hand dismissively. "No worries. Once Brock's out, he's out. He only wakes up to be fed." She smirked and looked at Tom. "He takes after his father."

"Ha,ha," Tom said, then smiled.

Ian, despite his current woes, also grinned. She'd pretty much hit the nail on the head with that one.

"Just walk us through it," Trisha said, tucking her flannel clad legs up beneath her, ready to listen.

"Right." Ian cleared his throat. "So, everything was going fine, her kids had gone off to bed and we were talking through a few things."

"Like what?" Trisha cocked her head.

Ian hesitated. While Pat had admitted to acting uptight over his family, that was as far as they'd managed to get before they'd been interrupted. He didn't want to share information that was based on only half the facts.

"Nothing worth talking about here," he said, shrugging his shoulders. "We didn't really get a chance to finish our conversation because her ex showed up and pretty much threw a wrench into the works."

"I can't believe you let him in," Tom said, bluntly.

"What was I going to do?" Ian countered. "It's Pat house, so I couldn't exactly start throwing my weight around. Besides, the guy's gotta be fifty years old; not to mention the father of her kids."

Trisha nodded and gave him a sympathetic look. "You're right. You were pretty much in a no-win situation."

"Exactly."

"So, the ex stormed the gates, then what?" Tom prompted.

"Then, it just went from awkward to chaos." Ian exhaled heavily as he relived it all in his memory. "Pat's kids came downstairs and there was a big fanfare about the guy showing up. Then, he loudly mistook me for one of her son's friends... Or, so he said."

"Get the fuck outta here!" Tom blurted, outraged. "What a prick!"

Trisha laid a hand on Tom's arm. "Whoa! Calm down there, Tiger."

Ian couldn't help himself and laughed. It was pretty much what he'd wanted to say to Stephen when he'd made a big show of apologizing over his 'blunder' and poor Pat had just blushed and tried to smooth things over.

"I swear," Tom said, shaking his head. "I'll gladly go over there and belt him for you. I don't care if he's fifty, he's an ass."

Ian laughed some more and sighed. At least his big brother was always in his corner. "Not necessary, but thanks," he said, appreciatively.

"What I want to know is," Trisha commented as she tucked her hair behind her ears. "Why he showed up in the first place. Did Pat invite him without telling you?"

"No. Absolutely not." Ian leaned back into his chair. "Her daughter was the one who created the so-called *surprise*. She claimed she thought it would be great if everyone was together during the holidays, to have a kind-of a trial run before her upcoming wedding next summer."

Tom groaned. "Holy crap. Poor Pat."

"Poor Pat and poor you," Trisha added, shooting Ian another look full of sympathy. "And, at Christmas to boot."

"*Now* do you get why I left?" Ian asked. "The thought of staying there, under the same roof as that guy, then waking up tomorrow..." He shuddered and shook his head. "I just couldn't do it."

"I totally get it," Tom said. "But, did Pat?"

"I hope so." He shrugged. "I did my best, in the few moments we had alone, to explain it to her. She seemed to understand, but I think she was so upset by all of the upheaval, it was just one more shitty thing added to the pile."

"Well," Trisha said, her voice kind. "I'm glad you came here. After all, even though he's only a few weeks old, it is Brock's first Christmas. It's really great he'll have his Uncle here to share it."

Ian swallowed against the lump that formed in his throat. Despite all of the crap he'd just endured, he knew he was still a very lucky man.

***

CHAPTER TWENTY TWO

Pat opened her eyes, rolled over in her bed and groaned. The clock on her bedside table informed her it was only seven in the morning, but, against her will, she was awake.

At least I'm not hung over, she thought, tucking her covers up under her chin. Probably more than the majority of the people who'd showed up at their impromptu New Year's Eve party could say.

"Bloody Stephen," she muttered to herself, wrinkling her nose in annoyance.

The party had been entirely his creation and it hadn't taken more than an hour for news of it to spread like wildfire to all of Crystal's, Kent's and Michael's friends. In a blink of an eye, the house had been crawling with youth and noise.

Pat sighed and sunk down further into her covers. She dreaded returning to the scene of the crime on the main floor; having a strong hunch it was exactly as she'd left it when she'd finally escaped to her bedroom long after the midnight hour had come and gone.

Whiskey crawled out from under the bed and jumped softly onto the duvet, padding over to join Pat in her warm cocoon. "Morning, Buddy," she said and made space for him to curl up against her stomach with a contented sigh.

Pat lay still and listened for sound of movement anywhere else in the house. Nothing. Maybe she'd be safe to go down and get herself a cup of tea without having to talk to anyone. And, by *anyone*, she meant Stephen.

"What am I going to do?" she asked the cat in exasperation. "Ever since he showed up, things have spiraled out of control. It's ridiculous! He's been here the entire week and now it's New Year's Day, that's enough."

Whiskey watched her intently and Pat felt slightly pathetic in her gratitude for his attention. However, it felt like he was the only one who had actually listened to her all week. Melanie certainly hadn't.

Instead of listening, she'd been on full attack pushing for Stephen's eviction. Every day that Pat had gone into the bookstore, Melanie had shown up at one point, gunning for his elimination from the equation. While Pat understood her motives, it was becoming exhausting finding new angles to defend her position. Not that she needed bother.

No matter how many ways she tried to explain that she was basically stuck between a rock and a hard place, Melanie wasn't buying it. If Pat told her that it was Crystal who'd invited Stephen and it would make chaos if she threw him out, Melanie frowned and told her to suck it up.

She also went one further and told Pat it was high time Crystal accepted that they were never, under any circumstance, going to play happy families again. To even let her think for one moment that it could happen was absurd.

"Ugg!" Pat exhaled and threw back her sage green quilt. Her brain was starting to hurt from all of her back and forth thinking.

"Time for tea, Puss and Boots," she told Whiskey as she slid her feet into fuzzy, blue slippers and reached for her yellow terry cloth robe.

He stayed put, moving just enough to allow his soft head to be seen from beneath the blankets, his eyes already closing as he returned to his slumber.

"Fine." She shrugged. "I'll go alone, as usual."

It was no use, the animal kept his own counsel and would not be guilted. Pat figured she could learn a lesson or two from his example.

***

"Holy crapoly." Pat's breath came out in a whoosh when she hit the landing at the bottom of the staircase into the kitchen.

It was worse than she'd imagined. Plates and cups were scattered haphazardly across the countertops; crumbs from snack foods were on the table and the floor; empty and half empty alcohol containers of various types - wine, beer, coolers - were on every surface, some tipped onto their sides to leave sticky puddles. It looked like some sort of frat house after a party filled with debasing debauchery.

"Where to start," Pat muttered, feeling the beginning of a headache behind her eyes that had nothing to do with lack of sleep and everything to do with her ex-husband. "Probably with tea."

"Pat?"

Pat looked up, surprised, when she heard Ian's voice calling her name from outside.

"Ian?" she called back, nearly tripping over her own feet in her eagerness to get across the kitchen.

"Yeah."

"Come in," she said, unlocking the door and pulling it open. "It's freezing, get in here."

Ian grinned and stepped inside, shutting the door on the frigid elements. Pat knew she'd missed him over the past week, but finally seeing him in person - tall, broad shouldered, strong and solid - made her heart clutch at the reality of how much she adored him.

"Happy New Year," he said, his voice warm and inviting.

"It's so good to see you," she said, half laughing at the mixture of joy and relief cascading through her. "How did you know I was up?"

"I was outside in my car and going to call you on your new cell, when I saw the light on and figured I'd take my chances."

Pat grinned. The new iPhone he'd given her had been so unexpected, but already in the space of one week she was amazed she'd lived without it.

"So," he said, stepping forward into her personal space and wrapping his arms around her waist. "It *is* the New Year..."

Pat laughed and immediately melted into his embrace, finally getting the kiss she'd so craved from the moment the clock had struck midnight. When they came up for air, she felt she had to ask, "But, what are you doing here so early?"

"Where else would I be?" he stated, matter-of-fact, his green eyes so honest and without a hint of guile Pat had to control herself from choking up.

She'd been listening to Stephen and the schmalzy charm oozing from his pores for so many days, she'd almost forgotten what genuine sincerity felt like. It felt fantastic.

"I don't know." Pat hesitated and shrugged her shoulders. "I guess I thought you'd be intent upon sleeping half the day away like everyone in this household. And, since we've basically been apart for the last week..."

"You understand why, right?" he said, looking directly into her eyes.

Pat felt shame wash over her and looked away. "Yes," she admitted, while keeping her gaze fixed on the kitchen and its mess. "But, the holidays are finally over and he'll be gone right away..."

"And, then, we'll see where we're at," Ian finished, straight to the point.

Pat snapped her eyes back to him, taken off guard by his direct, truthful statement. She'd never even considered that they didn't know where they were at, but in the light of day had to acknowledge he was right. They'd had such a bumpy ride in the past month that where they were was up for interpretation.

"So, anyway." He pulled off his gloves, set them on the hutch by the door and started picking up snack food wrappers from the table top. "Judging by this mess, I'd say you hosted a party last night?"

Pat winced at the tension in his voice. When she'd spoken to him the previous evening, she hadn't mentioned the party. In her defense, she'd had no idea the size to which it was going to grow and; thus, had chosen to keep quiet about it to try and quell any further awkwardness between them.

There had already been so many spontaneous 'family moments' thrown together during the week by her bullheaded daughter - out in public for everyone to see and gossip about - Pat just could not face any more explaining.

However, standing there and watching him toss empty foil packets into the trash, his shoulders stiff and unyielding, Pat didn't blame him for his anger. If their positions had been reversed, she would have been exactly the same. Oh Hell, who was she kidding? She'd be way worse.

"Yeah, sort of." Pat sighed and tried to smooth her wayward hair. "It was..." She hesitated, then stretched the truth. "The kid's idea. And, as you can see, it became a much larger gathering than I thought it would. I pretty much stayed in the background and escaped to my bedroom as soon as I could without being noticed."

Ian paused in his clearing and studied her face. Pat prayed she looked innocent, as opposed to riddled with guilt.

"Right." He nodded curtly and began collecting the bottles and cans for recycling. "Anyway, I've been thinking a lot about what you said, or tried to say, just before your..." He faltered at the idea of labeling Stephen. "*He* showed up at the door last week."

Pat stood very still, her breathing shallow as she listened. It seemed like a lifetime ago they'd been sitting snuggled up on the family room sofa, but instantly she remembered with alarming clarity what she'd been about to tell him about her insecurities.

"You said it wasn't Brock that was the issue, it was what he represented." Ian shook his head, his face puzzled. "I've thought and thought on your words and I'm pretty sure I've worked out what you meant, but then again I might be completely off base. Can you tell me, please? So we can at least clear that up."

Pat left the stack of dishes she'd been about to transfer to the dishwasher on the counter and wiped her hands on a dish towel. She had no idea how she was going to find the words to explain her still persistent fears about their age differences and her gut-churning worry he might suddenly want children - especially when so much time had passed - without sounding like a pathetic whiner.

"Before you start though, I want you to know that when I talked to Trisha and Alexa about it..." He stopped talking when he saw the horrified look on her face. "What? What is it?"

"Are you kidding me? You actually talked to *them* about what I said?" Pat was finding it difficult to catch her breath. Her living nightmare was going from bad to worse.

"I didn't betray a confidence," he said, frowning. "If that's what you're implying. I just needed a woman's perspective."

Pat sat heavily on a kitchen chair and rubbed her tired eyes. "And, what did they say?" she asked, wearily; deciding that, as it probably couldn't be get any worse, she may as well know.

"I told them what little I knew, pinned it on a co-worker's experience, and they said it sounded like the woman was feeling she was being placed second to the guy's family, not to mention the new baby, and would feel upset in that position."

Pat nodded. Of course that would have been his hypothesis, she'd given him so little to go on. How could he have known that seeing him with little Brock, not to mention willing Alexa, had struck terror in her battle scarred heart?

"Do you feel that way, Pat?" Ian looked at her with real concern in his eyes. "Because if you do, I want you to know that there's no way I'd place you second to my family, or Brock, or anyone else."

"No," she told him, truthfully. "I can honestly say I don't feel that way at all."

"Wow, honestly? That's a huge relief." He breathed a heavy sigh. "I was making myself crazy worrying that you were feeling slighted and that's why Brock seemed to bother you so much..."

"Morning!" Stephen came striding into the kitchen, making both Pat and Ian jump with his exuberant greeting.

"Jeez, Stephen," Pat chastised him. "Inside voice, please."

Stephen grinned and nodded. "Sorry. I just slept really well. It must be the fresh air, it's been a while since I've been back." He tightened the sash on his navy blue robe and looked around the kitchen. "Man, looks like a bomb hit the place, doesn't it? Any coffee started yet, or should I make it?"

"Nope. Help yourself," Pat replied, tightly, not really caring as long as he wasn't bothering her.

Ian watched with narrowed eyes as Stephen worked his way around the kitchen with well-worn familiarity. He reached into the cupboard for cups, pulled out a tin of coffee beans from its place tucked on an open shelf, swiftly checked the coffee maker for old filters, all without missing a beat - as though he'd done it hundreds of times before. Which, of course, Ian knew he had.

"Quite the party last night, hey young man?" Stephen addressed Ian as he turned on the tap for water for the coffee maker.

Pat gritted her teeth. If he called Ian *young man*, or said *your young buck* to her one more time...

"I wouldn't know," Ian replied, his nostrils flaring.

"What?" Stephen cocked an eyebrow and pulled a surprised face. "Didn't Pat invite you? I'm sure when we started planning—"

"*We* didn't plan anything, Stephen," Pat cut in, her words clipped. "It was the kid's party and you know it. Ian would have felt just like us, too old and in the way."

Stephen laughed and poured the water into the coffee maker. "Oh, come on Patty-cake! You're only on the upswing of the hill, quite acting like you're at the top and sliding down the other side!"

Pat's jaw dropped and she was speechless. The man had become so damned infuriating since they'd split up, she found him nearly unrecognizable.

"I should be off." Ian spoke between clenched teeth, derailing the conversation in its tracks. He pulled himself up to his full height and yanked on his gloves.

Pat looked up at him, at the tightness of his face as he watched Stephen moving territorially around the kitchen and felt her heart clutch.

Damn it to hell, she thought. *Why does it all have to be so complicated?*

"Are you sure you can't stay for one cup?" Stephen offered, always the generous host.

Pat wanted to reach out to his benevolent face and slap it. Hard.

"No, sorry." Ian shook his head and backed away toward the door like the place held unexpected danger. Which, for him, it probably did. "Tell everyone I said Happy New Year, okay Pat?"

Pat swallowed against the lump that had formed in her throat and nodded. "Okay," she said, trying to hold him with her eyes. "Call me later?"

Ian ducked his head as he pulled open the door, nodded briefly and made a swift exit, leaving nothing behind but a blast of chill air.

Pat wrapped her arms around her torso and stared for a moment at the space where he had been.

"You still take cream in your coffee?" Stephen asked.

***

CHAPTER TWENTY THREE

"How can this be?" Melanie demanded of Pat, her voice brittle. "Seriously, I don't understand how it is that a week after New Year's that man is still residing in your house!"

Pat was feeling much the same way. And, she was beginning to worry about her blood pressure. "I don't know! It just sort of happened!" She threw her hands in the air in exasperation and took off at speed toward some bookshelves that needed straightening.

Melanie followed.

"Then, why on Earth can it not *sort of happen* that he gets the hell out of your house!" Melanie started straightening books alongside Pat, needing something to do with her hands to keep from grabbing her friend by the shoulders and shaking her.

"Apparently he had time booked off after the holidays..."

"So?" Melanie stopped straightening and placed her hands on her hips.

"And, then, he made this big song and dance about family and the upcoming wedding and wanting to help me out while he had the time." Pat paused and took a breath.

"Oh, Jesus," Melanie said, rolling her eyes.

"And, basically, he just did what he always does; schmoozed his way into getting what he wants."

"What about the word *no*?" Melanie spat. "Ever heard of it?"

She knew she was delivering a low blow, but, she'd had it. She'd watched from the sidelines for way too long and was sick to death of Stephen and his crap and the way it turned Pat inside out and upside down, leaving her a wreck for her friends to clean up.

"I'm trying!" Pat yelled into the silence of the bookshop, stopping both women in their tracks.

Melanie softened her stance. "*Pat*," she said, gently, touching her friend's shoulder. "What's really going on?"

Pat let her legs go limp beneath her and sunk to the shop floor. "I've messed it all up, Mel." She began to sob.

"What? What have you messed up?" Melanie sat on the floor beside her, her eyebrows knotted together with concern. Pat had come such a long way, it was distressing to see her moving backward into tears and self-loathing.

"Stephen just bulldozed in and Ian fled." She wiped her nose on the sleeve of her blouse. "We've barely talked this past week, the last time I saw him was just after New Year's and I feel like I let it all unravel without even so much as a whisper of protest."

Melanie sighed. She wished she could fix things, wave a magic wand and make it all better.

"I didn't even tell him about my worries about him and babies, although I guess I can leave that concern in the dust." Pat wiped at the tears that had fallen across her cheeks. "Oh hell, it's probably for the best anyway. It's time I stopped acting like a teenager and accept that he didn't need a woman, and an older one at that, like me to clutter up his life with all of my baggage."

"Oh, please, be quiet," Melanie said, gently shoving Pat's shoulder. "He was lucky to have you and if he didn't know it, then he was a stupid fool."

Pat gave her a half grin and swallowed a sigh. "Spoken like a true best friend," she said.

"Spoken like someone who knows the truth," Melanie stated. She pulled herself upright and reached down for Pat's hand to help her off the floor. "It will work itself out," she said, confidently. "These things always do. Haven't we always said that life is just a series of stories strung together? Well, this is just one more story filled with pages to be turned."

"But, what if it I don't like the ending?" Pat questioned. "Will there be a better one behind it?"

Melanie didn't know how to respond. She was worried, seriously worried, that Stephen might carve a new niche for himself in Pat's world. The very idea made her want to lose her lunch.

"One page at a time," she counseled, trying to keep her voice chipper as she reached out and gave Pat a hug. "That's all anyone can do."

***

CHAPTER TWENTY FOUR

Ian walked back and forth across Tom and Trisha's living room, Brock nestled sleepily on his shoulder. He'd volunteered to watch his nephew while they stepped out to do errands and while he was loving the quiet time with the little guy, it was giving him too much time to think.

"You falling asleep, buddy?" Ian cooed at Brock, when he felt the baby's breathing grow rhythmic. "Guess I should put you to bed, huh?"

He padded into Brock's nursery and gently placed him into his crib, grinning when he stuck his thumb in his mouth the moment he touched the mattress. Ian sighed. It was a baby's life.

He turned on the baby monitor, crept from the room and gently closed the door. It was a small accomplishment, easing the little guy into a peaceful sleep, but after the week he'd had, he'd take it.

"Hey," Trisha called out, as she pushed open the front door. "We're back."

Ian smiled and walked through the kitchen to greet them in the front hall. "Just in time, he's down for the count."

Tom grinned and handed him the largest box of diapers he'd ever laid eyes on. "Way to go, Uncle Ian."

"Holy Moses," Ian said, amazed, while he tried to see around the box. "Is Brock going to go through all of these before he outgrows them?"

Tom patted him on the shoulder and laughed. "Sadly, yes."

Trisha carried her bags into the kitchen and placed them on the counter, then turned to Ian, a questioning look on her face. "So?" she said. "Anything?"

Ian shlepped the box in behind her and set it on the floor. "No," he said, shaking his head.

"Oh." Her shoulders sagged and she started pulling things from the bags. "I guess I was just hoping..."

Ian smiled. She had such a good heart. He'd been hoping Pat would call, too, so he understood her disappointment.

"What are you going to do?" Trisha asked. "I mean, if things keep going this way, what'll happen?"

Tom kept quiet and put things away as Trisha set them out. He knew the growing estrangement from Pat was killing his brother and he didn't know how to help.

Ian sighed and sat down on a bar stool. "I don't know. We've talked a bit and I have a feeling things are going to come to a head right away. Her ex is still there, she has to make some choices, right?"

Trisha nodded. "Yes, I think so," she said, smiling kindly as she handed the last box of cereal to Tom. "It's been long enough, I think she'll put things right."

"Yeah," Ian agreed, then couldn't help but add, "One way, or another."

***

CHAPTER TWENTY FIVE

Pat felt the calendar was taunting her. February fourteenth, Valentine's Day.

She'd been so busy over the last month, had been intentionally keeping herself so busy, that the day of romance had managed to sneak up on her. She'd even asked Sarah to decorate the store and had purposely stayed upstairs in her office as much as possibly to avoid the blatantly schmaltzy theme, but it came after her anyway. Phooey.

Also, Melanie, Travis and Gerry weren't helping.

"You *have* to." Melanie was using her most insistent voice, while she pulled another chocolate from the box on Pat's kitchen table. "Mmm, nougat," she murmured, after biting into the confection.

"What if I don't want to?" Pat asked, sipping her coffee.

"Then, you'll leave me no choice but to stay at home, all alone, while the rest of the world is out reveling in the company of others."

Pat rolled her eyes. "Please," she said, still not convinced.

"Don't you *please* like that," Travis piped up, sitting across from Pat and trying to keep his attention away from the chocolates. "Mel's right, isn't she Ger?"

Gerry, intently examining the guide that came with the box of candy, looked up and nodded. "Uh-huh, one hundred percent." He finally made his choice and reached for a milk chocolate square. "It's not right that you sit here by yourself and mope. And, it's even more selfish to ask us to give up our plans to mope with you."

"I'm not asking you to!" Pat blurted, her face indignant. "When did I once ask you to? Please, I beg of you, go and have your fun. Don't give me another thought."

"What if we have a get-together at our place?" Travis offered, his eyes sparkling at the idea. "Ooh, we could get our decorator on!" He started waving his hands around excitedly as he elaborated. "We'll string lots of streamers - red and gold of course! Hearts and bows and glitter will carry the theme. We'll get a love themed menu and—"

"*And,* invite some single friends!" Gerry chewed vigorously on his candy as he matched Travis in his enthusiasm.

"Whoa!" Pat held up her hand. "Stop the train. You're getting way ahead of yourselves. I'm barely single again. No fix ups here, thank you very much."

Melanie let them bicker while she weighed her options of how to get her way. Finally, she had it: out and out pleading. She would resort to pretty much anything at that point to get Pat out for the evening, otherwise her best friend was going to pull out her well-worn, flannel pajama bottoms, make a bowl of popcorn for her dinner and basically slip back into her alarmingly reoccurring pattern of working all day, then staying at home alone every night. With her cat. Scary stuff.

"I'm telling Duncan." Melanie folded her arms across her chest and glared petulantly at Pat. "And, he'll be so upset when he hears the news. Is that what you want?" She switched on her best doe-eyed gaze. "Poor guy, he has to be out of town for work and he's trusting you to be my date and keep me from being lonely on Valentine's Day. Are you seriously going to let him down?"

That one made Pat laugh and she finally gave in. "Okay, fine. You're really reaching now and I give you props for your effort. Not to mention, I want nothing to do with the shindig these two fools are proposing. I'll go."

"Yay!" Travis cheered, then reached out swiftly to slap Gerry's returning hand to the chocolate box.

Melanie ignored them both and beamed. Mission accomplished.

***

CHAPTER TWENTY SIX

"This is crazy," Pat remarked, while she and Melanie followed their hostess and threaded through the crowd of diners that packed the tables of the restaurant. "Who knew so many people actually went out on Valentine's Day?"

Melanie knew. That was why she'd called for a reservation in advance. "Believe it or not," she told her friend. "Many people do still believe in a little romance."

"Oh, there they are," Pat said, catching sight of Travis and Gerry already seated, their heads close together as they leaned across the table to talk. "Does that make us partners, now?" she teased, just before they reached the table, leaning into Melanie so as not to be overheard.

Melanie snickered. A joke. Excellent. There was light at the end of the tunnel.

"Just for tonight," she bantered back. "Otherwise, Duncan would never forgive me for tossing him permanently aside."

"Hello, gorgeous ladies!" Travis stood up to get Pat's chair, Gerry followed his lead for Melanie and they all sat down, pleased as punch with themselves for being together on a day set aside for love.

Pat grinned at her friends. She was actually feeling pretty good and it was nice to have an excuse to dress up for something besides work. "This place is something," she said, glancing around. "Have you eaten here before? What's good?"

"Nope," Gerry replied, while he and Travis shared a drinks menu across the table. "We're first timers here, too."

Melanie didn't answer. Her face had gone rigid and she was looking past Pat's shoulder with a fierce intensity.

"Mel?" Pat frowned. "What is it? What's wrong?" She craned her head to follow Melanie's stare and her breath left her in a whoosh.

"No, don't!" Melanie tried to stop her, but too late. Pat had seen them.

"Oh, double hell." Pat's pulse kicked up and she clenched her teeth. "You've got to be kidding me. What a huge, goddamned, cosmic joke."

She was referring to the table just behind them. Seated comfortably and companionably, only a few footsteps away, was the entire Gaffney clan. Ian, Tom, Trisha, their lovely baby boy and, of course, Alexa. Fantastic.

"What's wrong?" Travis asked, twisting around in his chair.

"Don't look!" Gerry, seated beside Melanie, hissed before raising his menu to hide his face.

"Oh, God damn!" Travis exhaled and turned back to the table, his face ashen. He put an arm around Pat's shoulder for support and added, "Just ignore it."

"What are the odds?" Melanie speculated, equally startled. "I haven't seen any of them, not a one, for at least a month and now here they all are."

"Should we go?" Pat pondered, unsure.

"No," Melanie stated, firmly.

"Absolutely not." Travis agreed.

Gerry nodded. "They're right. If we don't want them to notice us, we absolutely cannot do the one thing that will draw their attention to our presence."

"One thing?" Pat repeated.

"If we get up as a group and leave," Gerry told her, leaning in toward the table. "Don't you think it would immediate attract their attention?"

Pat nodded and reached out with a shaky hand to pick up her water glass. She sipped the cool liquid as images of she and Ian, at her house, came flooding back...

It was a week after the New Year and he stood in her living room, demanding to know what was going on. "Why is he still here?" he'd asked, his brow furrowed. "You said he'd be gone and he's not. Why? What aren't you telling me?"

"He's taken time off work," she'd tried to explain to him, just as she had to Melanie. He wants to show support for Crystal and stay a bit to help out..."

Once she'd stopped explaining, Ian had looked at her with such disbelief he didn't need to say out loud the words that they were both silently thinking. Words like, *what a steaming load of crap*. Instead, he'd gone for the jugular.

"Are you kidding me?" he'd said, incredulity in every syllable. "Are you telling me you can't see exactly what's going on here?"

"That depends," she'd replied. "What is it that you think is going on?"

"The guy wants you back."

He'd said it with such controlled loathing, her stomach had churned.

"It's so God-damned obvious he's regretting your divorce and now that Crystal's getting married, he's running back to try and mend fences. He's probably got some desperate idea in his head that he needs to put things right, so he doesn't have to face the possibility of dying along."

He was right. She knew he was right. From the moment Stephen had shown up, she'd been on the receiving end of his sudden change of heart. And, it probably hadn't helped matters that Ian was in the picture, fourteen years Stephen's junior, young and virile and clearly desiring to be with her. Stephen had rapidly transformed from ambivalent ex-husband, to attentive suitor - very startling and very unsettling.

Pat had no words for Ian. She had so much on her plate; juggling her work, him, wedding plans and Stephen, it had become a huge mess. How could she have, in good conscience, asked him to wait around - more or less sitting like a patient toy on a shelf - until she got everything straightened out? It would have been selfish, childish and mean.

And so, she had done what she'd thought was the kindest thing - let him go. It had torn her up inside, make no mistake. She craved him physically, mentally and emotionally - more than she had thought she would in such a short period of time. However, she'd been down that road before, with a whole lot more years invested, so she knew it would just be a matter of time before she would slowly pull herself out of the quicksand once more.

Telling him, finally saying the words, had been awful. He'd looked so hurt, so deeply betrayed, Pat had nearly started to panic and pull back. She'd never wanted to be the one to do that to another human being. She'd had it done to her. And, yet, she'd had to steel herself, knowing it was the kinder option.

It wasn't until he'd kissed her one last time and closed the door behind him as he left the house that she'd finally allowed herself to fully unleash the torrent of heartache that sat at her core, waiting for release.

And, it didn't end there.

Pat hadn't known she'd have so many tears to shed. Instead, she'd had some idea that after the breakup of her marriage she would be more hardened. She'd been wrong. Gut wrenchingly wrong.

The hole in her heart had felt huge and she'd clutched Whiskey to her chest and carried him around the house with her for days and days, shielding herself from the emptiness she felt inside.

Melanie had come and gone on a regular basis, bringing food and temptations, glaringly concerned for her best friend. Pat had been grateful and probably would have let that continue for a lot longer, had it not been for Stephen. His arrogance, his confidence that he could wheedle his way back into her life, had finally worked against him in the form of an apple pie.

It had been a Saturday evening and Pat had returned home from work feeling completely drained from being chipper and pleasant at the bookstore. She had gone upstairs, changed into her soft flannel pajama pants, washed her face and then snuggled Whiskey into her arms in preparation for the evening ahead. She'd had no idea where Stephen was, whether he was in the house or not, and hadn't cared. She just wanted solitude and a large piece of the gorgeous apple pie Melanie had baked for her in hopes of tempting her appetite.

"Pat?" Stephen had called out as she'd shuffled down the staircase, Whiskey held close to her chest. "We've really been spoiled this time," he'd said as she entered the kitchen. "Melanie has outdone herself."

Pat had taken one look at the scene before her - Stephen with a large serving of *her* pie on a plate, a messy bite already missing and a look of pleasure on his face - heard the *we* ringing in her ears and hit the wall. She completely lost it. Magnificently.

"God damn it all to hell!" she'd bellowed. Whiskey had stiffened in her arms and she'd released him to take cover in his basket. He was going to need it. "You self-centered son of a bitch!"

Stephen had looked at her, wide eyed and shocked. "What? What is it?" he'd said, having never heard such language out of Pat, not even when he'd left.

"You come in here, in *my* house." She'd waved her arms erratically to further her point. "Acting as though you have some sort of entitlement to this place. Interrupting *my* Christmas and New Year's plans—"

"The kids." Stephen had tried to interject, his voice wheedling. "Crystal—"

"Was full of shit," Pat had stated. "And, you should have known better. You should have at least had the courtesy to call me and ask me about coming here, instead of feeling it was your right to come waltzing in unannounced."

Stephen had tried to launch a defense. "I did it for you, Patty," he'd said, pulling out his pet name of old.

"Like hell," Pat had countered, without so much as a flinch. "You did it for *you*, Stephen. At least have the balls to admit that."

And, so it had gone on. Stephen had tried to present a case that showed him as caring and considerate and Pat had kept on slapping him back. It had been cathartic. She'd let him have it for not just the current situation, but for the past and everything she hadn't said then, too. Finally, he'd said uncle and conceded he'd overstepped his mark and had rapidly, the very next day, packed up his belongings and slunk from the house.

Since then, in the month that had passed, Pat had been working to acknowledge her part in all of it; coming to conclusions about herself and growing in the process. She was a stronger woman because of it and for that at least she was grateful...

"Pat?" Melanie jostled her from her thoughts, her face a picture of concern. "You're off in your own world and you look upset. We can leave if you really want. Who cares what they think. If you can't handle it, we'll go."

Travis, his arm still around her shoulder, gave her a quick squeeze and nodded. "Absolutely, Pattycake. It's just dinner. We can go out any old day of the week."

Pat swallowed and placed her water glass back on the table. She thought she could actually feel Ian behind her and wondered how it was possible he was not aware of her.

"I don't know," she said, her new found strength beginning to desert her. "Maybe it's for the best. We can avoid any awkwardness..."

"Oh drat." Melanie blanched and muttered under her breath. "Brace yourself."

"Melanie?" Trisha called over to their table, her voice full of friendliness. "Is that you?"

"I'm so sorry, she caught my eye," Melanie whispered to Pat, before raising her eyebrows in surprise at Trisha. "Oh, hey! Good to see you."

Pat's back was to Trisha and she sat ramrod stiff in her seat. Travis leaned into her, almost like a human shield and Pat silently prayed Trisha would keep her greeting short and leave them alone.

"How *are* you?" Trisha gushed, clearly delighted to see Melanie.

"Good, thanks." Melanie delivered a tight, closed mouth smile and attempted to keep things short and sweet.

"Is Duncan here?" Trisha looked around the room, as though she expected to see Duncan materialize.

"Jeez," Gerry whispered. "Can't the woman take a hint?"

"No, he's not." Melanie shook her head and ignored Gerry's muttering. "He's out of town at the moment."

"Pam?" Alexa piped up, joining the conversation.

Shit, Pat thought, feeling an electric charge shoot up her spine when Alexa opened her mouth. *I'm not up to this.* Her shoulders sagged beneath Travis' embrace and she sighed, wishing she was anywhere but there.

"It's okay," Travis soothed, holding tight and refusing to budge from his position as human shield. "You can do this. We're here with you."

"Oh, is that you Pat?" Trisha's voice had taken on a slightly shrill note. "I didn't realize it was you."

Pat twisted slowly in her seat, kept her face as composed as she was able and nodded at Trisha. "Hi," she said, giving a small wave to the table.

Ian stared. Stared so intently, so unflinchingly, that Pat felt her breath catch in her chest. What was wrong with him? Couldn't he at least pretend to play nice?

Melanie jumped in and attempted to smooth things over. "Look at Brock," she said, deflecting their attention to the small blonde boy in Tom's arms. "He's grown so much!"

Trisha immediately threw herself into the role of doting mother, smiling and bragging about her son. Tom went along with Trisha, helping to ease the tension, and Alexa... She wrapped a slim hand around Ian's bicep and cut her eyes at Pat before turning to whisper in his ear.

Pat felt sick. Physically sick. As though, at any moment, she could throw up the water she'd just gulped from her glass. She turned back toward her own table and looked into Travis' concerned face. "I don't feel very well," she told him, swallowing against her nausea.

"Gerry Carrion and Travis Walker!"

Gerry snapped his head up and looked around them, startled nearly out of his shoes at the sound of he and Travis' names being shouted over the restaurant din.

"What in Heaven's name," Travis began as he leaned around Pat for a better look at whoever was making themselves a public display. "Oh!" He exhaled, dropping his arm from around Pat's shoulders and jumping to his feet. "Denise Chang and Heidi Moore!" Travis clapped his hands with glee and reached out to grab Gerry's hand. "Look Ger, two of our favorite gorgeous creatures in the flesh!"

And, were they ever. Pat stared, wide-eyed, her upset deftly pushed aside by her surprise, at Denise and Heidi. They looked like entirely different women from the last time she'd seen them.

Denise was dressed in a stunning, plum colored, knee length mandarin dress adorned with a print of tiny gold flowers and leaves. Combined with her chin length, sharply cut black hair and expertly made up eyes, she looked like Chinese royalty.

Heidi, no slouch beside Denise, was wearing a knee length, midnight blue, empire waisted dress cut low in both front and back. Her fiery red hair had been styled in loose curls that framed her face, while gold chandelier earrings glittered from her ears.

"Still feeling nauseous?" Melanie asked, a huge smirk on her face as she watched the love fest going on before them.

"Happy Valentine's Day!" Heidi said, excitedly, before she and Denise started grabbing both men for hugs and kisses; all the while being observed by two identical men they'd dragged along behind them.

Pat blinked and shook her head. "Nope," she acknowledged. "You?"

Melanie laughed and jerked her head toward Ian's table. "Get a load of *their* faces," she said, highly amused. "They looked shell shocked."

Pat turned around again and saw it was true. Instead of going back to their own conversations, Ian, Tom, Trisha and Alexa were all sporting expressions of disbelief at the sudden chaos that had arrived adjacent to their table.

"And, *Melanie*," Heidi said, her voice affectionate as she disentangled herself from Travis and reached to grab Melanie's hand. "I've been dying to run into you! Davis loves the treats I buy from your shop and now I can finally introduce him to the woman behind the vision!"

"Davis?" Melanie raised her eyebrows at Pat and Pat shrugged her shoulders.

"Yes, *Davis*," Heidi replied, then reached over to pull over one of the twins standing at attention.

Ahh, Pat thought, remembering her evening at *Lucky's. Right. The twins.*

She wanted to snicker when Heidi introduced them to Davis, but knew the joke would be lost on everyone else. The only one who had witnessed Heidi and Denise's lascivious comments about their twin boyfriends was Ian. Somehow, Pat didn't think he'd want to share the joke with her now.

"And, *Pat.*" Heidi shifted her radar from Melanie and smiled warmly. "It is so good to see you out since..." She cleared her throat and raised an eyebrow. "Well, since you became a free woman."

Pat smiled. Heidi was trying to be kind and she appreciated it. "Thanks," she said, hoping to leave it at that. No such luck.

"Now that you are," Heidi continued. "Denise and I will have Davis and Daniel keep their eyes open for any single men at their gym, hmm?"

"Oh, well..." Pat laughed uneasily at the suggestion.

She assumed Daniel was the other twin and there was no question, judging from the fact that both men were solidly built with well packed muscles, they went to a gym. *However...*

"They own it," Heidi told her, while nodding at Melanie to include her in the conversation. "So, if you girls want to mix up your workout routines any time, just call them up and they'll comp you right in." She turned and gave Davis a lavish kiss on the mouth. "Won't you, Pumpkin?"

Davis grinned and nodded. Pat raised an eyebrow at Melanie and whispered, "Not so much a man of words, as action?"

Melanie snorted and picked up her menu. "Hey, guys," she said, hoping to interrupt what had turned into some sort of in-depth conversation between Denise and Travis and Gerry. "I'm starving, shouldn't we order?"

"Oh God!" Denise threw a hand over her heart. "She's right, you naughty brats! Quite chattering with me and get back to your dates!" She pushed her dark hair from her face and in doing so, inadvertently glanced over her shoulder to lock eyes with Ian at the next table. "*Well,*" she said, giving Heidi a nudge on her shoulder. "Look who's also here."

Pat caught her breath and looked at Melanie. "Oh God," she said, suddenly fearful of what was going to happen next.

Heidi turned to follow Denise's gaze and her mouth twisted up to reveal pure distaste. "*Ian,*" she said, her voice brittle. "You're here, too. Who knew?" Before he could reply, she added, "Guess you're getting a burger tonight, huh?"

"Oh, that's for sure," Denise chimed in, following Heidi's lead and letting her eyes travel over Alexa, almost sitting in Ian's lap, with naked contempt.

Ian frowned and Heidi offered her clincher. "After all, everyone knows it takes a *real* man to be able to handle steak on a regular basis."

Melanie coughed loudly and Pat blanched as Heidi delivered her blow, then spun on her heel to form a solid wall with Denise, Davis and Daniel.

"Holy Moses," Melanie said, beginning to snicker quietly as the two women gave their last goodbyes to Travis and Gerry. "No need for interpretation there."

Pat nodded her agreement as hilarity began to bubble up in her chest. "Oh man," she murmured, her shoulders shaking as laughter took her over. "You can't write this stuff."

Melanie needed no further invitation and dissolved into hiccupping giggles across the table top.

"Happy Valentine's Day," Pat said, feeling much, much better.

***

CHAPTER TWENTY SEVEN

"Seriously? Even after all of that," Tom said, shaking his head at Ian. "You're still smitten with the woman?"

Ian shrugged. It didn't make sense to him either, but there it was.

"It's been a month since you split up, man," Tom added, sitting down on his couch and supporting Brock while he tried to stand upright on his knee.

"Jeez," Ian said, smiling at Brock. "He's gotten so strong, already."

Tom grinned. "I know. Must be those strong Gaffney genetics."

"Got that right," Ian agreed, getting up from his chair and walking toward the kitchen. "I'm going to grab a beer, you want one?"

"Sure." Tom cooed at Brock, then offered another thought. "You *were* also basically cast as the villain of the piece by her friends at the restaurant last night.

Don't you think that's a clear indicator it's time to move on?"

"If only I could." Ian sighed and took two beers from the fridge. "Oh, and those women don't really count as her friends. They're just a couple of locals who seem to show up right when you least expect it."

Tom raised an eyebrow, nestled Brock into his lap and picked up a soother from the coffee table. "So, what's the game plan?"

"I'm not sure, exactly," Ian admitted, walking back into the family room and setting Tom's beer on the coffee table in front of him. "But, it doesn't seem to matter how much time has passed, I just can't get her out of my head. She's like a drug."

Tom nodded and offered the soother to Brock's open mouth. "Yeah, I felt that way about Trisha." He glanced at Brock and added, with an adoring smile, "And, look how well that's turned out!"

Ian smirked and sat down in the oversized arm chair. "I've talked to her friend a couple of times."

"Melanie?"

"Yeah."

"And?" Tom got up, tucked Brock into his arms and traversed the same path Ian had into the kitchen.

"Nothing, really." Ian reached for the bottle opener on the coffee table and popped the cap off his beer, then reached for Tom's and did the same. "I've just been asking a few questions about Pat, staying in the loop and seeing if she might be thinking of me, too."

Tom reached into the cupboard, pulled out a bag of barbecue chips and set them on the countertop. "So, what you're saying is, you've been indirectly stalking her?"

"Shut up!" Ian blurted, defensively, as he sat back, stretched out his legs and propped his feet on the coffee table. "It's not like that."

Tom laughed and pulled a green plastic bowl from a cabinet beside the dishwasher.

"Relax," he said, putting the bowl down on the counter and pouring the chips inside. "I'm just busting your chops. Did you find out anything?"

Ian took a swig of his beer and shook his head. "Not really. Just that she's been working all hours since we broke up, which I take as a good sign she's trying to avoid thinking about me."

Tom picked up the bowl, walked back into the family room and set it down between their drinks. "Yeah, that sounds about right. That's what I'd do. Hell, it's what you've been doing, isn't it?"

Ian nodded and grabbed a handful of chips from the bowl. "Yup. Pretty much."

Tom looked at him thoughtfully as he sat down and tucked Brock onto his lap. "You going to keep checking up on her?" he asked, having a feeling he already knew the answer.

Ian met his eye and shrugged. "She's my drug."

"Yeah." Tom nodded, grabbed his drink with his free hand and turned up the sound on the TV.

***

CHAPTER TWENTY EIGHT

"Funny thing," Melanie commented, her voice casual as she flipped through some magazines laying on the cash desk of Pat's bookstore.

Pat was setting up an Easter display near the front of the shop and paused in her work. "What's that?" she asked, taking a step back to examine what she'd done so far.

"I don't think Ian has totally forgotten you."

Pat's eyebrows shot up on her forehead in surprise.

"Ian?" she said, completely taken off guard. They hadn't mentioned his name since their fiasco at Valentine's Day. "What on Earth brings him into the conversation?"

"I'm just saying," Melanie continued as she flipped through the glossy pages and chewed on chocolate eggs from a bowl on the desk top. "Even though it's been a couple of months now since everything went kaput with you two, I think he still has you on his mind."

Pat put down the books she was holding and turned to stare at Melanie. "And what, pray tell, has given you that idea?"

Melanie stopped chewing and a guilty look swept across her face.

"Mel," Pat warned. "You may as well say it, you want to. And, if you don't, I'll just pester you until you do."

Melanie sighed. It was true.

"Okay," she ventured, watching Pat's face. "There may have been some times in the past couple of months that Ian might have come into my shop."

Pat said nothing, just stared at her, so Melanie fast-tracked; almost tripping over her words in her haste to get to the end. "Not to shop, but to ask me questions about you."

Pat was stunned. Her life since the awkward Valentine dinner encounter with Ian and his family had finally begun to settle into a manageable groove. She felt she was moving past it - after lots of ice cream, talks with Melanie, and running to exhaust her mind into submission. And, she was feeling positive about the strides she'd been making toward being an independent single woman, instead of a broken down mess. Now *this*?

"I don't understand," Pat told her.

"The truth is," Melanie admitted. "I've been feeling terrible, not telling you about how he's been showing up at my shop and asking how you're doing, if you've been dating, if you miss him. I've been feeling really uncomfortable, like I've become some sort of informant, and I don't like it. Which is why I'm telling you now."

"Why?"

"Why?" Melanie echoed. "What do you mean *why*?"

"Why did you tell me?" Pat folded her arms tightly across her chest.

Melanie frowned. "*Because*, I just told you—"

"No, you didn't. You told me how it's been uncomfortable for *you*." Pat clarified. "You never said *why* you thought I should know."

"Oh." Melanie stopped to think about it. "Okay, I guess you're right. But, it seems—"

"Because," Pat continued, interrupting her. "It comes across that you're giving me the information in much the same way a cheating partner would give information; for themselves and *their* guilt. Not actually considering how it could make the other person feel to hear it."

Melanie sat up straight. "Wait just a minute," she said, closing her magazine. "I did too want you to know for *you*, not me."

"I don't think so," Pat said, stiffly, unfolding her arms and picking up the books she'd laid down. "Because, I gotta tell you, knowing this has not made me feel good. Not at all. It's actually made me feel... I don't know, confused or something."

Melanie stood up and came around the cash desk. "I thought that might happen, which—"

"So, you wanted not only to clear your conscience, but to confuse me as well?" Pat interrupted her again and considered throwing the books down, not caring where they landed. "You *wanted* me to be confused and upset by the information?"

"No!" Melanie blurted, throwing her hands in the air. "Of course not! I *wanted*, or at least I'd *hoped*, that the information might actually make you feel good."

"How?" Pat whirled around to face her. "How could that make me feel good? Finding out, after all of this time has passed, that Ian hasn't actually moved on and is still thinking about me?"

"Are you hearing yourself," Melanie asked. "At all?"

"Yes!" Pat's hands clenched into fists as she tried to control her exasperation. "And, the point is, I don't want to know that he's thinking of me! At all! I've left that gate behind and would like to forget he's alive, if that's possible!"

"That makes no sense!" Melanie had become just as shrill, matching her tone.

"Yes, it does!" Pat could feel her heart beating and knew it wasn't just because she was upset. Every time she thought about Ian, her heart seemed to wake up and beat more intently.

"No, it does not," Melanie spat, her teeth clenched. "The only way that that could make sense is if you still have feelings for him."

Pat glared. Damn her for saying the very thing she'd been trying to avoid. "Okay, I'm done with this conversation. I don't want to talk about this, Melanie."

Pat turned on her heel and marched over to the cash desk. "I have too much here that needs my attention, not to mention at home with all of the wedding crap piling up fast and furious as we get closer to the whole shmozzle of a day. I don't need to have inane discussions about issues that are closed, done, finished."

Melanie watched in amazement as Pat spun around; sending Whiskey, tucked under the desk, flying up the stairs. She pounded up the stairs behind her cat, without so much as a backward glance.

Huh, Melanie thought. *So, she does still have feelings for Ian. Interesting.*

***

CHAPTER TWENTY NINE

"Hitting the club scene tonight, huh?" Tom said, a wide, teasing smile on his face. "On the *prowl.*"

Ian rolled his eyes as he pulled a sport coat over his black dress shirt. "Not quite."

"Leave him alone," Trisha admonished, from her seat beside Brock's blue and white highchair. "And, in case you've forgotten, he's going out with my sister. That could cramp his ability to pull."

Ian laughed. "She's got a point."

"Fine." Tom threw his hands up in exasperation. "You can't blame a guy for trying to live vicariously, when the topic of excitement around here is mashed sweet potatoes versus carrots."

Brock laughed suddenly from his chair and Ian watched Trisha's delight and, beside her, his brother's face as it softened into an expression of the mush he was lamenting. Yeah, poor guy.

"I think you're doing okay," Ian said, slipping on his shoes.

Tom pointed at him. "If anything good happens, I want a blow by blow."

Ian chuckled and walked toward the door. "You got it," he said, over his shoulder, before exiting the house.

***

"Calm down," Pat insisted, trying to focus on her task of mending a small tear in the back of Crystal's wedding dress.

"I'm trying," Crystal replied, even though she continued to fidget.

"Not hard enough," Pat remarked and then sat back on her heels. "Take it off. I can't do it with you moving around so much, so take it off and I'll get it done in half the time."

"Oh, God!" Crystal squeaked. "The time! What time is it?"

"Time for you to take a valium, or have a drink at least," Melanie said as she walked into Pat's bedroom. "Here." She offered a glass of white wine to Crystal. "You'll note that it's white, no worries about stains on your dress."

Pat smirked and caught Melanie's eye as she waited for her daughter to take a long swallow from the glass and then remove her wedding dress.

"Okay," Crystal said, handing over the cream-colored, chiffon dress. "I'm going to go and start picking out something for later."

Pat, her arms full of fabric, and Melanie, swigging wine from her own glass, watched her beetle out of the room.

"My God," Melanie said. "I wasn't joking about that valium. Were we that bad when we got married?"

"Probably," Pat said, holding up the dress and admiring its flowing lines and the sprinkle of crystals on the bodice and through the waist. "Can you believe this dress? I never would have thought Crystal would pick something Grecian inspired."

"And, yet," Melanie said. "It suits her perfectly. She's going to look sensational. Only one week to go, providing she survives her bachelorette party tonight."

"God," Pat groaned, then made quick work of mending a small tear where the satin ribbon around the waist had separated from the fabric at the back of the dress. "Don't remind me. How in heaven did we get roped into going again?"

"How could we not?" Melanie drained the last few drops in her glass and sprawled across Pat's king sized bed. "Duncan's going to Kent's party for goodness sake, how could we be the two old ladies refusing to join in on Crystal's night?"

"Those are the operative words," Pat told her, smoothing the dress and then covering it in its protective wrapping. "Old ladies. We're going to look so damned out of place in that club."

Pat shut her eyes for a moment, remembering her last foyer into a nightclub and how poorly that had turned out. "Women over forty do not belong in nightclubs. Ever."

"Well, we have no choice, so we'll just have to pretend we're a couple of cougars and make the young boys nervous as we watch them with lechery in our eyes."

Pat burst out laughing. "Yeah, until one of them says, 'Mrs. Keegan? Is that you? I didn't know you came here.' And, I turn three shades of pink with embarrassment!"

Melanie dissolved into giggles, overjoyed Pat was able to handle the cougar joke without a flinch. They'd put their last chat about Ian behind them, she didn't want to open any cans of worms in that department again.

***

"What?" Pat shouted, trying to be heard above the music thumping throughout the dimly lit room.

Melanie started to laugh and all Pat could see was her face contorting, her voice swallowed up by the crowd. Pat shook her head and shrugged, so Melanie held up her glass and raised her eyebrows in question. Pat nodded and happily followed in her wake to the bar.

"Wow!" Melanie shouted, when they were able to squeeze themselves into a tight space between two muscle-bound boys and waited for their drinks. "I had no idea the amount of kids that would be here. Apparently, I'm clueless as to the number of barely legal youth there are in this town. Makes me worry about Gina, when she comes of age. The thought of these boys, these young *men*, looking her over with drunken eyes. Blech."

Pat nodded sympathetically. She'd never had to deal with that worry. Crystal not only had her older brother to watch out for her, but there was also the fact that she and Kent had fallen for each other in high school. They were each other's first and only real dates.

"This is why, despite your apprehension about Crystal and Kent being too young, you should be counting your blessings. I have a feeling I'm going to have years of emotional upheaval to deal with when Gina throws herself into the fray."

Pat took the glass the tall, dark and handsome barman held out to her and thanked him. He grinned at her for a moment longer than was necessary and she felt herself flush. He grinned wider and gave her a wink, nearly making her spill her drink.

"Well, well," Melanie said, with a dirty chuckle. "Looks like Momma's not so far up on the dusty shelf as she thought she was."

"Stop." Pat warned and slapped her arm. "He was just flirting to get a larger tip."

"I don't know about that, Darlin'," Melanie teased, watching the barman continue to watch Pat. "Seems to me if you wanted, he'd be up for a little more than a slap and tickle at the end of his shift."

"Melanie!" Pat blurted and blushed again. "He's a child!"

Melanie took in the broad shoulders, faint laugh lines around his eyes and dark stubble across the so-called *child's* jaw line and shrugged. "Not really. He's more than legal and no one said you had to take him home to your mother. Just take him home!"

"You're impossible!" Pat told her, while having a hard time dropping her grin. While she would never do it, admittedly, she liked the idea that she wasn't out of the game quite yet. Maybe what her kids were saying was actually considered true; forty five was the new thirty five, after all.

"Oh, here comes Crystal." Melanie pointed to their left. "Get ready for it, she has that look in her eyes and she's going to insist we dance."

She was right. Crystal wanted all of her hen night girls out with her on the dance floor and Pat and Melanie let themselves be dragged along for the ride. It was actually rather fun dancing in a large group of women and not caring who was, or wasn't, watching. She and Melanie were laughing and falling into one another, thoroughly enjoying acting like teenagers together. Pat even noticed that they had attracted some admiring glances from more than a few young men. It was flattering, until one of them looked so much like Ian she did a double take.

"Oh-my-God," she said, losing the beat and grabbing Melanie's arm.

"What?" Melanie had been lost in the music and swiftly came to her senses. "What's wrong? Is it Crystal?"

"No." Pat shook her head, not able to tear her eyes away. "It's Ian."

"What?" Melanie spun around to follow Pat's gaze and sure enough, there was Ian - next to Alexa.

"I knew it!" Pat yelled, forgetting to even try and look like she was still dancing. She gave up and started to weave her way off the floor.

"What? What did you know?" Melanie demanded, following on her heels. "Pat? What did you know?"

Pat pulled her aside and leaned in so she could hear. "I *knew* he had a thing for Alexa! All that time he insisted he didn't, but he did! The bastard!"

Melanie stared at Pat, her expression confused. "Okay, so even if you were right," she said. "Why does it matter?"

Pat was taken aback. She'd been so intent upon what she had discovered, she'd never considered why she cared.

"Well, it matters because, umm... *Because* he obvious lied to me and that's just... Uhh..." She faltered and sighed. "You're right. It doesn't really matter. I guess I was just so surprised for a moment there..."

"Because you still have feelings for him," Melanie finished, firmly. "I don't care if you get mad at me again for saying it because I'm going to. I wasn't going to, but now I'm going to keep on saying it until you face up to it."

Pat watched Ian from the opposite side of the dance floor, completely unaware that he was in her sights and shrugged. "Fine. Even if I did finally face up to it, what good would it do now? Looks like that ship has sailed."

Melanie looked as well and watched Alexa laughing up at Ian; leaning into him as she spoke animatedly.

"He's better off," Pat said, dropping her gaze and looking down at her new red pumps.

"You don't know that," Melanie said, shifting her focus to watch Crystal and the girls still strutting their stuff on the dance floor.

"Yeah, I do," Pat remarked. "He deserves someone uncomplicated. Someone like *her*. Not a woman shifting into a new stage in her life, unsure of her footing."

Melanie peeked at Ian one more time. "Well, if that's true, he certainly doesn't look all that ecstatic about Ms. Uncomplicated. He looked a lot happier with Ms. New Stage of Her Life."

Pat frowned. "How can we know for sure, right? He's over there and we're over here, there's no way to tell other than marching over and demanding answers."

Melanie nodded. "And..."

"And, there's no way I'm doing that!" Pat said, firmly.

"Mom! Melanie!" Crystal called out, waving from the crush of writhing bodies. "Come back!"

Melanie smiled and Pat straightened her shoulders. "You in?" she asked.

"What the hell," Melanie agreed and grabbed Pat's hand.

They giggled and shifted their way through the young and nimble bodies on the floor, completely unaware that as they rejoined the hen party, Ian had spotted Pat. He did a double take, just as she had, and was mesmerized by how beautiful she looked. Her short, chestnut hair sparkled under the flashing lights, her black skirt showed off her lean, muscled legs and her smiling face as she tilted her head back and laughed with Melanie nearly tore his heart out.

"Another drink?" Alexa nudged Ian's hip with her own. He blinked and caught his breath as he pulled his focus from the dance floor. "There's a line up, but I am willing to brave it."

Ian glanced back at Pat, noted the obvious male attention she was attracting and nodded. A line up? He'd believe it.

***

CHAPTER THIRTY

"Oh my God! I'm so sorry!" Pat swerved her shopping basket at the last second as she came around the grocery aisle, just barely missing smacking right into a cart on the corner.

"No, no." The woman pushing the other cart was insistent. "I should have been watching more carefully! I've just been a bit out of it and have a case of baby brain going on..." She tapered off and her eyes grew wide as they met Pat's.

Pat watched the recognition hit the woman's face, smiled and said warmly, "Well, it was bound to happen, right? How are you, Trisha?"

Trisha's face relaxed and relief swept across her features. "I'm good. Tired, but good."

Pat laughed and pulled her cart to the side of the aisle. "How're Tom and Brock?"

"They're good, too," Trisha said, her face becoming thoughtful, then hesitant; as though she was weighing her words.

"Brock must be growing like a weed, huh?" Pat smiled some more in hopes that she'd see they could leave the past in the past.

"He is!" Trisha enthused. "It's hard to believe he's already 6 months old. Well, in theory it's hard. Physically, I'm all too aware."

Pat laughed. "I remember, believe me. Is he sleeping through the night, yet?"

"Not yet," Trisha told her, then covered her mouth with her hand when a yawn snuck up. "It's getting better and we're hopeful it'll be any day now."

"It's a stage," Pat soothed. "As I'm sure you've heard many times. It goes by—"

"Ian misses you!"

Pat stopped her soothing and gaped at Trisha.

Trisha wrung her hands together and shifted back and forth on her feet. "Look, I know I probably shouldn't say anything and it's been months since you two split up, but Pat, I'm telling you the absolute truth when I say he still misses you like crazy."

Pat watched her chest go up and down as she caught her breath and felt her own heart rate speed up. Maybe she'd been wrong when she had seen Ian and Alexa at the night club. Maybe they weren't as serious, or exclusive, as they'd appeared.

"Oh, God," Trisha said, looking very uncomfortable. "Please say something, Pat."

"I don't really know what to say," she said, truthfully.

"I don't blame you. If I was in your shoes, I'd feel the same way."

"What about your sister?"

Trisha frowned. "What do you mean?"

Now it was Pat's turn to feel uncomfortable. "Well, I thought I might have seen her and Ian together, and I know it's none of my business..."

"They hang out, it's no big deal. She doesn't own Ian, even though she likes to act like she does. Alexa is so flighty, it's like she's sixteen, instead of thirty." She shrugged and pushed her hair behind her ears. "Can I ask you something?"

Pat nodded, even though Trisha hadn't fully answered her question. "Shoot."

"Are you seeing anyone new?"

"Oh." Pat blinked, unprepared for the inquiry.

"Because if you are, that's great," she said. "However, if you're *not...*"

"What?" Pat asked, almost afraid to hear the answer.

"Well, I just think that you and Ian were great together, you know?"

"Umm," Pat said, more confused than before. Was Trisha trying to tell her that she wished she was with Ian, instead of Alexa?

"Don't get me wrong," Trisha added. "I know you guys had your stuff to work out. But, honestly, I don't think any of it was worth giving each other up for. I think it was just a case of timing. It was off then, but that doesn't mean it always will be."

Pat let her words wash over her and was shocked to discover they felt absolutely wonderful. After months of back and forth internal dialogue, Trisha's simple truth about timing felt like a sweet breath of fresh air.

"You know," Pat said, feeling lighter than she had in a long time. "You may just be right on that, Trisha. And, I guess, using your analogy, time will tell."

Trisha grinned and nodded.

***

CHAPTER THIRTY ONE

The shop bell rang and Pat looked up from her laptop where she'd been scanning inventory lists, to see a wild-haired gentleman stride through the door.

Thomas MacLeod, she thought, surprised, as she pulled glasses from her face. She hadn't crossed paths with the man in a very long time; years in fact.

Pat watched him and was pleasantly surprised to see he hadn't changed much at all. Still sporting his Albert Einstein inspired hair, still dressed in plaid and looking a lot like a disheveled professor and, she would bet money, still smoking like a chimney.

Thomas glanced around the shop, rocked back and forth on his heels and let out a large puff of air. Pat had seen it before; show time.

"Good afternoon," she offered, getting up from her stool and coming around the side of the desk. "Can I help you find something in particular, Sir?"

Thomas turned away from a bookshelf, his face a picture of relief. "Aye, you certainly can. I'm in need of a book. A book fer a small child. A wee gel."

"Okay," Pat said, trying not to grin at the sound of his Scottish brogue. "Let's start with her age, shall we? How old is she?"

"Right. Well, she's got-ta be around four? Maybe five?" He shrugged, then snapped his fingers. "Ah, right! Definitely four, she's nay in school yet. That'd make her four then, yeah?"

"Sure," Pat agreed, pleasantly. "If you say so, then four it is."

"You leuk familiar to me, lass." Thomas cocked his head as he stroked his salt and pepper colored, Van Dyke beard. "Have we met?"

Pat grinned. "Yes, sir, as a matter-of-fact we have. My name is Pat and my son, Michael, beseeched you for your assistant a number of years ago - gosh, it's got to be about ten years now - when he and his friends were making a motor powered go-cart." Pat chuckled as the memory came back.

Thomas nodded and smoothed back his unkempt, windblown hair. "Aye, I remember. Sharp as a tack, brown hair, a smile to charm the whiskers off a cat?"

"I'd say that pretty much sums him up," Pat agreed. "He was so thrilled with your help. It was Mister MacLeod *this*, and Mister MacLeod *that*, for days on end as he sang your praises."

Thomas sniffed and cleared his throat. "Well, you certainly donna need to be callin' me either Mister MacLeod, or Sir, for that matter. Thomas will do just fine."

Pat saw the flash of pleasure that had crossed his face when she revealed Michael's admiration. It was endearing to see a soft side in a man who looked so rough around the edges.

"Deal," she said. "So, what say we start looking for that book, Thomas, for the lucky little girl in your life?"

"I'd say I'm the lucky one, Pat." He winked and his blue eyes sparkled. "I've been wracking my brain aboot this gift and walking by your shop was clearly a stroke of Divine intervention. That, or just bloody good fortune I dropped me pocket watch ootside your door."

Pat chuckled appreciatively. "Oh, pocket watch aside, I'm sure you'd have found something if I hadn't been here."

"Aye, you're probably spot on. I think it's all aboot timing, personally," Thomas offered, sagely. "No pun intended."

Pat stared at him. Trisha had said nearly the exact same words. What were the odds that two people, worlds apart, would give her the same sort of message in less than a week? Very good, apparently.

"Absolutely," Pat said, wholeheartedly, feeling inspired. "Let's find that perfectly timed book, shall we?"

"Aye." He winked and extended his hand. "Lead the way, lass."

***

CHAPTER THIRTY TWO

"I'm gettin' married in the morning!" Gerry sang loudly.

"Ding, dong, the bells are gonna chime!" Travis leapt in.

Pat rolled her eyes as they dissolved into giggles, thoroughly entertained by just themselves. She might have spared herself a moment of jealousy at their intimacy, but she was up to her ears organizing complimentary take home gifts for the wedding guests and couldn't find the energy to spare.

They were funny, though, in their enthusiasm. And, Pat had to admit they'd carried her more than just a little bit over the past few months, not only in her relationship drama, but in wedding preparations as well.

"Oh, *fine*," she said, with a dramatic sigh, knowing it was what they wanted. "Pull out the stopper! Let's have a whopper! But, get me to the church on time!"

"Woohoo, go Pat!" Travis cheered, while Gerry whistled, and they all fell over themselves laughing.

"What's all the cheering and singing going on in here?" Duncan asked as he breezed into the family room with a large tray laden down with iced tea and donuts. "Aren't you people supposed to be working?"

"Bless you, you dear man!" Travis jumped up from where he was seated on the floor and picked his way through rows of crackled glass candle holders and miniature clay tea pots; bags of lemons; bunches of pink lavender and stalks of green mint. "Refreshments, just what we need. Is there booze in that iced tea? Because, I think we might be getting a little punch drunk."

"Or," Pat added, a wry smirk on her face. "You've just been sneaking a little too much punch and actually *are* drunk!"

Duncan laughed and squatted down beside Pat also seated on the floor, surrounded by pairs of flip-flops, miles of ribbons and stacks of woven baskets. "Can I help?"

"Oh God, really?" Pat reached out and squeezed his arm gratefully. "Would you? That would be so great."

Duncan shifted and sat down beside her. "It would be my pleasure. What can I do?"

Pat picked up a set of pink flip-flops and a length of yellow ribbon. "It's simple," she told him. "Just put the flip-flops together, bottom sides inward, and tie them with the ribbon so they stay as a pair."

"Sounds simple, alright," he said. "Not much chance of me messing it up and catching hell. I like it."

Pat chuckled. "Once you've tied them together as a set, place them in one of these." She gestured to the stacks of white baskets. "And, finish by adding a pair of yellow sunglasses from that bag beside the end table."

"And, we're making one of these baskets for every guest?"

"Every damned one." Pat verified. "Since it's a backyard wedding, Crystal wants to make sure everyone has access to comfy footwear and, if it's too bright during the ceremony, they have proper eyewear at their disposal."

Duncan shook his head and let out a low whistle. "Impressive. Sounds like she's really thought of everything right down to the minute details."

"I'll say," Gerry piped up, listening in on their conversation as he and Travis munched on the glazed donuts. "How do you think those baskets ended up so pretty, with the ribbons woven through them and the cutesy pictures of her and Kent attached to the handles?"

"You guys?"

"You'd better believe it." Gerry flexed his hands. "I swear the tips of my fingers were numb for a week."

"Oh, *please*," Pat said, raising an eyebrow. "You're not telling him where Crystal came up with the idea."

"You guys?" Duncan repeated himself.

"Well..." Gerry smirked and Travis snickered. "I saw the idea in a magazine and it seemed such a perfect idea for a garden wedding, so..."

"So, you ended up with numb fingers," Pat finished for him.

"Who has numb fingers?" Melanie asked, coming in through the front door. "Do I even want an answer to that question?"

"The baskets," Pat said.

"Oh." Melanie raised a hand to stop Pat elaborating and nodded in understanding. She'd heard the tales of woe already and didn't want to hear them repeated.

"Got yourself a helper there, huh?" She grinned cheekily at Duncan sitting beside Pat, dutifully pairing pink flip-flops and placing them into the waiting baskets.

"A volunteer, actually," Pat told her. "He's a good man."

Melanie raised her eyebrows. "Or, smart. They're bringing out the heavy stuff now, getting all of the chairs arranged in the garden."

"Oh boy." Pat stood up and brushed off the seat of her shorts. "Thanks for telling me. I'd better supervise this, or suffer Crystal's hysterics if they do something wrong."

She hesitated before leaving the room, torn between her many duties. Melanie waved her hand and said, "You go! I'll stay here with Duncan and help him get the rest of these done."

"Wonderful," Pat said, gratitude thick in her voice. "Thanks."

"Pah, don't give it another thought. Go."

Pat spun on her heel and silently repeated the mantra she'd created when she'd first gotten divorced, and used in every challenging situation since then.

Just one more day. Just one more day...

***

"Well, we did it," Travis said, his voice slightly shaky and tears in his eyes as he wrapped an arm around Pat's shoulder. "She's married now. We did our duty to give her the best wedding we could, the rest is up to her and Kent."

Pat looked up at him, one eyebrow raised. "How much have you had to drink?"

"Not enough to mend the stitch in my heart." He sniffed and tossed back the last of his hard lemonade in one go.

Oh, boy, Pat thought as she searched the yard for Gerry. Thankfully, he was in sight and Pat waved him over while trying not to buckle under the ever increasing weight of Travis' relaxing arm across her shoulders.

"Got yourself a leaner there, do ya?" Gerry teased as he walked over to them.

"Gerry!" Travis shifted himself from Pat and draped himself around his partner. "What now? What do we do *now*?"

Pat snickered and made her escape, leaving Gerry to mutter his assurances that they still had Michael to look forward to.

"It couldn't have gone better," Melanie commented, coming up behind Pat and offering her a tall gin and tonic.

Pat took the drink and raised it up. "You've got that right. Cheers." She brought the glass to her lips, took a long swallow and sighed.

"Shirley and Bud are no slouches on the dance floor!"

Pat snickered. Her parents were the least senior-like people she'd met. "It's all those cruises. Keeps them dancing into the wee hours."

Melanie smiled. "I have to admit, though," she said, lifting one of her feet off the ground and twisting her ankle back and forth. "I wasn't sure about the flip-flops, but they actually were a stellar idea."

Pat shook her head. "I know! Darn that Gerry for hitting one out of the park. Almost everyone's kicked off their shoes and all you can hear between songs is the thwack-thwack of the guest's feet."

"The pink does clash a bit with my dress," Melanie said, with a shrug as she indicated her red cocktail dress. "But, it goes with your mother of the bride togs."

"Crystal made me wear this," Pat said, looking at her own dress; strapless, knee length and daisy yellow. "I match the theme."

Melanie smiled and looked at the beautifully manicured garden. The maple trees and marquee were adorned with white fairy lights and pink and yellow paper lanterns. The crackled glass candleholders were alight, each housing a flickering, petal pink candle. And, the miniature clay teapots were the perfect vessels to display slices of lemon, threads of pink lavender and stocks of green mint. It was all tasteful and intimate, exactly as Crystal had wanted.

"Could be worse, I suppose," Pat admitted. "She could have made me wear pink and we know I look hideous in pink."

"She looks so happy." Melanie smiled affectionately when she caught sight of Crystal in her gorgeous, flowing dress, walking forward into Kent's waiting embrace.

Pat followed Melanie's gaze and watched her daughter and new son-in-law sway to the music. "Content, even," she added.

Melanie turned to look at Pat and cocked her head. "So do you."

Pat shifted her focus from the happy couple to Melanie and sighed. "You know what? I am. And, exhausted. And, relieved. But, most of all, I'm happy for Crystal and Kent that I was able to do this for them."

"Now you can put the house on the market, right?"

"Uh-huh. I already told Gerry." Pat took another long swallow of her drink, then yawned. "I just need a couple of weeks to decompress and then we'll get the sign on the lawn. He thinks it's the perfect time, the house should be appealing to families looking to get settled in before a new school year begins."

Melanie swallowed the last of her drink and took a breath. "So, since you haven't reacted yet, did you happen to see who Stephen is talking to?"

Pat frowned. "No. Why?"

"I didn't think so. Brace yourself."

Melanie pointed across the yard and Pat followed her finger, finally locating Stephen tucked into a corner of the marquee chatting animatedly with a tall, blonde man.

Pat squinted. "I don't have my glasses. Who is that?" she asked. "Did Stephen bring a friend..." Her voice caught in her throat and the air left her lungs as the man turned to his left and his profile came starkly into view. Ian.

Melanie watched Pat register him and placed a steadying hand on her shoulder. "He's been here for a while, laying low. Michael let him in. I didn't want to say anything earlier to throw off your game."

Pat looked at her, incredulous. "But, why? Why is he here?"

Melanie shrugged and then smiled as Duncan sidled up to join them, planting an affectionate kiss on her cheek. "I don't know. I haven't had a chance to say anything more than hello. Maybe you should go and ask him."

As though by some sort of invisible force, Ian seemed to sense they were talking about him. Either that, or it was a coincidence. Regardless, he stopped talking with Stephen and turned to meet Pat's stare.

"Oh, help," she muttered under her breath.

It had been such a long day, hell such a long half year - never mind that she'd had more than her usual two drink maximum. Pat didn't know if she was ready to meet him head on.

"Nope," Melanie said as she and Duncan pushed off when Ian made his move toward them. "Sorry, Sweetie. You're on your own on this one."

She gave a small, friendly wave to Ian before she and Duncan drifted toward the dance floor under the marquee. Ian nodded at them as he arrived to stand squarely in front of Pat.

"Hi," she said, woefully lacking for words.

It had been so long since she'd seen him up close and he looked so amazing, Pat felt unsteady in her flip-flops. She clutched her glass and wished she had something more substantial to hold in case her knees buckled beneath her.

"Hi yourself," he replied, his clear hazel eyes warm and friendly. "Congratulations on the day. The garden looks amazing and you look even more spectacular."

Pat blushed and dropped her eyes down to her pink painted toenails. "You, too," she muttered, trying to catch her breath. "You look well."

"I know you're probably surprised to see me here," he said.

"That's an understatement." She clarified.

Ian grinned, then his face became earnest. "I didn't know where else to find you..."

Pat raised an eyebrow. "Have you already forgotten where I work?"

"Ha,ha," he said. "I mean find you where I could actually have a conversation with you. I didn't want to show up at your door, unannounced, and yes I know, showing up at Crystal's wedding unannounced is pretty much the same thing..." He ran his fingers through his hair and sighed. "God, I'm making a mess of this. Can we talk, please?"

Pat cocked her head. "Aren't we doing that right now?"

"I mean *really* talk." His voice deepened as he took a step closer. "Somewhere else. Somewhere private. Where we won't be interupted."

"Oh," Pat said, wanting to smack herself for being so slow on the uptake. "Of course, inside. Follow me."

She gestured for him to follow her up the path to the house, past the kitchen and its chaos and into the sanctuary of her office. When she closed the door behind them, the room became dim and quiet and Pat was sure her nervous swallow was going to echo off the walls.

"This okay?" she asked, feeling more on edge than she had in a long while.

"Perfect," he told her, smiling in the soft light filtering through the sheer drapes on the window.

Pat sat down in her desk chair and tried not to fidget, hoping he would take the lead. Otherwise, she was about to feel very foolish, very fast.

"I'm not sure where to begin, so I'm just going to jump right in okay?"

Pat couldn't help herself and smiled at his choice of words. He'd said almost the same thing the first time he'd asked her out to coffee.

"So, I've been thinking about you," he said. "About us. A lot."

Pat nodded. She'd heard it from Melanie and then from Trisha, but she wasn't about to interrupt and tell him. Whatever he needed to say, she was going to let him.

"Now, I'll admit, I don't know if you've done any thinking about me—"

"Yes," she said, swiftly. "Yes, I have."

"Okay," he said, looking relieved. "So, the thing is, I don't want... Or, rather, I *know* I don't want...." He paused and took a deep breath. "Simply put, I can't live without you, Pat. I don't want to live without you."

Pat had no words. She felt just as she had the first time he'd revealed to her that he wanted to get to know her better. It was as though they'd come full circle and she was rendered just as speechless as she had been in the coffee shop.

"I'm not asking for an answer right now, but if you're willing..." He paused and swallowed. "I'd like to, *love* to, try again."

Pat clutched the arms of her chair as she digested his words. After months without him, what he was telling her was like music to her ears. Except for one, niggling detail.

"What? What is it?" Ian asked, staring at her. "Your face. Am I missing something?" He looked suddenly nauseated. "Oh, shit. Is there someone else? Is that it? You're involved and—"

"No!" Pat surprised herself with her force. "No, Ian," she said, softening her tone. "There is absolutely no one else. And, there hasn't been since we were together." She looked him in the eye. "Can you say the same?"

He frowned. "Of course I can. That's why I'm here."

"Really?" She pressed. "Because, you have nothing to lose by being honest."

His frown deepened. "I am being honest. I don't follow, what are you saying?"

Pat sighed. "I saw you."

"Saw me?"

"At the night club, with Alexa. And, even if you guys aren't serious, I still think it's something worth considering."

Ian's face cleared and he started to chuckle. "Oh," he said, his grin lighting up his face. "Okay, I get where you're going, but no. I absolutely was not *with* Alexa at that club."

Pat shot him a skeptical look. She'd seen them with her own eyes.

"Alexa was there, obviously," he continued. "But, she wasn't with me. She was with my buddy, Paul. It was a blind date, actually. Set up by me. I was there as support, to get things moving if they couldn't do it themselves." He shrugged. "Turns out I was very much a third wheel and it made for a long night."

Pat felt her knees start to tremble and was glad she was sitting. He hadn't been with Alexa. She'd been wrong. The enormity of that revelation, combined with her exhaustion and alcohol, made tears well up in her eyes. She looked away, so Ian wouldn't see them.

"Pat," he said, so softly she almost gave in to a small sob. "It's *you*, don't you get that? It was you from the moment we met on the path and that hasn't changed.

When I'm with you, when I'm not with you, you're with me. In my heart, in my thoughts, you take up all of the space and there's nothing left for anyone else."

A tear escaped and rolled wetly down Pat's cheek. She swiped at it and Ian gently placed a finger under her chin to turn her face toward him.

"I love you, Pat," he told her. "I'm sorry if that makes you cry, but I can't help it. I love you truly, madly, deeply."

More tears followed the first and Pat swiped furiously at her face. She still had to talk to him, had to tell him of the fears she'd held close to her chest way back when, before she could move forward.

"Okay," she said, sniffling and trying to gather some composure. "So, here's my truth for you. Do you remember when you asked me what was wrong, when you thought I was having a negative reaction to Brock?"

Ian looked thoughtful and nodded. "You said it wasn't him, it was what he represented, right?"

"Yes," Pat said, both encouraged and deeply touched he remembered her exact words. "That was it exactly and you need to know, that hasn't changed."

Ian shrugged. "Explain."

"You've never had kids, Ian." She pulled a tissue from a box on her desk, blew her nose and cut to the chase. "I have. And, as much as I loved that part of my life, it's done. Finished. And, furthermore, I know I don't want to revisit it. At least not until I have grandchildren."

Ian's face cleared as comprehension dawned. He couldn't help it, he started to laugh.

"Okay, not the reaction I expected," Pat said.

Ian laughed harder and, then, just as quickly, calmed down. "Pat, my gorgeous, smart, funny and sometimes over thinker. I don't care about that."

Pat was about to protest, but Ian held up his hand. "Please, save your breath. I've heard it all before from everyone in my family, all my friends, even perfect strangers." He sighed and rubbed his fingers across his chin. "It's not that I don't like children, I do. I think they're wonderful, adorable and amazing. But, that doesn't mean I feel the need to raise any of my own."

Pat turned his words over in her head. "Honestly? You're not just saying that."

"Honestly." He assured her. "I love being an Uncle, it's fantastic. My sister in the city has a couple of kids and they're a blast to hang out with. And, now, I have Brock to look forward to, but full time? I've just never had the bug."

"Well," Pat offered, as a slow smile began to spread across her face. "I guess that's it, then."

Ian raised his eyebrows in alarm. "That's it?"

"Yup," she said as happiness began to bubble up inside her. "All of my worries about younger women, about Alexa, about you resenting me for not giving you children, I can just let them go."

Ian's face broke into a huge grin and he reached out his hand to pull her up out of her chair. "Absolutely. Just toss them away into the rubbish pile where they belong. You're free."

Pat looked into his eyes and held his gaze until they both became slightly breathless. "Free to do whatever, or *whoever*, I want."

Ian moved a step closer. "That's how it works," he agreed, his voice husky.

"No time like the present, then." Pat chuckled as she reached for him.

He met her half way. "The present, the future, all of it," he said, wrapping his arms around her and pressing her against him.

"Timing," she managed to say, just before he bent close to take her mouth and seal their future with a kiss.

***

EPILOGUE

Pat wrapped her arms around herself, trying to contain her glee. The sold sign on the sprawling front lawn of the pretty yellow cottage made her want to whoop with joy. She kicked up the red and golden maple leaves that had fallen from the old trees in the yard to litter the path and silently declared that autumn was her favorite season.

Ian's BMW pulled up alongside the curb and parked behind her car and Pat felt all squirmy inside.

"Good things happen to me in the fall," she said, as he exited the vehicle. "I've decided that autumn is my favorite season."

He grinned as he strode purposefully around to the passenger side of his car. "Makes sense to me," he said, then pointed a firm finger at her. "Remember, you agreed. No peeking."

Pat giggled. "I did and now the curiosity is almost killing me."

He raised his eyebrows up and down, then waved a hand at her. "Go on, close your eyes. And, keep them closed and hold out your hands, just like we rehearsed."

Pat did as she was told. She pressed her eyes tightly closed, held her hands out in front of her like she was going to be given a casserole pan and felt excitement travel up her spine. What on Earth could the man be planning to add to the already wonderful reality of their new home?

"Okay, ready?" Ian's voice was closer, right near her ear.

"Ready."

"Brace yourself," he said and gently placed into her hands a bundle of warm, furry weight.

"Oh!" Pat blurted and her eyes flew open. In her grasp was the sweetest, cutest Jack Russell puppy she'd seen in a very long time. "Oh-my-goodness!" she squeaked as the puppy proceeded to cover her chin in kisses.

"Okay?" Ian asked, his voice slightly unsure.

Pat was speechless. The puppy looked so much like her beloved dog, Puck, she almost felt he'd been recreated like magic right before her eyes. Against her will, Pat felt tears begin to form in her eyes and nodded, overjoyed with her present.

"It's more than okay," she said, tears dripping down her face as she lifted the puppy up for a quick check. "*He's* more than okay," she clarified, snuggling him close.

"Now, we have our new home and our new *baby*," Ian teased, making her snicker.

"I wonder what Whiskey's going to think," Pat said, shifting the puppy in her arms and wiping the moisture from her cheeks.

"Oh, I'm sure he'll come around." Ian assured her, reaching out to stroke the soft fur.

"He needs a name," Pat said, gently scratching behind the pup's ears.

"Actually, on the way over, I was thinking about that. And, as a sort of hat-tip to your previous furry canine, came up with the name Jester. What do you think?"

Pat beamed. She loved it.

"Jester," she said, trying on the name. The pup perked up and turned his head toward her when she said it. "There you go. I think it's perfect."

Ian wrapped an arm around her shoulders, gazed at the ring glittering on the third finger of her left hand and nodded. "And, they lived happily ever after."

"*And*," Pat added.

Ian raised his eyebrows. "And?"

Pat looked at their new cottage and smiled. "And, they made sure they had Kent do all the heavy lifting."

Ian laughed. "Yes, they did."

***

THE END

ABOUT THE AUTHOR

Kathleen began storytelling in grade school and has many fond memories of passing summer afternoons, out on the swings in her backyard, creating tales that entertained her neighborhood friends.

Many years later, too many to talk about without seeming rude and nosey, Kathleen has channeled her imagination to the pages of her novels. She hopes you enjoy her tales and encourages you to feel free to read her stories on the swing set in your own backyard.

Kathleen now spends time in her backyard with her beloved husband, adored son and silly dog. They let her tell them stories and always laugh in all of the correct places. She's lucky, and she knows it.

Please visit Kathleen's website to find out more.

Connect with Kathleen Online

Website: www.kathleenkole.com

Facebook: www.facebook.com/KathleenKoleAuthor

Twitter: www.twitter.com/kathleenkole